COLD AS ICE CREAM

COLD AS ICE CREAM

AUNTIE CLEM'S BAKERY #13

P.D. WORKMAN

ISBN: 9781774680438 (IS Hardcover)

ISBN: 9781774680445 (IS Paperback)

ISBN: 9781774680421 (IS Large Print)

ISBN: 9781774680391 (KDP Paperback)

ISBN: 9781774680407 (Kindle)

ISBN: 9781774680414 (ePub)

pdworkman

Telepathy of Gardens

Delusions of the Past

Fairy Blade Unmade

Web of Nightmares

A Whisker's Breadth

Skunk Man Swamp (Coming Soon)

Magic Ain't A Game (Coming Soon)

Without Foresight (Coming Soon)

Zachary Goldman Mysteries

She Wore Mourning

His Hands Were Quiet

She Was Dying Anyway

He Was Walking Alone

They Thought He was Safe

He Was Not There

Her Work Was Everything

She Told a Lie

He Never Forgot

She Was At Risk

Kenzie Kirsch Medical Thrillers

Unlawful Harvest

Doctored Death (Coming soon)

Dosed to Death (Coming soon)

Gentle Angel (Coming soon)

AND MORE AT PDWORKMAN.COM

To friends who don't judge

CHAPTER 1

As soon as Erin got home from work, Orange Blossom was underfoot, meowing and yowling in greeting, winding around her legs, telling her all about his busy (or not so busy) day at home. Erin put down her purse and took off her jacket and picked him up.

"Hey. Quiet down. Relax. This is the time I get home every day, I'm not late."

He started purring, a loud rumble that filled the room. Erin pressed her face into the short velvety hair at the top of his head and scratched under his chin.

"There. You like that, huh?"

Marshmallow hopped out from behind the couch and nuzzled Erin's toes while waiting patiently for Erin to scratch his long ears.

Terry looked out from the kitchen. His jaw was dark with five o'clock shadow. He'd had an early shift and clearly hadn't shaved afterward.

"Whatever he is telling you about me, it isn't true."

Erin stroked Blossom's back, smoothing down his ruffled fur. "I think he's telling me about K9."

"You'd think he would be used to K9. Most other cats would have resigned themselves to a dog being around here by now."

Erin nodded. She could see K9 lying on the kitchen floor behind Terry, bored or tired after his patrol with Terry. Terry still wasn't back to working full-time at the police department since he had been attacked during an investigation. He was getting gradually better, but was still suffering from headaches, insomnia, and problems with concentration. Not something you wanted to worry about with your police force. K9 had been his partner for a long time and was used to patrolling all day.

"Maybe it's because K9 chased him when he was a kitten," Erin said, "back when we first met. K9 really scared Blossom, so maybe he was traumatized... instead of it being like a normal situation."

Terry raised an eyebrow. "I'd forgotten all about that," he said. "Funny. That seems like a long time ago."

"Maybe she has some kitty PTSD," Erin said, cuddling Orange Blossom up to her face again. "And here we are, just trying to get him to be friends with the person—animal—who traumatized him."

Terry rolled his eyes. "Well, something to think about. Are you hungry?" He segued to food, which Erin assumed was to avoid discussing PTSD any further. Neither of them was particularly good at discussing their feelings or their own symptoms. Terry had been mandated to undergo counseling through the police department following his attack; he probably wouldn't have chosen to do it himself. Erin had been to enough head-shrinkers in the past that she really didn't want to have to deal with another. She would do the best she could to deal with the nightmares and other issues that she had. At least after going through his own ordeal, Terry had stopped suggesting she get therapy. It seemed like a pat, easy answer, but it wasn't as simple as it sounded. It wasn't a matter of going to see a doctor, getting a prescription, and being okay. Even with intense, ongoing therapy, it could last for years and, while pills could help with the depression and some of the symptoms, they didn't fix the underlying problem with the brain.

"Yes. I don't know what you made, but it smells wonderful." Erin put Orange Blossom down and entered the kitchen. Marshmallow hopped along beside her, still waiting for attention. Erin looked at the red sauce bubbling in the pot and the various other pots and bowls on the stove and counter and smiled. "Wow, you went all out. This looks great." She bent down and petted Marshmallow. Terry wasn't an experienced cook, so she wasn't sure how any of the dishes had turned out, but he had obviously been pretty busy since he'd gotten off of his shift.

"I wanted to buckle down and make you a real meal for once. Not just a sandwich or warming up a can of soup. I keep promising to make you something, so…" He gestured along the length of the cluttered counters. "There you go. That's what I did. If you don't like it… well…"

"You must have been talking to Vic and Willie," Erin suggested. She remembered Vic getting after Willie and telling him that opening a can of soup did not constitute making her dinner. Not for a date night, anyway. Maybe other nights of the week it would be acceptable.

"Well, to Willie," Terry admitted. "We're going to do another fishing trip soon. He says it's a good time of year for…" Terry trailed off. "Hmm. I don't remember. But something is good this time of year. I don't think it really matters, as long as we have something to do while we sit around and relax. So no one calls us lazy. If you fish all day, then even if you don't come home with food, people still think that you've spent your day being productive. Not quite the same as if you just sit on the couch all day."

Erin nodded. She went to the cupboard to get out the dishes they would need. She cleared various items off of the table, which he had apparently used as a preparation area when he ran out of counter space, and set out the plates and cups. She cleared various open containers of ingredients as Terry started to fill serving dishes and take them to the table. That way, when they were done, there wouldn't be so much to clean up. Erin always felt more tired after she'd had a chance to sit down and eat. Best to get it done before the lethargy overtook her.

There were some odds and ends of vegetables left over from Terry making a salad, and she fed a few pieces to Marshmallow. Orange Blossom started to yowl and complain about how she was feeding Marshmallow and hadn't yet given him a treat.

"Okay, okay. Your treat is coming." Erin let herself into the pantry, but pushed him back and wouldn't allow him to follow her in there. A few weeks ago, she wouldn't have bothered, but since he had gotten sick, apparently after having eaten something he shouldn't have, she was far more careful about keeping him away from people food, whether it was something she thought would be okay for cats or not. He was only allowed to eat food that came in a package with a picture of a cat on the side.

And the crumbs that K9 left behind. Once Erin had slid a few treats across the floor for Orange Blossom to chase, she got a gluten-free doggie biscuit out of the cookie jar and gave it to K9. He lay with it between his paws, munching on it. Blossom saw that his adversary had also been given a treat and, after gobbling down his own, he slunk closer to K9 to see if he could snatch a few crumbs. It was the only time he would get close to the shepherd without hissing and puffing his fur out.

With the food preparation areas mostly cleared, Erin sat down to eat with Terry, looking over the variety of dishes that he had put together.

"This looks great," she told him.

Terry beamed.

CHAPTER 2

*S*he was happy that Terry was feeling well enough after an early shift to cook a meal for her. A few weeks before, that wouldn't have been possible. He had barely been able to get through his half-shifts, let alone do anything productive afterward.

They sat on the couch after eating, sharing details about their days.

Nothing exciting had happened, and that was perfectly fine. They didn't need any more crime or mysteries. Just routine, everyday baking and policing work. Muffins and parking tickets.

There was a knock at the back door, then the sound of the door opening and Vic's voice. "Y'all decent?"

Erin straightened slightly and smiled at her young employee. "What would you do if we weren't?"

"Well, I guess I'd go all the way back to the loft and entertain myself there," Vic drawled in her slowest backwoods Tennessee accent. "But it isn't like the two of you are ever doing anything… sensitive… out in the open." She chuckled. "Y'all know you could have drop-in visitors any time."

The blond young woman sat down on one of the easy chairs, smiling at her boss.

"Long time no see," Erin said. Vic had driven her home in

Willie's truck after they had closed Auntie Clem's bakery for the day. Erin's car had been wrecked before Christmas and she hadn't yet replaced it. Vic didn't have a car of her own, but frequently borrowed Willie's. And it wasn't like they couldn't walk to and from Auntie Clem's if they needed to. It was only a few minutes away. Though neither of the menfolk liked them walking in the predawn hours when they had to start baking to have fresh bread and muffins in the case by the time they opened up to the early-morning customers. Bakers began the workday very early.

"Where's Willie?"

"He took the truck out to one of his claims." Vic shrugged. "I didn't get any details. Something important in the world of mines and minerals."

While Vic sometimes went spelunking with Willie on days off, she wasn't involved in his mining operations. Willie always had a dozen different jobs on the go and he sometimes kept strange hours, especially if Vic used his truck during the bakery hours.

"How is the mining life?" Erin asked. "Things… going well?"

"I have no idea. He doesn't tell me about it. He keeps his head above water, so I guess it's going well. Or his other ventures are going well. I don't get into any of the business details."

Erin nodded. She rolled her shoulders and rubbed her neck, trying to work out a few knots. Terry pushed her hands away and turned her so that her back was to him, so he could rub her muscles. Erin closed her eyes and rolled her neck, trying to relax into it. His fingers were hard, digging down into the muscles and trying to massage away the tightness.

"How's that?" he murmured close to her ear.

Erin nodded. "That's good." She was sore but, even though it hurt, she knew it would help later. "I'll do some tai chi before bed. And then I'll be nice and relaxed to sleep."

Terry's fingers paused for a moment, but he didn't disagree. Both of them had difficulty getting to sleep, but discussing how difficult it was and the likelihood that either of them would be able to get to sleep when they wanted to would not be productive.

And neither of them wanted to talk about it in front of Vic, either. She always noticed when Erin had a difficult night anyway.

"There was some mail for you," Erin told Vic, nodding to the side table. Even though they had a separate mailbox for the loft over the garage where Vic lived, the mailman didn't always get the mail sorted properly between the two boxes. Erin and Vic just passed mail back and forth as necessary and weren't really bothered by it.

Vic stretched out one of her long, slender arms and managed to snag the pile of envelopes. She sorted through it, pulling out the couple of mail pieces that were hers. One of them was just a bill, Erin had noticed, but the other looked like a personal letter. It was rare to get actual personal postal mail, so she couldn't help but notice. Everybody used email and social media.

Although that wasn't entirely true. Erin remembered that Vic had also gotten postal mail from an old girlfriend, crazy Theresa, someone that they all wanted to avoid running into again. Ever. There were warrants out for Theresa's arrest after the murder of Bo Biggles and her attack on Terry and Jack Ward when they had gone over to talk to her about it. But so far, she was in the wind and no one had been able to bring her to justice.

Erin eyed the envelope nervously. She didn't remember enough about Theresa's handwriting to know if it were the same writing or not. Theresa had known about Vic's gender transition but had thought that Vic would still be interested in renewing their relationship. Even though Vic was already in a committed relationship with Willie.

Vic examined the letter in the green envelope. She glanced over it at Erin. "What's wrong?"

"Nothing."

"You look like you're in pain. Terry, I think you're massaging too hard."

Terry stopped. He leaned forward, trying to see Erin's face. "Are you okay? You need to tell me if I'm hurting you."

"No." Erin gently rubbed the sore muscles that he had been

working on. "It wasn't that. I was just..." She shook her head. "Nothing. I just wondered who the letter was from. Not that it's any of my business. Just curious."

Vic's brows came down for a moment, and then she understood. "Oh! No, it's nothing to be worried about." She worked her finger into the corner of the envelope and slit it across. "It's not from... her."

"Oh." Erin swallowed and nodded. "That's good. I was just wondering. I know there's nothing to worry about, she's not going to show up here or start anything... she would risk getting caught and sent to prison for a few decades. She wouldn't do that."

"Crazy Theresa," Vic intoned, shaking her head. "You can never be sure what that one is going to do."

Erin's stomach clenched. Vic must have seen a change in her expression because she hurried to change her words.

"She wouldn't come here, though, you're right. She'll stay far away from Bald Eagle Falls and anyone who knows that there are warrants out for her. Maybe she'll go north to Canada."

Erin rolled her eyes and gave a little laugh. "To Canada? She'd freeze."

"Good. Maybe a little chill would be good for her."

Vic herself hadn't been too impressed with the northern weather when they had taken a cruise to Alaska. Born and bred in Tennessee, her blood was too thin to appreciate the cooler weather. She'd been chilled the whole time she'd been north of the forty-ninth parallel.

Vic pulled the paper out of the envelope and unfolded it. Her eyes scanned over the page. "Oh, it's Clayton." She raised her eyes to Erin and Terry. "He was one of the group on the cruise," she said. "One of the people I met onboard."

"Oh." Erin nodded and tried to look happy about this. She *was* happy that it wasn't from Theresa. But she couldn't help feeling a little twinge of disappointment that one of the LGBT group that Vic had made friends with on the cruise was sending Vic letters. Vic was already with Willie and she already had a best friend in Erin. She could have however many friends she liked, but Erin couldn't help feeling like the men and women that Vic had become friends with on the ship were somehow trying to wedge themselves between Vic and Erin.

That was ridiculous, of course. It didn't affect her friendship with Erin at all. But Erin had grown up without many friends and felt possessive. Vic shared experiences with the LGBT group that Erin would never have. Erin knew about the challenges that Vic went through living among the cis men and women in small-town, Bible-belt Tennessee, but she would never understand it with the same depth and nuance of people who had lived through it. Erin could never fully be a part of that side of Vic's life.

She would have to settle for being Vic's friend and working side-by-side with her.

"So, how is Clayton?" Erin asked, trying to inject warmth that she did not feel into the question.

Vic's eyes moved over the page. She didn't look up to answer Erin. "Good…"

Erin leaned back against Terry, resting into his warm body. She waited for more information from Vic. Vic's voice was far away, not really engaged with the conversation as she read Clayton's letter.

Terry resumed rubbing Erin's neck and shoulders, but with gentle hands this time, soothing the sore muscles. Maybe he understood how disconnected Erin felt from Vic at times like that. She felt like the little girl left at home when the others went out to play. Erin scratched at a drop of bread batter that had dried on her slacks. She wasn't sure how it had managed to get past her apron. She always seemed to have a few spatters that made it to her street clothes.

"He's coming to Bald Eagle Falls," Vic said.

"Coming here? Why would he be coming here?" Erin answered too quickly before she thought through her answer.

Vic looked over the letter at her again, eyebrows quirked,

shaking her head. "Why not? There's no reason he *couldn't* come here."

"No, I didn't mean that. I just meant I was surprised. It's sort of out of anyone's way. Is he coming just to see you, or is he on his way to something else...?"

"There's some kind of contest. He knows that you and I got the tickets to the cruise as part of a prize package, so he says maybe we can give him some pointers on how to win..."

"We?"

"You and me. We did win it together."

"Did he say me? Or just you?"

Vic's eyes went back to the letter. "Does it matter?"

"No. Of course not. Just curious. I don't think he really wants my input, does he?"

"I don't know. I doubt if he really wants anyone's advice. It's just something to say. Small talk."

Erin nodded. "Yeah, I guess. What contest is it? I hadn't heard anything about a contest. Is it in the city?"

"I don't know. I haven't heard of it before. Not one of the big ones like the Pillsbury Bake-Off or something. There are little ones running all the time."

"I guess."

"Especially in the rural areas around here. It's entertainment. A good way to get people together. Have some fun, raise some money. Make people remember your name for the next time that they're buying groceries at the store."

The Fall Fair was the first baking contest that Erin had ever entered, but she had noticed since then little contests that popped up here and there.

"I think we just got lucky with our entry. It wasn't like I really knew what I was doing."

"It wasn't just luck," Vic disagreed. "We worked hard on that cake. It was the perfect selection for the Fall Fair."

Erin's cheeks warmed a little. Vic had been instrumental in picking out their entry and teaching Erin about the traditional way to make it, but it had been Erin's recipe and execution. They had both contributed. But she was glad that Vic didn't think it was just luck that had gotten them the prize.

"When is he coming?"

Vic looked at her phone face. "Uh… in just a couple of weeks. I'll have to give him a call and make sure he has everything he needs while he is down for the contest and make sure that he is going to come by for a visit."

CHAPTER 3

*E*rin had her massage and did her tai chi and got to bed in good time but, as she lay there cuddling with Terry, she couldn't seem to get her brain under control. She kept thinking about Vic and Theresa. And Vic and Clayton. Clayton was coming to Bald Eagle Falls. Erin's own territory. It was one thing to have to watch Vic making friends with other people and spend her time with them on an Alaskan cruise, but it was quite another to have to deal with it on her own turf.

"Are you okay?" Terry asked, running his hand over her back gently.

"Fine." Erin turned over and tried to find a more comfortable position.

"Do you need a painkiller? How are you feeling?"

Erin relaxed her muscles and tried to decide how her body felt. It was taking a lot longer to recover from the car accident than she had expected. She hadn't had any broken bones or permanent injuries. She hadn't stayed at the hospital overnight. But the doctor and everyone else involved had been amazed that she had gotten through the accident so unscathed. The doctor had warned her that she probably had soft tissue injuries and would have to be careful and give herself lots of time to heal and recover.

Still, Erin had thought that it would only be a few days, and then she would be able to go back to normal. But it had been several weeks and, even though the bruises had faded, she still found herself tiring easily. She had a lot of aches and pains she hadn't had before.

Her joints were hurting. Erin wondered if it meant that a cold front were coming in. Could she now predict the weather by her aches and pains like some of the older people? Maybe she was coming down with a flu bug.

Or maybe it just meant that she hadn't fully recovered from her injuries yet. Erin sighed. How long was it going to take?

"I'm sore," she admitted, "but I don't know if I want to take anything."

"You don't have to… but if it would make you feel better, help you to get to sleep…"

She sighed. "Yeah. I suppose I should probably try. I thought I would be over this by now."

"I know." His experience had been the same, Erin knew. He had thought that he would be able to recover quickly from his head injury and get back on the job and everything would be back to normal. But they were both struggling, waiting for their bodies and minds to heal.

Terry slid out of bed and she listened to him as he padded down the hall to the bathroom and got her a painkiller and a cup of water. He was good to her. It was nice to have someone around, checking to make sure she was okay and looking after her needs.

Erin eventually managed to get the sleep that she needed and wasn't too tired when she got up in the morning. Terry had eventually retired to the couch so that he wouldn't wake her up with his restless tossing and turning and had fallen asleep in front of the TV, as he had too many times since the attack. But it was the only way that he could distract his mind and eventually fall asleep. He didn't have to be awake as early as Erin, so his body wasn't ready for sleep as early as Erin was.

She quietly moved around the house, getting her morning tea and toast and taking care of each of the animals. She knew that Terry had the day off, so it didn't really matter if she woke him up. He could sleep later if he needed to. But just because he had the opportunity, that didn't mean that he would be able to, so she did her best not to wake him. She heard him murmur or move a few times, but he just readjusted and didn't fully awaken.

She texted with Vic to coordinate their departure for the bakery, and met her around the back of the house once they were both ready to go.

"Mornin' sunshine," Vic greeted. She yawned. "How did you sleep?"

"Pretty good."

"Another day, another dollar."

"Let's go make some bread," Erin said, smiling. "We're taking the truck again?"

"Yeah. Willie is going to walk over and pick it up later."

"We could just walk to Auntie Clem's."

"You know how he feels about that."

Erin shrugged and shook her head. "Yes."

They climbed up into the truck and Vic revved the engine. Erin winced, worried that it was too loud in the early morning. She didn't want Mrs. Peach complaining about them waking her up before dawn. But she'd already had that discussion with Vic more than once, so she kept her mouth shut and just started to mentally prepare her list of tasks for the day.

They were through all of the holidays, and Erin felt like it was time to add a few new offerings to the regular cycle of baked goods at Auntie Clem's. Adding fresh new experiences to the menu was a way of keeping people coming back for more. If she wanted to attract the people who didn't have to eat gluten-free or allergen-free and could pick up their baked goods from the bread aisle at the grocery store or at a bakery in the city, then she had to have something to offer them. Something more interesting than what they would find at the grocery store.

"How about lemon poppyseed loaf?" she asked Vic.

"That would be nice," Vic approved. Erin didn't need to tell her she was thinking about what else to add to the menu. Vic understood that part without being told. "A nice fresh taste. Good for breakfast."

"Yeah. We've been doing lots of earthier flavors, pumpkin and sweet potato and savory spices. Something a little lighter. And pretty. I love the color of a good lemon loaf."

"Good idea. I like it."

The early-morning hours zipped quickly past as they discussed other flavors and foods to try while they mixed batters and filled the ovens and then the display case before the earliest customers got there.

Erin loved the rhythm of getting everything ready in the morning. She had a number of employees who worked part-time to help them cover the busiest times and to make sure that she and Vic both got some time off to have personal lives, but Erin liked it best when it was just her and Vic working side-by-side, familiar and anticipating each other's actions.

Erin turned the sign over to "open" and unlocked the door for the customers who were already outside her door waiting. Cooler air blew into the bakery, and the sweet and spicy fragrances of the fresh breads escaped the shop to attract foot traffic as people headed to their work or school but just couldn't resist popping into the bakery for something delicious to start their day.

"Mmm," Mrs. Snell sniffed at the air and closed her eyes. "This is the closest thing to heaven I can think of. Fresh bread, cinnamon—I could just drink it all in."

"It's pleasant," Lottie Sturm agreed, scowling, "but heaven? That's a bit sacrilegious, don't you think?"

"Oh, I don't mean it that way," Mrs. Snell said, her cheeks flushing. "I just meant… it's such a lovely way to start the day. Of course… it's not heaven. I don't even know if people eat in heaven, do they?"

"Of course they don't," Lottie said authoritatively. "How could we eat as spirits? We won't have bodies and have to sustain them like we do here. That's just one of the things we have to put up with during mortality."

Mrs. Snell didn't look encouraged by this. "But I enjoy eating so much. Don't you think that we might still eat our favorite foods, even if we don't have to? And never gain weight however much we eat…?"

"Gluttony is one of the seven deadly sins," Lottie reminded her.

Mrs. Snell nodded sadly. Erin was worried that she would be discouraged by this and wouldn't want to buy the food that she normally did, concerned about the sin of being greedy.

But Mrs. Snell bought more than she usually did. Maybe Lottie had achieved the opposite, instead convincing Mrs. Snell that she would need to get in all of her earthly pleasures while she still had the opportunity. Erin handed her the bag, giving her a warm smile and wink.

"You enjoy that now, Mrs. Snell."

"Oh, I will, dear. I will."

Lottie herself didn't seem to be discouraged from pursuing her earthly pleasures either, getting more than just her daily bread, ensuring that she had a good amount of chocolate on the menu as well. Vic rang everything up at the register.

"Those double-chocolate chocolate chip cookies really are sinfully delicious," she told Lottie, making change for her.

Lottie gave her a baleful look, maybe not sure whether Vic was teasing her or had just picked her words poorly. "We all need to sustain ourselves," she said obliquely.

Vic gave a little laugh after Lottie left. "Some people wear their religion on their sleeve," she observed, "but then they don't seem to follow their own counsel."

Erin glanced around the bakery, not wanting to say anything

about it in front of the rest of the customers. An atheist herself, she was acutely aware that many of the church-going people in Bald Eagle Falls said they believed one thing while living another way altogether. Erin never had understood how they could divorce their religious beliefs from their behavior.

CHAPTER 4

The morning rush had ended. Erin moved back into the kitchen to put some cookies into the oven. Once done, she rejoined Vic at the front of the shop. "What do you think about—"

Erin's gaze shifted to the door as the bells announced the arrival of another customer.

A middle-aged man, not particularly striking in appearance. A little on the short and heavy side, dark hair, a bulldog mouth. Small fans of upward wrinkles around his eyes.

Erin's jaw dropped open. It was Chef Kirschoff from the Alaskan cruise.

Vic looked up to see if Erin were going to finish her sentence and, seeing Erin's expression, followed her gaze to the door. It took her a moment longer to recognize Chef Kirschoff than it had taken Erin. He wasn't wearing his whites and tall chef's hat, but just regular street clothes. And Erin had spent more time with him.

"Chef Kirschoff!" Erin exclaimed, excited to see him.

"Hans," he corrected. "We are not in my kitchen this time! I'm just Hans here."

"It's so good to see you! Why didn't you tell me you were coming? I can't believe this!"

Vic was laughing at Erin's star-struck reaction. "I think you have an admirer!" she told Kirschoff.

Erin didn't consider herself a demonstrative person, but she hurried around the counter to shake Chef Kirschoff's hand and, when he reached out to give her a friendly hug, she accepted, squeezing him back and then releasing him to step back and look at his face.

"What are you doing here?" she demanded. "Why didn't you tell me you were coming?"

"I wanted to surprise you. I was afraid that someone would tip you off ahead of time, but it looks like I was successful."

"Yes. Who would tip me off?" Erin turned and looked at Vic. "Did you know?"

"That Chef Kirschoff was coming? No, I didn't know that part."

Erin blinked and tried to process this. "That part?"

Vic laughed again. She and Chef Kirschoff exchanged looks. Kirschoff made a gesture for Vic to explain.

"Well, I told you that Clayton was coming here for a cooking competition."

"Right. You told me that." Erin looked back at Kirschoff. "Are you judging the competition? Or competing in it?"

"I am one of the organizers. I am not judging or participating."

"And you decided to have it in Tennessee?" Erin shook her head. "Why?"

"I found several willing sponsors." He shrugged. "I thought that since you came to me in Alaska, I would come to you this time."

"You picked Tennessee because I'm here? Really?" Erin shook her head at the thought. It didn't make sense that he would choose Tennessee to hold a cooking competition just because he wanted to see her again. He could email her. Video conference with her.

Call her on the phone. He didn't have to have a cooking competition as an excuse to see her again.

Kirschoff beamed at her. "Are you interested?"

"Interested… in competing? I don't know. What kind of food is it? When is it? I haven't had a chance to prepare anything."

"I want you and Vic to be judges. You wouldn't have to prepare anything ahead, just make sure that you could take some time off to attend and judge the entries."

Erin looked at Vic. "Judges. I don't know… do you want to?"

"We don't have to both agree," Vic pointed out. "We can each decide individually."

"Yes, of course," Erin agreed. Maybe Vic didn't want to be a judge, but she didn't want to prevent Erin from going. Vic might not want to be in the spotlight. "If you don't want to, that's okay."

"Oh, I'm going to be a judge," Vic said as if it were a foregone conclusion. "But you don't have to if you don't want to. It's up to you."

Chef Kirschoff laughed heartily. "Welcome aboard!" he told Vic. He looked at Erin. "And you, Erin? Can I convince you to be a judge as well?"

Erin shrugged. "Well… it sounds like fun. But what kind of food is it? What's the theme? Because if it's haggis or something like that, I might change my mind."

"The theme is CO2."

"CO2?"

"Carbon dioxide." Kirschoff grinned rakishly.

Erin still didn't understand how the theme of a cooking contest could be carbon dioxide. "How exactly…? I have no idea how you cook with CO2. Are there CO2 burners? Like cooking with natural gas?"

"The opposite. You can freeze with CO2—dry ice—or you can use it to carbonate drinks."

"So, ice cream and coke?" Vic asked.

"Ice cream and soda," Kirschoff agreed.

"Oooh," Erin breathed. "That could be dangerous."

Kirschoff quirked an expressive eyebrow at her. "Dangerous?"

"I could put on twenty pounds. You'd have to roll me back in here."

"You only have to taste the products," Vic pointed out, "you don't have to eat a whole bowl of each one."

"Maybe you don't. I'm not sure I would be able to stop myself."

"Well then, you're right… this could be dangerous."

Word of the cooking contest (or chilling contest, to be more accurate) spread quickly through Bald Eagle Falls and the surrounding areas. Everyone was talking about the generous prizes and the fact that some of the judges would be local celebrities. Erin wasn't sure how she felt about being called a celebrity. People knew her by business and because she had won the grand prize at the Fall Fair. But also because of her involvement in solving some of the local crimes that had occurred over the previous months. She didn't exactly like being known for the way she had stumbled into those cases.

But it was good to get her face and name in front of people to get free publicity for Auntie Clem's bakery, so she couldn't shun the spotlight. She just wasn't sure she was a celeb.

Everyone had family recipes that they thought would win the grand prize for sure. They all wanted to know what the rules for the contest were. Sales increased at Auntie Clem's as people came by to gossip and to get on the judges' good sides.

Erin and Vic wanted to treat Chef Kirschoff to dinner, so both called their partners to see if they would come along. Erin's heart sank as Terry's phone rang and rang without him answering. He was normally good about answering his phone even if he was on duty, though Erin tried not to call him if he was on shift. It was only when he was asleep or not feeling well that he didn't answer right away.

Or if he was in the middle of an investigation or an arrest, of course. But he wasn't on duty. Erin watched Vic talking on the phone with Willie while she waited for Terry to answer. Vic wasn't exactly frowning, but Erin didn't think she was getting very far. Willie often had other plans. He and Vic were independent and didn't necessarily see each other every night.

Erin started to pull her phone away from her ear to hang up the call when she heard Terry's faraway voice. She put it back to her face.

"Terry? Are you there?"

"Erin. What's wrong?"

He sounded groggy. She had awakened him. "I'm sorry. Nothing is wrong. I just wondered if you wanted to go out to supper tonight. Chef Kirschoff is in town. Vic and I are going to take him out."

"No." His voice cracked and faded, and she didn't think it was just the cell service. "I'm not up for that tonight."

"You don't sound good. Is it your head?"

He cleared his throat and took a few extra seconds to answer. "Yes," he agreed finally. "My head. It's really bothering tonight."

It was still mid-afternoon. "Did you take something for it? Do you need me to come home?"

"I can look after myself, Erin. I took a pill… I just need to sleep now. That's all. Go out with Vic. Have a nice time."

"Are you sure? You'll need something to eat and you won't be in any shape to fix yourself anything."

"I'm sure it will be better later. Just go ahead without me, okay?"

"If you're sure. I just want to make sure… that you're going to be okay. Will you call me when you get up later and let me know how it's going?"

"Sure," he agreed, and hung up.

Erin kept her phone at her ear for a few moments, even though she knew he was already gone. He didn't sound good. She wasn't sure she should go out anywhere without him. He wouldn't remember to call her back, and he wouldn't call her if he needed something. He was stubborn and macho that way. He was perfectly fine with insisting that Erin needed to take care of herself, but he would be at death's door before asking for her help.

Erin lowered the phone. Her eyes met Vic's across the room.

"Is it just us girls tonight?" Vic asked, reading her body language.

"Yes. Us and Chef Kirschoff. But I wonder… maybe we should pick another night. He's going to be here for a few weeks, we don't need to run out and do it tonight."

"You sound worried. Was Terry upset?"

"No. I woke him up. He sounds like he's feeling pretty rough. He said to just go ahead without him, but maybe I should stay home with him tonight. We can go out another night."

"If you want. Do you want to call Hans and let him know?"

Erin didn't know if she'd ever be able to think of Chef Kirschoff as just Hans. His chef persona was so much a part of how she perceived him. He wasn't just a normal, everyday Hans.

"I don't know what to do."

"Well, why don't we leave it for now. You can touch base with Terry later on and see if he's any better. If you think you need to be home with him, then go. We'll let Hans know then. He can still eat out tonight. Any of the restaurants are good."

There weren't many dining choices in Bald Eagle Falls, but they put on a pretty good spread. And even a chef didn't need to have gourmet food every night. Kirschoff wouldn't mind if they were forced to reschedule.

"Okay… or you could go on your own if I need to stay with Terry…"

Vic rolled her eyes. "Probably not a good idea. Me and Chef Kirschoff out to eat together… the rumors would fly like feathers in a twister. I might not care what the gossips say… but there's no need to feed them." She looked uncomfortable, her cheeks pinking up.

She might say she didn't care what the gossips said, and she was good at just moving on, but Erin knew that the things people said about her did bother her.

"Right. I wasn't thinking. You're right. That wouldn't be a good idea."

"We'll go home after we close," Vic told Erin. "You can pop in and see how Terry is. If you think he's okay on his own, we'll go out with Hans. If he needs you, we'll just reschedule for another night."

"Okay. That sounds good," Erin agreed. She slid her phone back away and went to the front of the display case to wipe down the fingerprints and tidy up before the after school/before dinner rush. Vic retreated to the kitchen to make sure that everything was in order there.

CHAPTER 5

When Erin stopped at home, Terry was in front of the TV and startled slightly at Erin's entrance.

"I thought you and Vic were going out." He frowned, a crease appearing between his brows. "Didn't you call me earlier to say that the two of you had to do something together? Or was that another day? It's easy to get confused when..."

"Yes, we were going to go out with Chef Kirschoff. But I wanted to check in with you and make sure you're okay first. You sound like you're doing better, do you want to come?"

"Chef Kirschoff?"

"Yes."

He rubbed his forehead. "Isn't that the name of the chef on the cruise?"

"Yes. You're not going crazy. The chef from the cruise. He's here in town. He's running a cooking contest and he's asked Vic and me to be judges."

"What's he doing here?"

"I guess he decided Tennessee was a good place for this contest."

"Bald Eagle Falls?"

"It's actually going to be in Whitewater Junction, but he's

asked us if we'll judge. The entries will be from all over the area. Like with the Fall Fair. Anyone can enter."

"Are you entering?"

"No. I'm not going to enter anything. I'm going to help with the judging." Erin studied his face, trying to decide if he was getting it, or if she should just give up and try again when he was feeling better.

"Oh. Okay. That's kind of weird."

"It gets stranger—the contest isn't actually a cooking contest, it's for preparing food with CO2."

"Carbon dioxide? How do you cook food with carbon dioxide?"

"That's what I asked too. But they don't. They freeze it with dry ice, or they carbonate beverages with it."

"Oh." He nodded. "Sweet."

Erin giggled. "Did you just make a pun when you've got a migraine?"

"I guess I did."

"Can I get you anything? Bring you a pill or the cold pack?"

"No. I just put it back in the freezer and I'm at full dose." He gave her a warning look. "Don't think that means it's worse than usual. I just decided to be a big boy and take my prescription instead of complaining that the pills don't work."

"Okay." Erin held up her hands. "I'm not saying anything."

Orange Blossom was sleeping on the top of the couch behind Terry. He stretched and yawned, looking at Erin. He gave a long yowl.

"I'll give the beasties their treats. Do you want anything from the kitchen?"

"No. I'll eat later… before I take another pill."

He was doing everything he was supposed to in order to take care of himself—taking a nap, using the ice pack, taking the pills he was supposed to with food so that they wouldn't upset his stomach. Erin couldn't think of anything else she could do for him.

"Do you want me to pick you up something at the restaurant?"

"Which one are you going to?"

"I don't know yet. Chinese, maybe."

"Well, you know what I like… if there are leftovers, bring them home with you."

"Okay. I will." Erin leaned down and kissed him, then went into the kitchen to take care of the animals.

Vic was still sitting in the truck waiting to see if Erin was going to need to stay home with Terry or not. She pushed the door open when she saw Erin coming back out.

"Does this mean he's doing better?"

"Little better. Up from his nap. Took his pills. Told me to just go ahead with the dinner, so…" Erin shrugged. "We might as well."

"Glad to hear it! Climb on in."

A few minutes later, they were at the Chinese restaurant and met Hans. He had on a coat and was flapping his hands near his face. "I dressed way too warm for this weather. I knew it was nice here, but it was winter when I left home!"

"It's winter here too," Vic pointed out. "Where is it you live?"

Erin had only pictured him on the cruise ship. It seemed bizarre that he might actually have a house and live in one place like a normal person, only going on cruises when he was hired for those jobs.

"Colorado," Kirschoff explained, flapping his coat to cool off his body. "We get *real* winter there. Not whatever this is." He gestured toward the door.

Vic opened her mouth to argue the point. Erin raised her brows. "Do you remember how cold you were on the cruise?"

"Well… yes."

"You're always saying that I complain about the heat when it's mild. Well, the same goes for you when you went to a colder climate. You thought it was really cold when someone from there would think it was just pleasant autumn weather."

Sally, one of the waitresses, ushered them to a booth and handed out menus. "Just give me a shout when you've decided what you want."

Hans removed his coat and tugged his collar away from his throat. "I'm glad that we're doing this in the winter. I'd hate to see your weather in the summer."

Erin nodded sagely. "It gets a mite warm," she told him, imitating Vic's accent.

They both laughed.

～

Once the table was spread with food and everyone had exclaimed over and discussed the dishes, Erin turned the conversation to the competition.

"We need to know what the contest rules are going to be," she told Kirschoff.

"You will have plenty of time to read through the rules closer to the time," he told her, making a brushing-away gesture. "Tonight is just relaxing and fun."

"A lot of people are talking about entering the contest. I need to know whether people qualify or not."

"Anyone qualifies. Anyone who wants to try to make something for the contest is welcome to do it. They just have to fill out an entry form."

"But not everybody can take part, can they?" Erin said. "What about friends and family of the judges? What about employees at Auntie Clem's? Or employees of any of the sponsors? Are they allowed?"

"We are going to be very open." Kirschoff drew his hands apart to indicate something large. "We don't want to be cutting a lot of people out because of their relationships. To be honest..."

he went on delicately, "I don't think that you are going to find anyone on the mountain not related to one of the judges, one way or another."

Vic laughed merrily. "That's one way to put it."

Erin remembered Mary Lou telling her that if she was related to Clementine, she was kin to half the mountain. After reading through some of Clementine's genealogical research, Erin realized that this was not an overstatement. The families living in Bald Eagle Falls had, for the most part, lived there and intermarried for many generations. Erin saw names that were repeated over and over again in the family tree charts, and they were names that she knew from her neighborhood and the customers at the bakery. Erin would never have gone so far as to call them inbred, but many families had lived in or around Bald Eagle falls for hundreds of years. They came, they saw, they stayed.

"So, no, I don't think we are going to have rules saying that the entrants are not allowed to be friends, families, or employees of the judges or the sponsors," Kirschoff reassured her. "Everybody is going to be. We have multiple judges to help fend off any accusations of impropriety."

"I think you're going to get a lot of entries," Vic said. "A lot of people were talking about it today. If even half of them follow through and make something for the competition, it's going to be big."

"I hope so," Kirschoff agreed, with a firm nod. "It should be the talk of the mountain for months to come. We are going to put on a competition like no one has ever seen here before."

"How are you going to do that when you only have a few weeks to prepare?" Erin challenged. "You have to get the word out, and venues booked, get the press there… is it going to be bigger than the Fall Fair? Bigger than the 4H rodeo? We may be small, but there are a lot of fun events going on around Bald Eagle Falls. People draw together and everyone contributes."

"There is a lot to do, but we've got the money and the staff to do it. Most of that is already planned, it's just a matter of starting the ball rolling."

"Did you hear that a bunch of the group from the cruise are going to come watch?" Vic asked Erin. "Not just Clayton, but a lot of them."

Kirschoff raised his brows with interest.

"No, I hadn't heard." Erin smiled encouragingly. She was sure that Vic would be happy to see all of her friends again. And Erin didn't need to feel like they were going to take Vic away from her, because she and Vic were judging the competition together. Vic would have to be careful not to show them any favoritism.

But Erin couldn't help feeling just a little twinge of jealousy at hearing that Vic's new friends from the cruise were going to be invading Bald Eagle Falls.

Bald Eagle Falls was her territory.

She felt just the tiniest twinge of jealousy. That was all.

$\mathscr{E}$rin kept an eye on the clock to make sure she was home in plenty of time to get to bed and get enough sleep before going back to the bakery the next morning. She always had to be careful to give herself enough time to settle in and get to sleep. Her sleep had been poor ever since finding Mr. Ingersoll's body. And worse yet since Terry had been attacked. Characters on TV might be able to roll with punches finding a newly dead body every week, but Erin found that her exposures to violent crime made it harder to deal with, not more used to it.

Of course, they had ordered a lot of dishes to sample and there were plenty of leftovers. She and Vic split them up to take home to their men. Chef Kirschoff didn't want any to take back to the motel with him.

"No midnight snacks for me," he told Erin, patting his stomach ruefully. "I will not be the chef who indulges too much and ends up weighing three hundred pounds."

Erin nodded her understanding. At her height, she had to watch what she ate very carefully. Every extra pound looked like two. Or more. Vic's height and faster metabolism were far more forgiving. "Your feet will thank you," she told Kirschoff. "I don't know how some of those cooks manage to stay on their feet all day."

"Yes, you're right," Kirschoff agreed. "The more you weigh, the harder it is to prepare food and supervise in the kitchen. You can't do everything sitting on a stool. Working in a kitchen involves lots of movement, going from the cold room to the kitchen, the sink, the different stations, and the restaurant. You are constantly moving from one place to another, and I don't know how anyone carrying an extra hundred pounds or more can do it."

So Erin had plenty of leftover Chinese food for Terry when she got home.

She found him on the couch again—or still—but no longer watching TV. He had fallen asleep sitting up and was listing to one side. Erin knew that she wouldn't be able to shift his position without waking him up; she had tried before. He was going to have a crick in his neck when he eventually did wake up. And that could potentially make his headache that much worse again.

She tiptoed past him to the kitchen but, as soon as she crossed the threshold into the tiled area, Orange Blossom hurried in, meowing loudly, as if he hadn't been fed all day. Of course, Erin knew better. He often tried to tell Terry that Erin had forgotten to feed him, and Terry had fallen for it a few times before he realized that the cat lied. Erin had fed Blossom before she went to work and when she had returned home. She would give him just a little more dry food before she went to bed and, hopefully, that would keep him quiet for the night and he wouldn't be complaining and asking for more if she had to get up to the commode or if Terry were back and forth.

"You be quiet," she whispered to Orange Blossom, quickly putting the Chinese food container in the fridge, hoping to get to the pantry to freshen Orange Blossom's dish before he woke Terry up.

"Erin?" Terry called out sleepily. "Are you home?"

"Yes, in the kitchen." Erin poked her head out the doorway to wave to him. "Sorry, I tried to keep him quiet."

"He works better than a burglar alarm."

"Oh. Speaking of which, I haven't armed it yet. If you're getting up, would you mind…?"

"Do I smell ginger chicken?"

"You sure do."

"Then I'm getting up."

Erin smiled. She went back and retrieved the Chinese food from the fridge. She heard Terry groan as he pushed himself up from the couch. He went to the front door and armed the burglar alarm and then joined her in the kitchen.

"How was your dinner?" He was rubbing his forehead slowly. His head was obviously still bothering him.

"It was good. So nice to see Chef Kirschoff again."

"Aren't you two on a first-name basis?"

"Yes… but I can't help thinking of him as Chef Kirschoff, even if I manage to call him Hans to his face."

He nodded and sat down at the table. Erin handed him the box of Chinese food and a fork. He opened it up and started picking out the pieces of ginger chicken.

"Mmm. I'm glad you didn't eat all of this."

Erin sat down with him, sighing. It felt good to sit down with him at the end of the day. She didn't realize how much she worried about him while they were apart until she could be with him and know that he was okay. She wondered if he felt the same way about her when they were apart. Though she had mostly healed from her physical injuries after the car rollover, he knew she still struggled with emotional issues.

"You look tired," he observed. He rubbed his eyes and yawned.

"You look a little tired yourself."

"I don't know if I'll be able to go back to sleep, or if that's it for the day."

"You should try, though. You obviously needed the extra sleep."

He nodded. "I will… but I don't know if my body will let me

sleep any more. It seems like it wants to sleep when I should be awake and won't sleep when I want to."

"I know. The doctor said sometimes that happens with head injuries. It's just your brain's way of trying to heal."

He picked out a few more pieces of chicken. "I wonder if that's just something they say to any symptoms a patient is having. 'Oh yes, that's normal, it will probably go away eventually.' I'm not sure they really know anything. They certainly aren't doing anything to treat it."

"You have sleeping pills."

"Yes… and you know how you feel about taking the sleeping pills they prescribed for you."

Erin shrugged. She hated the way they made her feel. Even if they worked, she still felt so groggy and muddled in the morning that it wasn't worth it. She would rather feel tired in the morning than have that gross, hungover feeling.

Terry didn't react the same way to the pills as she did, but he had his own reasons for not wanting to take them.

CHAPTER 7

$\mathcal{A}$fter work the next day, Erin went with Terry in his truck to pick up some supplies from the grocery store. She was working from a list, but she stopped when she saw a familiar slim, neatly-dressed woman with a helmet of gray hair.

Mary Lou Cox was in the dairy aisle and Erin didn't know whether to avoid her, greet her, or pretend that she hadn't seen her. She stopped and Terry bumped into her.

He looked up from his phone and glanced around. "What is it? Did you forget something?"

"Uh… no. I just…" Erin motioned at Mary Lou.

Terry raised his brows, not understanding her reluctance at first. He hadn't been around when Mary Lou had reamed Erin out for mentioning her son Joshua to Officer Terry Piper during his investigation of a rash of burglaries before Christmas.

Erin hadn't meant to implicate Joshua. She had just been worrying over something someone else had said to her but, as a result, Terry had invited Joshua to the police department to ask him what he might know about the burglaries.

She had told Terry that Mary Lou was upset about it, but she hadn't given him any details. Mary Lou had stopped coming to the bakery and had not had a civil discussion with Erin since then.

Mary Lou had been a friend, and Erin didn't know what to do or say that would help the situation. She had done her best to support Mary Lou through her difficult times; her husband having to be committed to an institution, Campbell being arrested on drug charges, and then… the problems with Joshua.

Erin looked around, trying to decide what else she could get while Mary Lou was in the dairy aisle. She could come back for her dairy ingredients later. She started to turn the buggy around. Terry put his hand on it to prevent her from going back. He looked at her steadily.

"Don't run away."

"I don't want a scene. I don't want to cause any trouble."

"You're not causing a scene or making trouble. You're here to buy groceries, just like everyone else. Don't let someone else push you around."

Erin looked down at her buggy, swallowing. She knew it was cowardly to keep avoiding Mary Lou. But she didn't like conflict. She had come to hate all kinds of conflict when she was in foster care. Raised voices or threatening body language sent her running for the hills. Growing up hadn't changed the way she felt, even if she didn't physically run away anymore.

She did not want to be in conflict with Mary Lou. Or anyone.

"Come on," Terry said gently. He tugged the cart forward, stepping ahead of her to guide her along. Erin didn't have to listen to him. She could pull back. She could let him take the cart and she could turn around and go to another part of the store. Or out to the truck. Or home.

But she knew he was right. She shouldn't let Mary Lou's anger keep her from completing her tasks. Sooner or later, she had to face the other woman. It wouldn't be at the bakery or at the First Baptist Church, but they were bound to run into each other sooner or later in a small town like Bald Eagle Falls.

She reluctantly let Terry guide her forward. Erin picked up the butter and cream cheese that she needed. They continued down the aisle to the cream and milk. Mary Lou saw their approach.

"Evening, Mrs. Cox," Terry greeted.

Mary Lou's nostrils flared. She smoothed her tunic-shirt over her hips, looking the two of them over. "Officer Piper," she said crisply.

Erin looked intently at the refrigerated shelves.

"Nice night," Terry offered.

"Lovely."

Erin swallowed. She just wanted to get out of there. She grabbed a carton of cream, even though it wasn't the brand she usually got, and reached for a gallon of milk.

Terry and Mary Lou both looked toward her, not saying anything to her. Erin avoided looking at their faces. Her eyes were hot with tears and she was finding it hard to catch her breath. She put the supplies in her basket and pushed it forward, pulling it out of Terry's grasp. She rounded the end of the aisle and hurried down the next one, even though she didn't need anything there.

"Erin."

She ignored Terry's call and kept going. On the next aisle, she stopped and looked at the packages of sugar, but tears blurred her vision, keeping her from seeing anything more than the product names in big, bold type.

Terry touched her back, taking care not to startle her. "Erin. It's okay. Everything is fine."

"Mary Lou was a friend. I know she's always been a little cool; she doesn't share her feelings easily. But I was there for her when Campbell was arrested. I was there when Roger…"

"I know. You've been a loyal friend to her. And time will heal this rift. So she's upset about Joshua being questioned. Most of the children in town ended up being interviewed, even the young ones like Peter. She'll get past it sooner or later."

"But that doesn't mean she'll get over being mad at me. She was really angry about me talking to you about Joshua. And I… just don't know what to do about that. I don't know how to fix it."

"It's not your responsibility to make her get over it. If she's holding on to that anger, it's going to hurt her, not you. She's the one who will suffer from those negative feelings."

Erin swiped at a couple of tears that leaked out onto her cheeks. "And she's the only one suffering?"

Terry took her head between both of his hands and kissed her forehead. He used his thumbs to wipe the tears away. "You have a tender heart. It will work itself out eventually. Let it go and don't stress about it. I promise it will all be worked out eventually."

Erin sniffled. She put her hands over his for a moment. Then she nodded, took a deep breath, and pressed onward.

She had mostly gotten herself together by the time she reached the cashier at the front of the store. Sue Anne scanned her items through, smiling and chattering about the weather and inconsequential things. She paused as she ran through the last few items and leaned forward, closer to Erin.

"It was so nice to see you at the candlelight service at First Baptist on Christmas Eve," she told Erin. "I was hoping that we might see more of you…"

"Uh… no." Erin shook her head. She glanced at Terry. "I was just… I wanted to join Officer Piper there, share it with him. But I'm not going to start going regularly." She paused, weighing her words. It wasn't the first time since Christmas she had faced these questions. The citizens of Bald Eagle Falls, even the ones she barely knew, were remarkably persistent in their expectation that she would convert to Christianity and start going to services at First Baptist like all of the respectable women. "I'm still an atheist," she told Sue Anne. "That hasn't changed."

Sue Anne sighed and shook her head. "You'd make a great Baptist," she said, as if she might be able to tempt Erin into it. "Maybe someday…"

Erin and Terry picked up the packed grocery bags from the counter.

"Don't hold your breath," Erin advised.

otices had been published and, if everyone hadn't already been talking about the contest, they were now.

In addition to the actual food preparation and judging, there were a number of community events being held for the children: science experiments, a family dance, an eating competition, and a traditional Tennessean BBQ.

"I'm going to make wild raspberry ice cream," Bella Prost told Erin excitedly. She was one of Erin's employees. Erin had been worried she wouldn't be allowed to enter the competition because of their relationship. But Chef Kirschoff and the official rules had assured her that there was no problem with any of her employees joining the competition, so Bella was excited to work out what she was going to do. "You can make the ice cream a few different ways —you can use the dry ice to freeze the ingredients by chilling them from the outside of the bowl, or you can actually stir dry ice into the ingredients and freeze them that way. Then it kind of bubbles and carbonates and makes the ice cream light and foamy."

"I don't know if I would want to eat it if dry ice was stirred in," Erin said uncertainly. "If a piece didn't dissolve, you could burn your mouth, couldn't you?"

"Well, yes, you have to make sure that it all dissolves. But it's not that hard to do. And it's not against the rules. If it was really dangerous, it would be against the rules."

Erin nodded. "I didn't say it was. I just haven't heard of people making it that way before. It always makes me nervous when they put it in drinks to make them fog."

Bella nodded. "No one is going to get hurt in this competition," she promised.

All day, people were coming through the bakery, talking about who was entering and what they were going to make. Erin was asked her opinion constantly, which she wasn't sure was proper. They really shouldn't be asking her about her preferences, thinking that they could get ahead of the other contestants by knowing what she liked or didn't like.

As it was, Erin would eat pretty much anything, having learned as a child to eat whatever was served to her, and then as an adult experimenting with different cuisines and cooking methods. She'd made her share of disasters. And when she was poor, barely making ends meet, she had to eat what she made, good or not. She didn't have the option of just throwing it out. So she'd learned to eat anything that wasn't absolutely inedible.

"I think everyone in town is joining the contest," Vic told Erin during a lull when they were both in the kitchen, taking baking out of the oven. "Or if they're not entering something, then they're helping out with the other activities. It's like a circus!"

"It sure is."

The bells over the door tinkled, and Erin looked through the doorway to see who had come in. She looked for a moment at the new faces, trying to place them. Not anyone she knew from Bald Eagle Falls, yet she thought that they were vaguely familiar, as if she had seen them somewhere else.

Then it came back to her, and she realized that she had seen them before. On the Alaskan cruise.

"I think your friends are here," she told Vic.

Vic left the cookies that she had been arranging on the cooling rack and went out to the front. Erin heard her squeal as she saw the friends she had made on the cruise.

"Wow! You're here!" Another squeal. "All of you!"

There were hugs and back slapping and a few kissed cheeks as Vic made her way around the group, greeting everyone. Erin waited until the excited reunion cooled a little, then went out to say her hellos. She poked her head out tentatively, not wanting to interrupt anything. Vic saw her.

"Oh, and you guys remember Erin, right? Erin, all the gang from the cruise…"

"You're going to have to remind me of your names," Erin said. "I don't remember them all, and with everything that happened back then…" There were a lot of reasons she hadn't memorized everyone's names.

"Okay, I'll go through them," Vic said, "but everyone should remind you the next few times they talk to you. Because getting all of the names at once is a bit overwhelming."

Erin nodded gratefully. She knew she wasn't going to remember them all without a few reminders, no matter how many memory tricks she tried to use.

"This is Clayton," Vic said, putting her arm around a boy with a red knit cap and a pale, angular face. He was a couple of inches taller than Vic was, and she was tall for a girl. "He's the one who wrote and said he was coming. He's going to enter something into the contest, right Clayton?"

He nodded seriously. "Yeah, you bet. It's gonna be cool."

All of the treats were going to be pretty cool. Some of them frozen. Erin nodded and shook hands with him. He had long, spidery fingers and a firm grip. "Nice to see you again."

"This is Melanie," Vic motioned to the girl standing next to

Clayton in the group. She was a black woman in a flared plaid skirt and a green blazer, with no jacket. Very chic.

Erin vaguely remembered her from the cruise. She nodded again. "Melanie."

"And Jack," Vic introduced the heavier man next in line. He had some scraggly whiskers on his chin like he was trying to grow a beard, but it wasn't coming in very well.

Jack smiled a greeting. "They/them."

Erin blinked. "What?"

"My preferred pronouns. I'm nonbinary."

Erin had only a vague idea of what Jack meant by this, but nodded as if it were clear. "Okay…"

"I love cooking. Can't say I'm much good at it, but I'm going to take a run at the contest too."

"Great. I look forward to tasting what you come up with."

Jack grinned as if she'd given them the best compliment ever. She smiled back and looked at the next person in the circle.

"Norman." The imposing-looking man thrust his hand forward with such force and suddenness that Erin jumped, flinching back.

"Oh. Sorry. Hi, Norman."

He took her hand in his, and then sandwiched it with his other hand, giving her a hearty two-handed shake. "It's so good to see you again, Erin. How have you been since the cruise? I know you weren't feeling really well at the end there. Everything back to normal now?"

Erin nodded. She didn't know how normal she could claim to be now, but she was definitely feeling better than she had been while she was on the cruise. Things had gotten pretty dicey toward the end.

"Yeah. Good. I'm good."

Vic introduced the last few people in the group, but Erin had already reached saturation point. If she tried to remember all of the names, she was going to forget the first few that she had learned.

"Well, it's so cool that you all got back together here. It's neat to see relationships that started somewhere like on a cruise continue afterward. People get so busy and go their different directions, but you guys have all kept in touch and are doing something else together again. That's amazing."

Everybody was smiling and chatting with each other; they had an easygoing, casual manner that Erin envied. She always felt like she had to try so hard at relationships or they wouldn't work out. But there didn't seem to be tension between members of Vic's group of friends.

"I'm glad that you're all here for the contest," she offered. "I hope you have a good time and do really well."

Vic promised her friends that she would meet them after closing for drinks and dinner, and they set out to explore the town. As Vic and Erin prepared for the afternoon rush, Charley came in through the front door, at a hurried pace, perpetually late. Erin hadn't been expecting her, so she didn't know what Charley thought she was late for. Maybe it was just habit.

"Hey, partner," Charley greeted. "How is my favorite half-sister?"

Erin shrugged. "Same as usual," she said cautiously. It wasn't like Charley had any other half-sister. Not living. At least, not that they knew of. With all of the family secrets Erin had unraveled, nothing would surprise her anymore.

Charley pushed back her hair, longer than Erin's but the same dark brown color. "How are things coming along with the contest? Everybody is talking about it."

"They are," Erin agreed. "You'd think these parts had never seen a cooking contest before."

"Well, it is a big one," Charley pointed out. "You can't sneeze at a two hundred and fifty thousand dollar grand prize."

Erin felt her jaw drop. "Is that what it is? I heard that the prizes were going to be good, but I didn't know they had been announced yet."

"I don't know if they have been officially announced," Charley said loftily, "but I have it on good authority that the top prize in each category is two fifty G's. That's not anything to sneeze at."

"No. It's not."

Charley leaned on the display case, getting closer to Erin. And she couldn't exactly tell Charley not to lean on it when she was Erin's partner in the business. Charley had been there for Erin when Erin had thought she was going to lose Auntie Clem's. Erin couldn't let herself forget that. Not that Charley would have let her.

"I'm going to enter," Charley confided.

"In the contest?" Erin looked at Vic, wondering if she could object. But Chef Kirschoff had already told her that anyone could enter the contest. Even Erin's half-sister and partner in the business. So there wasn't anything Erin could say about it. "That's great."

"Yeah. I figure I've already got one of the judges in my pocket," Charley said with a laugh.

"Which one?" Vic asked dryly.

Charley laughed loudly. Erin couldn't help smiling at Vic's comment.

"Don't you go repeating that to anyone," Erin warned Charley. "I don't want people accusing me of favoritism. Even if you're technically allowed to enter the contest… I might have to recuse myself from casting a vote on your entry."

Charley sobered up. "All entries are blind, so you won't even know which one it is."

"That's probably a good thing," Erin admitted.

"I may just surprise you. I'm a good cook, you know."

Erin had always assumed that she got her culinary skills from her father's side of the family—she had inherited Clementine's storefront from her father's side after all. As a little girl, she had 'worked' with Clementine in her tea room, but neither of her parents had shown any interest in baking or cooking. But Charley was her mother's daughter, and she did seem to have a knack. Even though she had known nothing about gluten-free baking before partnering with Erin, she had quickly caught on and was proficient when she put in a shift. She was a night owl, so Erin and Vic had quickly learned not to put her on a morning shift. But as long as they didn't schedule her before noon, she would usually get there.

"You are a good cook," Erin agreed. "But you're going to have some pretty heavy competition."

"As long as I don't have to compete against you or the chef, I think I've got a pretty good chance."

CHAPTER 9

There wasn't a lot of time to prepare for the competition. Erin didn't know much about carbon dioxide or making carbonated beverages before the competition was announced, but she was learning a lot.

"There are a few ways to carbonate drinks," she told Terry as they relaxed on the couch. He wasn't anywhere near as interested as she hoped he would be in all of the details, but she needed to talk through the processes to firmly entrench the details in her brain, and he was, at least, being a good sport about it. "Of course, the traditional way of making them didn't involve pumping CO2 through flavored water."

"I don't imagine so," Terry agreed with a serious nod. "So what did they do?"

"Fermentation. Just like with wine or beer. Yeast converts the sugars, creating carbon dioxide, and that produces the fizz."

"I see. I prefer the higher-proof stuff."

Erin chuckled. "So do a lot of people. But you can't exactly give that to children. Or drink it while you're on the job. So the new way of producing soft drinks is to inject carbon dioxide right into it, rather than relying on a chemical reaction. It's faster and there is no danger of producing something that's going to make granny drunk."

"Too bad."

She favored him with a glare. "You're not taking this seriously."

"Sorry." He wiped the smile from his face and gave her a flat, blank stare. "Continue with your story, ma'am."

"Those are the first two ways that you can make a carbonated beverage for the contest."

"And the third way?"

"Putting solid carbon dioxide directly into a drink."

He considered that for a moment. "Putting dry ice in."

"Exactly. It reacts with the water and bubbles and makes fog and is very dramatic. So some people entering the contest will do that."

"Very dramatic. Too bad they didn't do it for Halloween."

"That would have been a lot of fun," Erin agreed. She had thought of that herself. "We could have had all kinds of witchy drinks. Although, maybe the Christians wouldn't like that. They can be pretty uptight around here about anything witch-related."

It wasn't the first time they had discussed the fact, particularly since Adele, Erin's groundskeeper, happened to be a practicing Wiccan, something those in the know kept from becoming public knowledge. They didn't want Adele run out of town, as she had been from other towns.

"True. Might not have been able to spin that. Too bad, because it would have been a cool Halloween activity."

Erin pushed a stray lock of hair back over her ear. She looked at the notes she had made as she had taken her crash course on carbonation.

"So, they're allowed to use any of the three methods for the competition?" Terry asked.

"Yes. That means that the people who are doing fermentation get a head start. They need a couple of weeks longer than the rest of the contestants to get their brews going."

"Are they all in different classes, or do the fermented drinks get judged against the carbonated ones?"

"They are all together, to get the grand prize."

"Two hundred and fifty thousand dollars."

"Yeah."

"That will be a nice little injection of cash into Bald Eagle Falls. So many people have had such a difficult time lately."

"If someone from Bald Eagle Falls wins. It could be someone from one of the other towns or outlying areas."

"Well, with two of the judges coming from Bald Eagle Falls, hopefully the Bald Eagle Falls entries will have a *bit* of an advantage over the others."

"We won't know which entries are from Bald Eagle Falls. It's all supposed to be judged blind."

"And you haven't heard what anyone around town is going to enter."

"Uh… well, yes, I guess I have."

"There you go."

"But that doesn't mean that they'll be the only entries. If someone is making a raspberry ice cream, that doesn't mean they'll be the only raspberry ice cream entry."

"I suppose," Terry agreed. He shifted his feet, forcing K9 to move. "Come on, buddy, you don't need to lie right on top of my feet."

K9 groaned and moved away slightly but, after Terry settled again, K9 readjusted, and Terry's feet were soon nestled snugly under K9's body again.

The official kick-off ceremonies for the contest wouldn't be held until the week that everyone would be submitting their entries but, since the fermented drinks had to be started early, Erin and Vic had a dinner with the other judges and officials in Whitewater Junction where the contest would be held.

Erin hadn't been to Whitewater before, even though it wasn't far from Bald Eagle Falls. She always drove the opposite direction, into the city for supplies.

It was a nice little town, similar to Bald Eagle Falls in many respects. Though, of course, it didn't have a gluten-free bakery. Sam Litwin, the mayor of Whitewater, was curious about the bakery, and how Erin had managed to keep a specialty bakery like Auntie Clem's making a profit.

"We sell a lot of stuff to people who do not have to eat a special diet," Erin explained to him. "The majority of our clientele don't have any dietary restrictions."

"Ah." Sam nodded. He pushed up the sleeves of his dress shirt and tugged at his collar, looking uncomfortable. "So you sell regular baking too. I wondered."

"No. Everything we sell is gluten-free. And most of it is free of the top ten allergens as well. And we have some that are vegan, or low carb, or that are appropriate for people with diabetes or other special requirements."

"But if you only offer gluten-free baking…" Sam trailed off, frown lines between his brows. "That means that everybody has to buy gluten-free, or go somewhere else."

"Yeah. And it's easier for people to just buy at the bakery anyway, even if they don't follow a special diet, because otherwise, they have to go into the city. Or just buy factory-made stuff from the grocery store."

"And that doesn't bother people?"

"There was some resistance at first," Vic contributed. "But people get used to it. Like everything else in a small town. You can either buy locally or spend extra time and money to buy things in the city. Some people will buy up baking when they go into the city and store it in the freezer until they need it, but…"

"That's not as nice as buying freshly-baked bread," Sam finished. "Although… I don't know what the gluten-free stuff is like. Maybe people prefer frozen stuff from the city to having to eat the gluten-free baking. I've heard…" His cheeks flushed noticeably. "I've heard that it isn't the best stuff. It can be gritty or tough. Or falls apart the minute you touch it."

"Depends on the recipe and who is making it," Vic told him. "We've got some really great recipes. You wouldn't even guess that they are gluten-free. And if you can't tell the difference, why would you drive into the city to get wheat bread?"

"Hmm." Sam nodded. He picked up his glass and had a drink. "I suppose. I think it's amazing that you've been able to keep that bakery open—let alone make a profit from it. That really is extraordinary. Especially in today's economy."

Erin nodded, her face warm. "Thank you."

"Economy?" Chef Kirschoff's voice was raised over the buzz of conversation at the long table. "Who's talking shop? We're supposed to be getting to know each other, not talking business."

Erin's face got hot. She looked away, embarrassed at being called out. Chef Kirschoff looked down the table and saw her. "I know it's hard for business people to get together and not discuss such enthralling things as the economy, but you're here to have a good time and get to know each other on a personal level. You're not here interviewing for a loan. Let's talk about food!"

"We were," Vic protested. "You just heard one word out of the whole conversation."

"Try to keep that boss of yours in line. I know it's impossible to tell Erin Price what to do, but do your best…"

Erin put her hands over her flaming cheeks. "I was just answering the mayor's questions…"

"She's right," Sam said, lifting his hand in acknowledgment. "It was my fault. I'll stop talking about business."

Kirschoff gave them a broad grin and nodded. He turned his head to talk to someone down the table in the opposite direction. Erin rubbed her cheeks, even though she knew that wouldn't remove the flush of embarrassment.

"Don't worry about Hans," Vic laughed. "He's just teasing."

"I know, I know!"

"What's even more impressive about your business is that it

was already burned to the ground once," Sam contributed, clearly not worried about following Kirschoff's instructions. "Most businesses would have gone under at that point. How did you keep it afloat?"

Erin glanced down the table at Chef Kirschoff to make sure that his attention was still elsewhere and dropped her voice to try to keep him from hearing that they were still discussing business. What else was she supposed to talk about? She worried about Auntie Clem's Bakery almost every waking moment, and Sam asked her a direct question about it. If he wanted to talk about her business instead of the contest or more personal information, that wasn't her fault.

"I would have gone under for sure if it weren't for Charley."

"Who is he?"

"She. Charley is my half-sister, and… well, to make a long story short, she inherited the other bakery in town, the one that would have been my competition. She was going to run it as a competing business… which probably wouldn't have been very good for me. But she doesn't have any business experience and, after Auntie Clem's burned down… she offered to become my partner. She had the space, so we didn't have to buy another property or rebuild. She injected some capital into the business, and I got money from insurance for the fire. So we managed to keep it going. But I couldn't have done it without her, even though Auntie Clem's had been doing pretty well before that. We just wouldn't have survived a rebuild."

Sam nodded. He buttered a roll and tore pieces off of it while they waited for the main course to be served. "Now, you can't eat this, can you?" he indicated the roll in his hand.

Erin smiled. "Actually, I don't follow a gluten-free diet. I can still eat anything I want to. I started the bakery for other people. People who don't have that choice."

"Then why don't you do both? Gluten-free and conventional? If you don't have to eat gluten-free, don't you think it would do better if you had a wider offering?"

"No. You end up with problems if you are cooking both gluten-free and gluten products in the same pans and equipment. Even having wheat flour particles in the air can be a problem for some people. And the amount of gluten in a crumb of wheat bread could be enough to make someone with severe celiac disease sick. If I want to serve the people who are severely affected, not just people who decided to try a gluten-free diet to lose weight or because it is a fad, then I have to keep the kitchen completely gluten-free. No gluten flours of any kind on the premises, nothing with gluten being cooked in your pans or mixed in the bowls."

"That seems pretty extreme. You could just wash them in between."

"It's not worth the risk. People in the area know that my bakery is completely gluten-free, so they can trust it."

Waiters arrived bearing plates and started to place them along the table. Erin sat back and waited for hers.

 rin and Vic had taken several days off from Auntie Clem's, knowing that the dinner and other events that were planned for the judges and other officials would end up running late into the evening. Erin would need several days to get back on track after staying up late just one night.

She was yawning through the welcoming speech and a tall, severe-looking woman reading through the competition rules at long, tedious length. Erin was doing the best she could not to fall asleep in her chair, but she kept catching her eyes closing and her head tipping down, then bobbing up suddenly. Keeping her up late, feeding her, and then reading long, boring rules was a perfect recipe for putting her to sleep—something she needed to remember the nights that she had insomnia.

She got to her feet, blinking hard to try to wake herself up. Vic's eyes, focused off somewhere in the distance, turned to her questioningly. "You okay?"

Erin nodded. "Just need to walk around, or I'm going to fall asleep."

Vic grinned. "Tell me about it."

Erin went to the back of the room and wandered slowly along

the back wall. But her eyes were still closing even as she paced back and forth. She left the room and went out to the lobby, then out the hotel's front door.

The air was cool and refreshing. She wasn't wearing a jacket but, having grown up in the north, she had better cold tolerance than Vic. She took a few long breaths of the cold air, waiting for it to wake her up. She yawned and breathed all of the air out in a steady stream. A few minutes in the fresh air, and she should be more awake.

"I don't think I could listen to that hot air balloon blather on for another minute," a voice said at her elbow.

Erin jumped and turned quickly. A woman was leaning against the building, a cigarette between her fingers. She gestured toward Erin with it.

"Out for some fresh air?"

Erin never could understand smokers saying that they were going out for fresh air when they wanted a smoke. When they would clearly be smoking polluted air.

"I don't smoke."

"I didn't either before this started," the woman joked. "What was that, like twenty years ago?"

"It has been a long night," Erin agreed. She looked at the woman's name badge on her lapel to see if they were both there for the same event, or whether the woman was there for some other lecture.

Beryl Batcombe. It sounded vaguely British. She was part of the CO_2 cook-off—or cool-off, as they were now calling it. She had dark hair and eyes, a slightly round face and well-aligned teeth. She was wearing a knitted raspberry-colored hat. She was taller than Erin, heavier, a solid-looking woman who would have been at home doing chores on a farm. Her eyes were narrow and fierce.

"I'm Erin," she introduced herself, holding out her hand. "I'm one of the—"

"One of the judges," Beryl finished for her, blowing smoke in her face. "Yes, dear, so am I."

Erin backed away from her, turning her head to the side and giving up on the idea of shaking hands. She tried to decide whether she needed to stay there and talk to Beryl because she had started the conversation, or whether she could find somewhere else to stand where she could get some actual fresh air.

"Sorry, I haven't met everyone yet. I know Chef Kirschoff wanted everyone to meet and get acquainted, but it's kind of hard with the long tables they had us at. You can really only talk to the people beside or across from you."

Beryl nodded. "I don't think it's been very well-organized," she said brusquely, "Too fast to get everything done properly. You need people who have done this before, many times, to be on top of all of the details. An event like this should have six to twelve months of run-up. Having only a few weeks… that's just crazy."

Erin had to agree. When she was planning an event with a lot of moving parts, she started well ahead of time. She would have lists written down and reference material in a binder. If she'd been pulling together a big event, she would definitely have started six months or further out, as Beryl had suggested.

"So are you from Whitewater?" she asked Beryl.

"Yes, I'm one of the locals. And you're from Bald Eagle Falls. But you're a transplant."

Erin hesitated. She didn't really feel like explaining, but she didn't want Beryl thinking that she was an outsider. She was as much a part of Bald Eagle Falls as anyone else.

"My family is from here. I lived here as a child. But when my parents died, I was put into foster care and I ended up mostly growing up in the north. I came back here after my aunt died. She left me the storefront where I started Auntie Clem's Bakery." Erin shrugged. "So… I guess I was a transplant for a while, but now I'm not. I left and then came back. I have… roots in these mountains."

"Ah. Well, there's no reason they shouldn't have picked you to help judge the contest. You *have* judged a contest before, haven't you?"

"No… I've entered contests before. But I've never been a judge. This is something that's new for me. Kind of exciting."

"You've never been a judge before." Beryl sighed audibly. "And what about the other judge from Bald Eagle Falls, you work with… *them* don't you? This… Vic person?"

"Yes, I work with Vic. She's a great cook. Good hard worker, and always there to help me out when I need something. We've been able to hire on some more help at Auntie Clem's now but, back in the beginning, it was just me and her…"

"Her," Beryl repeated flatly.

Erin shook her head. "What?"

"Her? Vic is a her?"

"Yes, Victoria. Sorry, I should have said that. It can be confusing if people think Vic is short for Victor."

"She's one of those kids that's all loosy-goosy about her sex, though, isn't she? Born a boy, but now she's decided to play at being a girl?"

Erin ground her teeth. She kept her mouth closed as she counted slowly to ten, giving Beryl what she hoped was a scathing glare. "Vic is transgender," she said. "I'd appreciate it if you'd use that language. It's not something to make fun of or for any of us to make light of. If you knew Vic…"

"Oh, I saw her at the dinner. Very pretty. Very convincing. But that doesn't change anything. That doesn't make her something she isn't."

"If you have a problem with it, maybe you should withdraw from judging the contest. If you feel like you couldn't work with a transgender person. If you can't show Vic respect, it would be best to back out now and give them time to replace you."

"So you're militant too," Beryl observed. "Well, now I know where you're coming from. I'm not going to back out of the contest. I worked hard to get this position, unlike others. If it's going to be a problem for you and *Victoria* to be on the panel with me, then maybe you are the ones who ought to step down."

Erin shook her head. Her anger at the way that Beryl talked about Vic instantly wiped out the drowsiness that she'd been feeling earlier. *No one* had the right to treat her friend that way.

Vic could tell something was wrong when Erin returned to the hall where the presentation was being held. Erin made her way back to her seat, her lips pressed tightly together. Vic raised her brows and mouthed, "What's wrong?"

Erin shook her head and sat down. It wasn't the time and place for that conversation. And if she started to talk about it, she was just going to get angrier. Best if she could get a little distance from it and relax for a few minutes. She listened carefully to the woman who was talking about the contest and their vision behind it. It was still just as dry as it had been before Erin went outside and, no matter how hard she tried to concentrate on it, it was still boring and didn't distract her from her anger at Beryl Batcombe.

It was torture but, eventually, they were released from their imprisonment. A big sigh went up from the assembled audience and everyone bounced quickly to their feet to talk with each other or get out of the stiflingly hot room. Vic put her hand on Erin's arm and, as they walked toward the door to make their escape, leaned in to whisper in Erin's ear.

"What is it? What happened?"

"Nothing. I'll tell you later."

"Tell me now! What was it?"

"At least let's go back to our room. I don't want to talk here in front of everyone else." Erin and Vic both looked around, but no one was hanging around them who appeared to be eavesdropping on their conversation. No one looked like they had the least interest in what Erin had to say.

"I think you're safe," Vic said dryly. "All anyone cares about right now is getting out of here and raiding the minibar in their rooms."

Erin wasn't a drinker, but if she were… She might even have been tempted by the overpriced bottles in the minibar. As it was, maybe if there were some chocolate in there…

Vic led the way back to their hotel room. They nodded to other officials for the contest in the elevator. Erin was too overwhelmed to remember anyone's names or why they were there. Their faces and names all ran together.

A few more elevator stops, and they were on their floor. They were the only ones who got off on the third floor. Vic found their room and swiped the key card.

"Well? Spill! What lit your hair on fire?"

"There is this other judge. Did you meet her? Beryl Batcombe."

"Beryl. No. I saw her, but we didn't talk. She was too far away from us."

Erin nodded. "Well, be glad. Do everything you can to avoid talking to her."

"That bad?"

"Yes."

"What did she say?"

Erin rolled her eyes toward the ceiling. That was the tricky part. Vic knew she was angry and Erin wouldn't get away with not giving her all of the details. But Erin hated to tell her the way that Beryl had been making backward comments about Vic's gender identity.

"She was just talking… being rude."

"What did she say? She sure got you riled up."

Erin sighed. She recounted Beryl's words and insinuations quickly, wanting to get them out of the way. Vic didn't act hurt or offended. She just rolled her eyes.

"People are going to talk," she said. "You know how it is in Bald Eagle Falls too. People are ignorant and uneducated, or they're willfully trying to hurt or irritate me. I don't care. I'm not going to give them the satisfaction. Beryl Batcombe can spin her wheels trying to talk crap about me, I'm not going to pay any attention. The only person it is going to reflect badly on is herself."

"I don't want her spreading that kind of talk around. I know that it's not exactly a secret, but I don't want people chattering on about it and nothing else. Why should anyone care about your identity, or Clayton's, or anyone else's? What difference does it make to any of them?"

"You know how people feel around here. They don't under-stand gender identity and they just want to convince me of the error of my ways. Repent and go back to the church. Put aside my foolish, childish ideas and find my way back to the truth."

"How can it be a sin to be who you are? What's wrong with that?"

"You don't have to convince me." Vic laughed. She went over to the minibar fridge to check it out. It was, unfortunately, not well-stocked. Vic poked through the nuts, candy, and tiny bottles, looking for a bedtime snack for the two of them. "You didn't happen to bring any bread and jam, did you?"

Erin sat down on one of the beds, then flopped back on it. Her body was tired, even if her brain was revved up again. "Unfor-tunately, no. But we could probably order something from room service if you're hungry. A peanut butter sandwich. Toast and jam."

"No. I don't want anyone cooking for me this late."

Erin grabbed the price list for the minibar off of the bedside table. "A sandwich would probably be cheaper than that stuff."

Vic took it from her and shook her head at the prices. "Good grief. Well, we can stay within budget if you have a packet of M&M's and I have a package of nuts. How does that sound?"

"It sounds like we should have brought snacks." Erin chuckled. "But, it's probably best if I avoid anything extra for the next couple of weeks. I want to be able to get through the contest without putting on any weight."

"I think you're too worried about it. You don't have to eat a whole bowl of anything. Just little tastes. You could even be like a wine taster and spit them out again."

"Yuck. I don't think so."

"We could all have spit buckets. You just taste the ice cream, and then spit it into the bucket and go on to the next one."

"Stop. No. No way."

The next morning, they were gathered for a tour of the restaurant that they were going to be using for food preparation and judging. Erin kept a sharp eye out for Beryl Batcombe but didn't see her.

"I don't think she showed up," Vic said, catching Erin's searching gaze. "She must have gotten drunk on her minibar and slept in this morning."

Or maybe she had decided to take Erin's advice and back out of the judging.

But Erin doubted it. She looked around one more time. Whatever the reason, Beryl appeared to have ducked out on the tour. Chef Kirschoff looked at his watch then finally shrugged.

"We're one short, but we're going to need to get this tour done if we're going to stay on schedule. She'll have to catch up on the rest later."

Erin heard him say something under his breath that sounded suspiciously like 'old bat,' but was probably just her name.

"Let's begin then," said the perky brunette who seemed to be some kind of party planner. There was a whole cadre of people taking care of all of the logistics. Erin supposed that the rest had been hired by the contest's chief sponsor, a company that sounded like a law firm, but Erin thought it was actually one of the big food service corporations.

"If everyone will follow me," the perky woman suggested. Everyone fell into place close behind her. She led them from the hotel to the sidewalk in front of the restaurant, Buttermilk Biscuits. They waited for her to tell them why Buttermilk had been picked and how its ambiance and reputation would contribute to the contest.

"My name is Sherry Vail," the woman introduced herself. "I know that you're all eager to get started today to get a full picture of why this contest was set up and how it is going to operate."

People looked around, but no one exactly agreed with her. They were eager to get it over with, anyway.

"Buttermilk Biscuits is one of the oldest restaurants in the Whitewater Junction area. Built in 1939, it is a great example of some of the ethnic cuisines that helped shape the Tennessee culture…"

Erin could barely focus on what Sherry was saying. Who cared how long the restaurant was there or how it had influenced the cuisine? They were going to eat ice cream and drink carbonated soft drinks. That wasn't exactly haute cuisine.

She looked around at the other businesses and buildings on what she assumed was Main Street. It was similar in a lot of ways to Bald Eagle Falls. Small, with the colorful, narrow buildings built right against each other, many of them with awnings to keep the brutal summer sun off of customers on the sidewalk. It might be a little older than Bald Eagle Falls, but not by a lot. Maybe there was a little more history there, or maybe the historical buildings had just been better preserved.

Vic caught her looking around at everything else and grinned, understanding her distraction. "Let's get a move on," she said under her breath. "The woman could talk the spots off a leopard."

"Maybe Beryl has the right idea. Maybe we should have stayed away this morning. It would be a lot easier to just say that we had slept in or got called in to Auntie Clem's."

"Shh," someone nearby hushed them like they were being noisy in a library. "Listen."

Erin and Vic looked at each other, both trying not to make the other laugh. It was such a ridiculous situation. They were adults, after all, not children who didn't know how to behave. They were there to get the details on the contest, not to be lectured on the local color.

Erin shifted her feet back and forth. What would she make for the contest if she were one of the contestants?

That got her brain going, and she was surprised when Vic tapped her arm to get her attention because everyone was going into the restaurant. Erin blew out her breath and followed the group. At last. She hoped that there was something hands-on, so she didn't have to keep listening to people lecturing.

They even made cooking boring. And Erin was never bored with cooking.

Her hopes were dashed when Sherry stopped everyone and continued her lecture, indicating the restaurant's decor, talking about the items on the menu, both traditional and new. They could have read about any of that in the papers that they had been given. In fact, most of what Sherry said was in the written materials, but she was intent on boring them to death by repeating every detail.

Erin inched her way toward the kitchen. It wasn't like she was budging into line. She just worked her way around the edge of the group so that she would be the closest to the door when they finally got on their way to the kitchen.

Sherry's voice went up and down, still perky, trying desperately to keep everyone's attention. But she had already lost it long ago. Everyone else seemed to be just as bored as Erin, shifting their feet, wanting to get on with the tour.

"Okay, we'll go into the kitchen now," Sherry directed,

motioning to the door Erin was standing close to. "Uh, Miss Price…"

She happily took the lead, pushing open the swinging doors and entering the kitchen's sacred realm. She realized that they weren't going to be in there to taste everything, though they would be allowed to check things out as the entrants were preparing dishes. There were cameras to provide top views, but sometimes there was nothing like getting close to the action.

Sherry began describing the various amenities of the kitchen.

"Is she serious?" Vic murmured. "We all have eyes. We can see how it's set up. It isn't like we've never seen a commercial kitchen before."

"I know," Erin agreed. She didn't want Vic voicing her complaint too loudly and being overheard. Or just getting shushed again. She looked around while Sherry talked, imagining how everything would look when there were multiple contestants preparing food in the kitchen.

There was a large, shiny door close to Erin, which she assumed was a freezer or cold room.

As Sherry told everyone about the ovens and where to find the cutlery, Erin tested the handle on the freezer. It was not locked. She pulled it harder. The mechanism made a noise that was too loud in her own ears. She didn't want everyone to turn around and ask her what she was doing. Erin turned her back to it, smiled, and waited a minute or two to make sure that everyone's attention was back on Sherry and hadn't been distracted by Erin's movements.

Of course, Auntie Clem's Bakery didn't have a freezer or cold room. They baked. The few frozen treats that they made were frozen in the small freezer of the kitchen fridge. It would have been great to be able to go into a cold room during the summer when the kitchen was sweltering hot from the combination of baking, the Tennessee climate, and running back and forth, looking after everything. She could just imagine being able to step into arctic temperatures in the middle of the day to suck all of the heat right out of her. It would be heavenly.

Erin gave the freezer door another twist, but found that she had already turned it as far as she could. She gave it a tug. It didn't come the first time. Erin didn't turn around to face the door, but gave it another pull. The door moved an inch. It wasn't open all the way, but she could feel the cold air starting to fall around her hand. Erin turned around and pulled the door slowly toward her.

The interior of the freezer was white with frost. Erin hadn't been sure whether the temperature would be turned down all the way past freezing, or whether they would be keeping it warmer, just a cold room for produce and food that was prone to spoilage. Definitely sub-freezing. Erin opened the door farther and looked at the shelves lining the cold room walls to see what they already had ready to go.

She wasn't usually that snoopy, but she had a thing about kitchens. And she was there to look around. It was part of her job, after all.

But there was something wrong.

CHAPTER 13

At first, she didn't know what it was. Her eyes skipped past what shouldn't be there, staying focused on the foodstuffs.

It could have been anything. A mannequin that was used during some kind of promotion. A few bits of clothing that someone had left behind by mistake.

Erin forced her eyes to focus. Forced them to stop looking at the rest of the freezer room and to focus on what she didn't want to.

She could still hear Sherry talking, going on as if Erin hadn't opened the door, that nobody had happened to notice her eagerness to get a look at everything that was behind the scenes.

Erin no longer wanted to see what was behind the scenes. She wished that she was standing outside the restaurant, bored while Sherry went on about its importance in Whitewater history and the shaping of the cuisine in that part of Tennessee.

Erin wasn't the first one in the freezer. She wasn't the only one who had apparently wanted to get a sneak peek before anyone else.

Beryl Batcombe wasn't back in her hotel room sleeping off a

drunk. She hadn't decided that she wasn't prepared to judge beside Erin and Vic and had backed out and gone home.

She was in the freezer. Just where she would be if she had been with the tour.

Erin could feel Vic behind her, pressing in for a look.

"No," Erin told her. "Don't come in here. Go back."

"I just want to see. We need to move in so that people can get in behind us."

"No." Erin blocked Vic's entrance.

"Erin, we're ready, Sherry said to come and have a look…"

"Vicky. No," Erin said firmly.

Vic frowned. "What's wrong?"

"You need to go out. No one can come in here."

"Sherry said we could now."

"No." Erin swallowed. "You need to go get help."

"Help?" Vic's face paled. "Erin, what is it? What kind of help? Do you need something…?"

"Beryl is in here."

"Beryl?" Vic tried to see around Erin. "What's she doing in there?"

Then the penny dropped. Vic's face became a mask. "Oh, no."

"Yes. See if they have EMS. Or a volunteer fire department. Or just… a doctor."

"Is she okay, Erin?" Vic's voice told Erin that she understood perfectly well that Beryl was not okay, even if her words were several steps behind her brain.

"No. Get the others out. And tell them we need help."

Vic turned, pushing back against the people who were pressing in on her from behind, trying to get in to see the freezer. There were protests. No anger, but certainly confusion. Vic pushed them along, repeating that no one was allowed to go in there and that they needed a doctor.

～

Erin was the only one in the room. Erin and Beryl. Erin wasn't sure why she didn't leave the freezer with everyone else. It wasn't like there was anything she could do for Beryl. But she felt like she couldn't leave the woman alone, no matter what state she was in.

Vic guarded the door from the other side. Erin knew she was having to put up with a lot more crap than Erin. There was no one to get after Erin but Vic herself, if she had wanted to. Instead, Vic stood in the doorway acting as gatekeeper. She kept the door open a few inches. Erin didn't have to worry that she was going to get trapped inside with Beryl. She would be able to get out again once help arrived.

There were new voices in the kitchen outside the freezer.

And this time, it wasn't going to be Terry or one of the police officers that Erin knew so well from Bald Eagle Falls. It wouldn't even be Stayner, the new cop she was still trying to get to know. Young, inexperienced, and somewhat blundering.

She would have been happy to see even Stayner.

Instead, the men who came into the freezer room were completely unfamiliar to her. She hadn't even met them once.

The first cop was older. Lines of experience creased his face. He was heavy, taller than Erin but shorter than Vic, his uniform wrinkled like he'd been sitting at a desk most of the day.

He shifted his heavy duty belt as he entered the freezer, lifting it up and then settling it down again. He looked around the freezer warily. His eyes went first to Erin and then to Beryl.

"What happened here?" he questioned. He took several steps toward Beryl.

"I don't know," Erin whispered, her throat dry.

"Something happened," contributed the younger cop who came in behind the first. "Looks like we've got a body."

"You're not qualified to declare a death," the first cop reminded him. He looked down at Beryl, frowning. He didn't reach down and touch her. Erin thought he should check her pulse, but he didn't. "Get Dr. Manuel on the phone."

"But she is dead," the second cop pointed out. But that didn't stop him from pulling out his phone and swiping through it to find the number he wanted. He waited for a minute, the phone pasted to his ear, as he waited for the call to connect. "Dr. Manuel…? I need him, please." He listened to the answer, seeming neither surprised nor angry at the answer. "I know he's probably in with a patient. But we have an emergency situation here."

A little more cajoling, and he apparently managed to convince them to interrupt the doctor for him. They all waited, no one talking.

"Dr. Manuel. Sorry to interrupt you like this, but we have a situation. Over at the Biscuit. No, I know no one is supposed to be cooking yet. That's not the problem."

There was the buzz of a response from the phone. Erin couldn't make out the words, just the impatient tone.

"There's a woman in the freezer."

Another pause as he listened to the reply.

"She's dead."

The younger cop grimaced as he listened to whatever the doctor had to say.

"I know she's not officially dead, that's why I'm calling you. We need you to check her out and do whatever needs to be done…"

More waiting, more words.

"I'm sorry. Can you come, though?"

Eventually, he convinced the doctor to make the trip to look at the woman in the freezer.

He arrived a few minutes later, dressed in a white lab coat and stethoscope and carrying a small bag, looking as iconic as if he were dressed up as a doctor for Halloween. He saw Erin first, then apparently decided that she wasn't the one he was there to see to, and looked around the freezer, his eyes eventually landing on Beryl.

"Well, that's something you don't find in your freezer every day."

He walked over to her, took her pulse, and listened to her chest for a heartbeat or breathing. He hung the stethoscope around his neck again.

"There's a saying. They're not really dead until they're warm and dead."

"What kind of sense does that make?" the younger cop demanded. The older one shook his head at his attitude toward the doctor.

"It means that we have to get this woman warmed up before I can declare her dead."

"But she's obviously dead."

"'Obviously dead' doesn't cut it when someone has been frozen to death. There have been cases where a heartbeat has been reestablished after an accident like this. Usually in children, but there have been cases of adults surviving as well. And I'm not going to take the chance or open myself up to a lawsuit. Taking the time to warm her up is not going to hurt anything. So let's get it done."

The first cop looked down at Beryl's body. "What do you want to do? You want us to carry her out of here? Turn off the freezer? Put blankets on her?"

"We need to get her out of here."

"We might be destroying evidence."

"We'll just have to be careful. But we need to get her out of here before we can decide that she's permanently dead."

Erin stood there watching as they navigated around Beryl, looking at her position and the various angles, and came up with a plan to pick her up and move her. The older cop apparently had back issues, so the doctor and the younger cop were nominated for the job. He made his first attempt to pick up Beryl's legs and let go again.

"Ugh. She's definitely dead! I can feel ice crystals crunching. And she's in rigor."

"Are you the doctor now? Frozen stiff is not the same as rigor. Grab her and let's get this done."

The younger cop picked up Beryl's legs a second time, and they moved toward the exit door.

CHAPTER 14

The older cop's name was Coleman, and he was the one who directed Erin to the police station and told her not to talk to anyone on the way. She exchanged looks with Vic, but obeyed, heading to the police station where she would be expected to give a statement.

There was an actual police station in Whitewater, different from Bald Eagle Falls, where the police department had a few offices at the civic center. The Whitewater police station was a small red brick building away from Main Street and the shops. Erin looked around, feeling disconnected from her surroundings. She didn't belong in Whitewater Junction. She didn't know anyone there. She was going into an unfamiliar police department to talk to unfamiliar police officers about the death of a woman she had only just met. She wanted to go back to Bald Eagle Falls and talk to Officer Terry Piper.

She just stood there, looking around, feeling anchorless.

Eventually, she shook off her torpor and forced herself to walk in through the front doors. There was a uniformed female officer at the front desk. Her hair was pulled back, but it was curly and tendrils were sticking out here and there. The uniform was not well-fitted; a large men's shirt rather than one cut for a woman's figure. Her name tag said M Sommers. She gave Erin a smile and raised her brows.

"How can I help you?"

"Uh—Deputy Coleman sent me over here. About the woman… in the restaurant."

"Oh, are you one of the people with the contest? He said some of you would be coming over." Sommers looked at her watch, then turned around and looked at the rooms behind her, as if everything were full and she didn't know how she was going to fit Erin in.

"Did you know the… victim?"

"I met her last night. Just had a short conversation with her."

"And what was it that happened today?"

"I was the one who… was the first one in there, and found her."

"Ah, okay." Sommers nodded her understanding. "You're an eyewitness. We're going to want to keep you on your own until you've had a chance to make your statement to make sure your recollection isn't influenced by someone else. I'm sorry, it's not much fun to sit all by yourself, but I'm sure Deputy Coleman won't be too long. He'll want to question you as soon as possible."

Erin shifted uncomfortably. "I don't know anything. He's going to know just as much as me from looking at the scene. Probably more, because of his training. I don't know anything at all."

"I'm sorry. Come on back here, and I'll get you a hot beverage while you're waiting. You're probably chilled after being in that freezer, and then the weather outside."

She gave a shudder. Erin smiled. Sommers had to be a native Tennessean, or from somewhere even hotter, if she thought it was that cold outside. Sommers directed her to a little gate through the counter, unlocking it with a button. She escorted Erin through.

"You don't have any weapons, do you?"

"No. I don't have anything."

Sommers didn't bother to check. She was very trusting, for a policewoman. She took Erin to a glassed-in office with a table and a couple of chairs and motioned her to take a seat. Erin sat down, her stomach tight with anxiety.

"Would you like coffee or tea?" Sommers asked.

"Tea, please."

"Coming up. You just relax in here and I'm sure Deputy Coleman will be here in no time. You can tell him what you know and be on your way."

"But I really don't know anything."

"Then it will be even quicker, won't it?" Sommers gave her a stern smile, then left the room, pulling the door shut behind her. Erin heard it click into place and had a pretty good idea that she was now locked in.

At first, a glass-walled interrogation room seemed like a pretty bad idea. She could just see a prisoner punching a hole in the glass or picking up a chair and launching it through one of the walls, bringing the whole thing down in a shower of broken shards of glass. But of course they would have made sure that it was some kind of armored glass that a person couldn't put a fist through easily. Erin looked at the chair across from her. Both the chairs and the table were anchored to the floor. So no throwing a chair through it, either.

Sitting in the middle of the glassed-in room, Erin was visible to everyone working in the cubicles of the police department. Everyone walking by could see her. It wasn't like in Bald Eagle Falls, where there was only a narrow window. Anything an interviewee did in the glassed-in room would be visible to everyone else, as would anything anyone did to the interviewee. No one could pretend not to see police brutality. And anyone who should not be there would be noticed immediately.

Erin fidgeted for a while, watching the people outside of her fish tank, waiting for Deputy Coleman to show up. At first, she thought he would only be a few minutes, like Sommers had suggested, but that had clearly been wrong. Sommers brought

Erin her tea. Erin sipped it slowly, making it last but, eventually, the tea was all gone and there was still no sign of Coleman.

Erin decided that sitting there doing nothing, just waiting for him, was making the time pass even more slowly. If she occupied herself instead of just sitting there, the time would go by much more quickly, and she wouldn't feel like she had wasted her entire day.

She opened her purse and sifted through the contents. She always had pens and notepads, or at least scraps of paper, with her. She knew she should get more organized. If she wasn't going to use her phone like Vic thought she should, she could at least get a dedicated planner to keep track of things and centralize it all in one location. Maybe when she got back to Bald Eagle Falls, she would do that. Or the next time she was in the city. The stationery store would have a lot more options than the little general store in Bald Eagle Falls. Though she did like to support the local businesses as much as she could.

She pulled out several blank sheets of paper and folded them over and smoothed them so she had a good surface to write on. She started to make notes on the contest and what she had learned so far about the rules and the different events that were being planned, and anything she ought to plan for those events. She wasn't the organizer of the contest, but that didn't mean she shouldn't be organized. And if she could tie some of the events in with promotions at Auntie Clem's Bakery, she would be able to get more visibility and sales.

That worked for a few minutes. But Erin couldn't stop thinking about Beryl and how she had looked when Erin had discovered her in the freezer room. She had looked like a sculpture, pale blue and covered with frost. Not like something real. The room and the body were bloodless, like Beryl had known she needed to keep it hygienic for food preparation. What had happened? Had she been looking for something and gotten confused when she got too cold looking for it? Had she been drunk or tired and thought she would just sit down and take a break for a few minutes? Maybe the door had been stuck. But Erin knew it hadn't been stuck. It hadn't been difficult to open. If someone had been trying to get out, she had only to put her shoulder to the door to push it open if it had been sticky.

Beryl hadn't been very nice, but Erin still felt bad for any friends or family. It was never easy to lose a loved one. And if Beryl hadn't had any family or friends… well, that was even more tragic. Then Erin felt bad for walking away from her the night before and not realizing that Beryl was reaching out desperately for attention and validation, not just being obnoxious. Maybe she couldn't help it.

A lost life was a lost life.

CHAPTER 15

Of course, Erin was assuming that Beryl had passed away. The doctor had said that he couldn't declare her dead until she was warm, but did that really mean there was a chance that she could recover? It seemed highly unlikely to Erin, but then, she wasn't a doctor.

What if they could revive her? Would that event change her life, or would she go on as before? What would it be like to be on the same panel with a judge who had just been frozen to death and then been reanimated? That was a creepy thought.

But maybe it wouldn't be any different from working with anyone who had been through a recent illness. Erin had experience caring for people who were older or had gone through an illness or accident and needed assistance taking care of themselves. Not as fun as baking, but it had been rewarding to know how important her work was to those people and their families.

Maybe the reason that Coleman hadn't yet returned to the police station to interview her was that he was waiting to see if Beryl could be revived.

Erin started another list of things she would need to do when she got back home. Not just the regular everyday things, but looking into whether she had enough life insurance that the bakery could keep running if something happened to her. Erin wasn't sure who would run it if she met with an accident. Charley, she supposed. Charley was the co-owner, so she was the one who would take over if something happened to Erin.

But would Charley keep it running? Did the existing employees know enough about baking gluten-free goods and running a business to keep it going if something happened to her? Or would Charley convert it to a conventional bakery?

Or sell it and start another venture somewhere else?

There was a knock at the door, and Erin looked up, startled. She had finished her tea quite a while ago. She had finally been able to put Beryl's frozen body out of her mind as she had been thinking about the long-term future of Auntie Clem's and what she needed to do to ensure that there were people ready and willing to take over if something happened to her.

But seeing Coleman's face brought it all back in a rush. She pressed her hands to the table to stand up but, in doing so, rocked the unsteady surface and her cup spun across the glossy surface intent on self-destruction. Erin grabbed at it and nearly knocked it over the edge, just managing to save it at the last moment.

She held the cup in her hand, splashed with dribbles of tea, and tried to catch her breath. She looked at Coleman with an embarrassed grin. So much for looking like a mature, graceful woman. He would think she was some nut; some crazy, clumsy nut who had turned up another body and couldn't give him the information he wanted.

"Uh—hi. Sorry about that. I didn't mean to…"

"Miss Price. Please, have a seat." He motioned back to the chair she had just bounced up out of. "Would you like a refill on that?"

Erin put the cup down with an unsteady clink. She wiped her hands on her pants. "No. I'm good. Thanks."

"Great. Thank you for coming in. I'm sorry to keep you waiting for so long."

"Oh, I'm sure you had good reason. How is… I mean… did the doctor… Beryl…"

"He's still working on bringing her core temperature up to where it needs to be to, uh, declare her. I have to say, though, that I am not optimistic, and I am treating this as a death investigation until I hear otherwise."

Erin nodded. That was about what she had expected. She settled herself back into the uncomfortable seat. "I don't really know anything."

"Well, I understand that. But we need to run through this anyway, so if you'll indulge me…"

"Of course. I'll help if I can, but…"

"All right." He pulled out a notepad, licked his finger, and turned to a fresh page. "Why don't we start at the top. How did you know Ms. Batcombe?"

"Well, I didn't, really. I just met her last night for a few minutes, but we talked for maybe five minutes. Not long enough to get to know her."

"Where and how did you meet?"

"We had a dinner and event last night. She was at that. I didn't talk to her at the dinner, but I went out for a bit of fresh air, and she was out there smoking. She introduced herself and we talked for a few minutes. That's all."

"What was your impression of her?"

Erin stalled. "What do you mean?"

Coleman studied her. He creased and smoothed a corner of the notebook page. "Where was she smoking?"

"Out front, against the front of the building. A little ways away from the doors."

"Had she had much to drink?"

"Oh." Erin thought about it. "I don't really know. She wasn't slurring or unsteady. But I don't know what she is normally like, so I can't say if she was more talkative than usual, or if she was… more emotional… or anything…"

It was possible that the way Beryl had been talking about Vic was just due to drink. Some people got mean when they were drunk and said things that they never would have considered saying sober. Erin hoped that it had just been because she'd had a bit much to drink.

"Do you think that she… got stuck in there because she was drunk?" Erin asked Coleman.

"We're just at the beginning of our investigation. We don't know anything yet. Just exploring the possibilities."

"Maybe she was drunk, and that was why she went in there… or why she stayed when she got cold. I was trying to figure it out."

"It is a strange situation. People who have had too much to drink often don't realize when they are getting cold. Or if she had something else to keep her mood up or to help her to stay awake… we will investigate whether there were any substances in her bloodstream that might have altered her perception of her environment or her body's signals."

Erin nodded. Meth, she knew, made people overheat. She didn't think Beryl was a meth user, but you couldn't tell in the earlier stages. The soccer mom down the street might have a meth addiction. Someone who wanted to lose weight. It had initially been designed to help soldiers stay awake and alert.

"When did you get to the restaurant today?" Coleman asked.

"I'm not sure what time it was. The woman giving the tour would have a better idea. We gathered at… eight-thirty. We waited for everyone to get there. Beryl didn't show up, so we waited for a little while for her, then started without her. There was some general stuff, and then walking down the street, stopping outside the restaurant while she talked about…" Erin squinted and sighed. "I don't know. Architecture. Local cuisine trends. It was all a little… um… high-brow."

"Boring?" Coleman suggested, the corner of his mouth curling up.

"Well, yes. Incredibly boring. I was really eager to get inside, to see where the competition would be held, the real nuts and bolts."

"Then y'all went into the restaurant, and you went to the kitchen."

"I stayed with the group. There was a bit of information in the main dining hall, and then we were allowed to go into the kitchen, all together. Not just me."

"But at some point, you became separated from the group."

"Not separated," Erin protested. "I was still right there, listening with everyone else. I just… tried the handle on the cold room door. I wanted to get a peek at it."

"I see." He didn't say anything else, looking at her, waiting for her to fill the silence.

Erin didn't say anything right away, not sure what she should say. Coleman scribbled some notes in his notebook, looking down at the page and then up at her as he considered.

"What did you notice about the door?" he asked eventually.

"Notice about it? It was… big, heavy, had a good seal. What do you mean, what did I notice?"

"What made you decide to open it before the tour guide said to check it out?"

"Just curiosity. I wanted to see everything, get a feel for the place. How the contest was going to be run. What it was going to be like when it was full of contestants and everyone else. I just… was bored and wanted to see something more."

"What did you notice about the locking mechanism on the door?"

"The lock?" Erin cast her mind back, trying to picture it. Imagining the movements of her hands, and the way the door had looked, mapping everything out in her head. "Was there a lock? I don't know if there was one."

"Wouldn't a freezer in a place like that have some security? What about when the contest entries were being stored in there? There must have been a way to keep it safe."

Erin shook her head. "I'm sorry. I just can't think of anything. Maybe there was a lock, but I didn't notice it."

"So how did you open the door?"

"It wasn't locked." Erin shook her head. She could feel the handle in her hand, the smooth, cool metal of the lever. "I didn't have to turn any locks. I just turned the handle. It was a little sticky for a second, but that's all. And I wouldn't even say it was stuck, I just had to give it a bit of a pull, because it was... sealed."

Coleman nodded. He made some more notes to himself.

"A freezer like that, they have to make it so that you can't be locked in, don't they?" Erin asked. "Aren't there laws... that there has to be an override, a release from inside or something. Just like the trunk of a car; they all have emergency releases inside now so that someone can't be accidentally locked inside."

Or on purpose. There weren't very many circumstances in which a person would get accidentally locked in a trunk. A small child, maybe, but not an adult. How many movies showed abductees or murder victims thrown into a trunk?

"There are safety features," Coleman agreed. "We will be looking into that. What was required and what was in place. We're not looking to place blame, but we do want to figure out what happened here. It's a very tragic case, you don't want to see something like that happen again."

"Did she have family around here? I feel so bad for her family and friends. So sudden and unexpected."

"Death often comes when we don't expect it," Coleman opined.

Erin shifted restlessly. "That's everything I know. I didn't know Beryl, and I don't know what could have happened last night. It's very sad."

"Have I heard your name before?" Coleman inquired, lifting one eyebrow. "We'll need your ID, of course, to fill out the official paperwork. But your name sounds familiar. I'm wondering where I might have heard it before."

Erin swallowed. She wasn't about to tell him about the other cases that she had been peripherally involved in. "I don't know. I guess you must have heard about my bakery in Bald Eagle Falls. Auntie Clem's Bakery? Most people have at least heard about it. There aren't a lot of places around here where you can get quality gluten-free baked goods."

Coleman's lips pursed. "I don't think that was it. Well, I'm sure it will come to me. If you could get out your driver's license, I'll take a copy of it, and I'll get Meribel started on the paperwork."

"Oh. Okay." Erin opened her purse and scooped out her wallet. It took her a minute to find her driver's license. It wasn't only her purse that needed to be sorted out, but even the wallet was stuffed too full of things that she didn't need to keep on her all the time. She had to learn to leave things at home if she wasn't going to need them right away. But she preferred to have her things with her. After going so many years with few possessions, she liked to have as many things on her person as possible. She found the edge of her driver's license behind another card and pulled it out. "There it is."

She handed it across the table to Coleman. He picked it up and studied it. Erin's face got warm. She hoped she hadn't let it expire. Coleman smiled and nodded and left the room.

The glass walls allowed her to watch him after he left the room, going out to the front of the police station where Erin had come in and handed her license to M Sommers. Meribel. For a few minutes, he talked with her; much longer, Erin thought, than needed just to give her instructions to copy the driver's license and get a witness statement form for Erin to fill out.

She was going to be there for a long time. She knew it. They were going to want a lengthy formal statement, even though she had done nothing more than to open a door and discover Beryl Batcombe's frozen body. But he wanted to make sure he had all of his bases covered. If Erin didn't tell him everything he wanted to know, it would be harder for him to follow up with her once she had gone back to Bald Eagle Falls. But not impossible. She had a cell phone and email.

CHAPTER 16

It was late afternoon, and Erin was tired and hungry when she finally got out of the police station. Her head was pounding and she wanted to lie down for a nap. But she also needed something to eat. And she couldn't eat and sleep at the same time.

She had seen Vic and some of the others at the police station. They had come and gone relatively quickly, filling in their forms at the front counter and not having to have personal interviews with Coleman. Erin imagined that those who knew Beryl better might have to spend longer with Coleman or his staff, but the people who were from out of town and who hadn't actually seen or discovered the body didn't have anything important to tell him. They just happened to be involved with the contest, there was no other connection.

Erin expected to see Vic in their hotel room. Reading a book or checking email on her phone, or watching daytime television. But it wasn't Vic who was waiting for her when she got back to the hotel, it was Terry.

"Oh!" Erin was surprised. She looked around for Vic. "I wasn't expecting you to be here."

"Are you okay?" He pushed himself up from the bed and stepped in close to enfold her in his arms. "How are you?"

"I'm okay. I mean, I don't feel good right now, but…"

Well, she wasn't dead like Beryl.

"Come here," he walked her over to the bed and lowered her to it. They sat side by side and he looked into her face. "I've been so worried about you. Vic said she'd seen you at the police station, and you looked okay, but I've been worried…"

He didn't say that he was worried she would have a breakdown. That seeing another dead body would be too much for her.

"No, no. I'm fine." She met his gaze. "It wasn't anything like…"

She didn't need to finish the sentence. Anything like Ingersoll's death. Anything like finding Terry bound and unconscious. She would be okay. It wouldn't haunt her dreams.

But how could she know that? She hadn't been as shocked and traumatized as when she had discovered Mr. Ingersoll. But that didn't mean it wouldn't follow her into her dreams. It might be added to the horrors that she dreamt almost every night.

She didn't think it had been that bad.

"There was… no blood," Erin explained to Terry. "It was just… she was there… and you could tell looking at her… she was sort of blue-gray and there was frost…" She stopped before describing the delicate frost sticking to Beryl's eyelashes. Frost was always so pretty and she loved how it clung to the trees in the early morning. She looked away from Terry. "It was different."

Terry rubbed her shoulders and the back of her neck. "Okay. We'll leave it at that. But whenever you want to talk about it… we can. Whatever you want to tell me about it."

Erin nodded. "Yes. Of course."

"What can I get for you? You must be dead on your feet."

"I haven't been on my feet. I've been sitting. Why would that be more exhausting than actually being on my feet all day at Auntie Clem's?"

"I think anything related to being questioned about a sudden death is going to be exhausting. It's an emotional thing. And you've been at the police station for hours. I didn't know if I should go over there and ask after you. I didn't want to throw my weight around, but there was no need for them to keep you for so long."

"You know how it is with police work. Lots of tedious sitting and waiting."

"Followed by bursts of heart-stopping insanity."

"Well, luckily, no insanity today. Just the tedious sitting and waiting. And paperwork."

"You can't uphold the law without plenty of paperwork."

"So I'm finding."

"The police officer's nemesis. Do you want something to eat? A hot shower? A nap?"

"Mmm. All of the above."

"Which do you want the most? Or first?"

"I think I'd better eat."

Terry got up and walked over to the mini-fridge, but his mouth turned down when he took a peek inside. "Whatever happened to actually having quality snacks in a minibar? I'll go down to the restaurant and pick something up for you. What do you want?"

"I don't know what they'll have."

"Anything you would order from the family restaurant at home. Do you want a full-blown dinner? Or something smaller?"

"No, nothing that big. A sandwich, maybe."

"With fries? Do you want grilled cheese or something grown-up?"

"Mmm, you know, grilled cheese sounds really good."

"And the fries?"

"I'd better not have fries."

"You sure?"

Erin nodded.

"I'll go get you a sandwich, then. It will probably take half an hour, you want to have that hot shower while I get it?"

"Yeah, that sounds really good."

He gave her a quick kiss and snapped his fingers to call K9, who had been snoozing next to the bed, to his side. Then he was gone.

Erin headed to the bathroom, filled the tub, and poured some of the hotel shampoo into the water to make bubbles. A bubble bath was even better than a shower. She closed her eyes and soaked in the hot water waiting for Terry's return.

Erin was feeling much better after her grilled cheese sandwich and soak in the tub. She felt human once more. She had changed into her jammies and was cuddling with Terry on the bed while watching some old noir murder mystery on TV. Despite her experience, the dramatic danger of the movie didn't bother her at all.

There was a tap on the door. Erin knew who it was. She'd heard that tap on her back door enough times to recognize it. She slid off of the bed and let Vic in.

"How are you?" Vic asked, giving her a brief hug.

"Better now."

"You're okay? I was so worried about you, but you looked like you were holding it together when I saw you. You looked pretty calm. Just bored."

Erin rolled her eyes. "Yes. So far, this 'vacation' has been pretty tedious."

"It will get better," Vic assured her. She looked past Erin to Terry. "And how about you, Officer Piper? How are you tonight?"

"Fine, Vic. Come on in and visit for a while."

"I don't want to interrupt anything…"

"We're just watching TV."

"Maybe for a few minutes, then," Vic agreed, smiling. She sat down on the chair for a chat with Erin. No matter how much time they spent together, they always found things to talk about.

They'd been talking for a half hour when there was another

knock on the door. Erin frowned. She hoped it wasn't the police again. She didn't want to have to deal with them again.

She was much slower to get up and get the door this time. She opened the door and found Chef Kirschoff standing there, with a small white dog in his arms. She blinked at him.

"Oh! Hi, Chef Kirschoff. Hans."

"Erin. I was so sorry to hear about what happened… you finding poor Beryl that way."

Erin stepped back, motioning for Kirschoff to enter, though it was getting a little crowded in the small hotel room.

Vic saw the dog and jumped up. "Oh! You have a puppy! Isn't he the cutest thing!" She reached out and scratched the dog's ears and crooned in a baby voice.

The dog nuzzled her and whined, enjoying the attention. K9's head went up and he stared at the interloper.

"He's not mine," Kirschoff explained.

Vic continued to stroke the dog's ears. "Whose is he, then?"

"He's—he was—Beryl's."

"Oh, no…" Vic leaned forward and kissed the top of the dog's head, covering his ears with both hands to keep him from hearing anything upsetting. "Oh, how sad. What's going to happen to him? Was she married?"

"No. She lived by herself. I don't know if there is any next of kin…" He shifted the dog closer to Vic. "I need someone to look after him. I didn't know who to ask."

He fumbled the white dog into her arms. Vic looked surprised, but she cuddled the puppy close, putting her cheek against him. "Oh, poor thing. I don't know." Vic looked at Erin. "Maybe *you* should…"

"No, I've already got two pets, three animals in the house when K9 is there. I can't take another."

"But…"

"He looks pretty happy right where he is."

Vic looked down at the dog. "I can't take a dog. I can't commit to…"

"It's not forever," Kirschoff said. "Just until they find someone else to take him."

Vic scratched the dog's ears. Erin could tell there was no way Vic was going to say no.

"What's his name?" Vic looked at Kirschoff.

"Nilla." Kirschoff grimaced. "Short for Vanilla Scoop."

CHAPTER 17

There had been more activities planned for the judges, staff, and officials over the weekend, but Erin found that everything had been called off. Or rescheduled, at least, while the contest organizers sorted out the wrinkles that Beryl's death had put into the contest plans.

The entrants who were making fermented drinks for their contest entries mixed up and bottled their creations under the supervision of the contest officials. The drinks would need to sit for a few weeks before the judges could taste them and decide which would go on to the next round. It was all done with a decided lack of ceremony, but Erin didn't hear anyone complain about having the pomp put aside in the wake of Beryl's death.

So in another day, Erin was headed back to Bald Eagle Falls with Terry. Vic had decided to take advantage of the fact that they had the hotel for a couple more nights, and invited Willie to stay with her for a bit of a vacation. And, Erin supposed, to introduce him to Nilla.

Erin was glad to get home.

Melissa heard that Erin was back, probably through the police department, where she worked part time. She showed up on Erin's doorstep with a covered dish. "I thought you probably wouldn't feel like cooking," she offered, reaching out with it until Erin took it from her.

"Thank you, that was very thoughtful. You're right… I don't feel like doing very much of anything but eating and sleeping right now."

Melissa nodded, standing there on the doorstep and waiting to be invited in. Erin finally relented. "Come in and set a while. How are you?"

Erin put the dish in the fridge and returned to the living room to sit down with Melissa.

Melissa leaned forward, eager for the details. "So? Tell me all about it. Was it awful? The police in Whitewater aren't releasing many details. I was hoping that we'd be able to get more, seeing as we're sister cities and you're associated with the police department through Terry. But I couldn't find anything out."

"It wasn't that awful," Erin said. "I mean… not like Mr. Ingersoll or Angela Plaint. It was just… like she'd died naturally. No violence."

"But it's not natural to end up dead in a freezer."

"No. But it wasn't like she was killed and stuffed in a freezer as a hiding place. She just… something happened while she was in there. I don't know what. Maybe she'd had too much to drink, or she didn't realize how tired she was and just closed her eyes…"

"I can't believe you found another body."

"But it wasn't a murder," Erin pointed out. "Just a tragic accidental death."

"Maybe. Maybe *not*."

"It wasn't murder this time." Erin smiled and shook her head at Melissa's thirst for drama. "I'm sorry, this one was just your normal, everyday, froze-to-death-in-a-cold-room."

"Did you know her? What was it like when you found her? You must have been shocked to find her there. Or maybe not anymore… maybe it's old hat now."

"No, it is not old hat," Erin said firmly. "It was still a shock. I couldn't believe it at first… but then I guess… it becomes easier to handle. I knew what to do. To keep everyone else out, to call the police. I didn't go in any farther or touch anything…"

"Of all the bad luck." Melissa shook her head. Erin wasn't sure whether Melissa was lamenting Erin's bad luck in finding a body or that Melissa had never found one herself. She'd missed out on Bo Biggles. That could have been her instead of Clara.

"Yes." Erin looked at the face of her phone. She didn't feel much like visiting and was hoping that Melissa would take the hint and leave. Then Erin could rest her eyes for a bit. Have a sleep.

"Of course, we're still cleaning up the mess after the last discovery you made," Melissa said with a little chuckle.

It took a minute for Erin to realize that she meant the burglaries, not the last body she had stumbled across.

"I guess you are… is it moving along? You know who the ringleader was, and I assume you've gotten information from some of the others. Do you think you have all of the names of the people who were involved?"

"I don't think you ever do in a case like this," Melissa said, tapping a finger on the arm of the chair she was sitting in. "I think that there are always going to be a few names that don't come out, or perps throw red herrings at us; the names of people who don't exist, or of people they knew were not involved. Just to throw us off the trail. Even with people you're sure are involved, you still have to have the proof. A gut feeling and overhearing something someone said just isn't enough to make an arrest. You end up letting some people go even though you know they were involved."

Erin rubbed her knee. She didn't like that. At least one of the people involved in the burglary ring had tried to kill her. What if that were someone who ended up evading the police net?

"It's okay," Melissa assured her. "We'll get all the big players. But whether we'll ever find out the names of all of the students who were involved…"

"What if they come back after me because of my involvement?"

"Kids? I don't think you need to worry about kids."

If Melissa didn't think that teenagers could be killers or cause harm, she was sadly mistaken. Adults, with brains that had matured, were less likely to do her any serious harm. Teenagers could be impulsive and unpredictable. And they could use violence without fully understanding the consequences of their actions.

Erin eventually saw Melissa on her way, but not until Melissa had exhausted several other avenues of inquiry and entertainment. Erin felt almost as exhausted as she had after Coleman had questioned her. Melissa had a friendlier manner than Coleman, but she was an expert interrogator. Erin had done her best to deflect Melissa's questions and hoped that she hadn't given anything away with her answers. Not that she knew anything to give away. But she felt like Melissa had gleaned more from their conversation than Erin had meant to give.

After Melissa was gone, Erin decided to turn her attention to her meditation. She had been practicing tai chi for some time now, and it was becoming easier to remember the forms and routines and to lose herself in the practice, letting her mind and body relax. It was still a struggle to keep herself from thinking about what needed to be done at the bakery or what she needed to write down and add to her lists. Still, she focused on each of the movements and managed to stay reasonably focused on relaxation and an open mind.

There was the sound of a key turning in the lock. Erin relaxed her stance and watched Terry enter.

"Hi, honey."

He looked her over. "Are you just starting or finishing?"

"Finishing. Good timing."

He walked in through the door, K9 at his side. "I thought you would be too tired for your tai chi."

"I need something to help me relax. Especially after... Melissa."

"Oh, has she been over here?" He rolled his eyes. He gave Erin a peck on the cheek and sat down on the couch, looking more tired than he ever had after a double shift in the old days.

"She came to pump me for more information on the body in the freezer. I think you guys have done yourselves a disservice by keeping her in an administrative position. She should be in the interrogation room."

"She knows how to get information out of people, that's for sure. And how to use the information and rumors that are swirling around to construct new rumors. I get tired just thinking about how much time and energy she puts into chasing after gossip."

Erin turned her head experimentally, making sure that her neck and shoulders were relaxed.

"Did she bug you more about church?" Terry asked.

"No, that one didn't come up this time, thankfully. I guess stories of dead bodies are good for one thing, anyway. They keep her distracted from my personal life."

"I'm sorry that there's been so much talk about you and your religious views because of that. You did something nice for me, and everybody is reading far too much into it."

"It doesn't seem to matter how much I tell people I'm not converting to Christianity, they think I must be lying."

"Why would you? And wouldn't lying about it sort of run counter to any kind of conversion...?"

"I haven't found Christians—at least the ones around here—to be terribly logical about their beliefs." Erin shrugged. "Maybe they think I don't know about the commandment not to lie."

"Well, as you stick to your guns and they see that you haven't suddenly started going to church, they'll fade out a bit."

"Hope so," Erin agreed. She headed for the kitchen. "Melissa brought a casserole. Do you want some?"

"Sounds good. I was going to see if we could get something delivered. But casserole is fine. Comfort food."

"I don't know what kind it is."

"Doesn't really matter. I grew up on them."

"Okay. I'll put it in the oven and make something to go with it. A salad or some veggies."

"You don't need to do anything. You're off duty. You can just eat the casserole and not worry about anything else."

"I have to watch what I eat, though," Erin touched her belly. "That casserole is going to be all carbs and cream. I need to focus on less calorie-dense foods."

"I'll cut up some vegetables for you, then." He sat forward on the couch to get up.

"No. You've been working. You need a rest. I've just been at home all day. I can manage."

"You're recovering from a trauma."

"I'm over it." Erin said it even though she knew she hadn't yet fully recovered from the shock and disbelief of finding Beryl's frozen body.

Terry gave her a skeptical look, but he shrugged and let it be. She supposed he'd come to the conclusion that if she wanted to cut up some vegetables that badly, she could go ahead.

$\mathcal{E}$rin was glad to get back to Auntie Clem's Bakery where she belonged. There, she could lose herself in her work. She could serve the people who needed a gluten-free or specialty diet and give them the sustenance—and treats—that they needed and deserved. It made her feel good that she could make a contribution to the community that way.

Things had been a little different since Christmas, but she thought that was just her own outlook. She needed to focus on the positive and not be so sensitive to the way that people looked at her or the slight dip in sales since Christmas. Of course people had bought more before Christmas and were now cutting back until their spending was back on track. A lot of people had either had their Christmas presents stolen or had contributed to fundraisers to help make up the losses for those who had.

The community had pulled together to help each other. That proved that people were good at heart. And that was how she should see them.

Erin stacked muffins on a tray to take out to the front and then arranged them in the display case. It was the quiet part of the afternoon. Things would pick up a bit when school let out, both with kids stopping by for a post-school snack and moms grabbing a few things for dinner.

Though she hadn't had as many school kids lately.

Or as many moms.

Erin tried to push the negative thoughts out of her mind as she arranged the baked goods.

She heard the tinkle of the bells at the front door and looked up with a smile on her face to see who it was.

It was Mrs. Foster, the mother of Peter, one of Erin's favorite customers, and his sisters. She was now heavily pregnant. Erin didn't know what her due date was, but she thought it might be the last time she saw Mrs. Foster for a few weeks.

Erin preferred it when Mrs. Foster came with the whole family so the kids could get their free kid's club cookies. But lately, she had been coming in by herself when the older kids were at school and Traci was, Erin assumed, in preschool or Mrs. Foster had swapped babysitting with someone else.

"Hello, Mrs. Foster," Erin greeted, standing up and rubbing her back for a moment.

"Miss Price," Mrs. Foster greeted. When she was with the kids, she usually said 'Miss Erin.' The southern way of being friendly yet respectful. 'Miss Price' was cooler, and Erin felt a little sting at the words.

"You're looking well," Erin said, forcing the plastic smile to stay on her face. "Doesn't look like it will be long now."

Mrs. Foster rested her hand on her bulging belly. "No, I don't think we'll have to wait much longer for this little one." She sighed, then looked at the baked goods in Erin's display case. She listed off the items she needed, and Erin silently gathered them together. Vic was in the kitchen taking care of some other tasks while it was quiet.

"It's been a long time since I've seen Peter," Erin said tentatively. "I hope I see him again soon. Everything okay with him?"

Mrs. Foster looked at her for a moment. She shook her head.

"Peter is fine. But I don't think you'll be seeing him anytime soon."

Erin wondered whether she should ask more questions, or if she didn't want to know the answers. If Peter was fine and Mrs. Foster didn't plan to bring the children by any time soon, then it was because she didn't want them to see Erin or vice versa. "He's such a smart kid."

"A little too smart for his own good, maybe. But he is just a child, and I don't want him around people who might do him harm."

Erin blinked. "Harm? I wouldn't ever do anything to hurt Peter."

"You may think that, but your actions don't bear it out. Twice now, he has had to talk to the police because of something that you have said. I don't want him involved with the police. I want him to have a normal childhood and not be brought under suspicion by the police or people wanting to know what he's been saying to them."

Erin was tongue-tied. She tried to think of what to say. She couldn't argue the truth of what Mrs. Foster said. Peter had held key pieces of information in a couple of investigations. He was very observant and, while he didn't always know the significance of what he knew, his keen eye had been relevant to the police department's investigations.

"I never intended…"

She nodded. "Like I said. You might not have thought about what you were doing, but your actions show that you are not putting Peter's safety or well-being first."

Erin stood at the cash register and tried to remember what she had just put into the bag for Mrs. Foster. Her brain had stalled, stuck on the realization that Mrs. Foster thought she had put Peter in harm's way by her actions.

"I'm sorry."

Mrs. Foster nodded. She stood there, one hand on her belly, waiting for Erin to finish ringing her purchase through. Erin looked in the bag and, with numb, clumsy fingers, punched in the numbers for her purchases.

"I… Is there something I can do…?"

"No, I don't think there is. I would just like you to stay out of Peter's life. Stay away from the school. Don't talk to him on the street. Don't talk to him at all if I am not supervising."

"Okay."

"It's my job to protect him. And if there is ever anything you think he can contribute to a police investigation…" Mrs. Foster licked her lips and shook her head. "You come directly to me. But that isn't ever going to happen again, is it?"

"I… I really don't know. I don't know what's going to happen in the future."

"You come to me. Not to the police."

Erin nodded. She took Mrs. Foster's money and handed over the bag of baked goods.

"I'm coming here because not coming here to get food that Peter can eat would be punishing him for your actions, and he didn't do anything wrong. But that's the only reason. If he didn't need this food, if he was able to eat gluten or I was able to get good gluten-free baking somewhere else, I wouldn't be here."

Erin nodded wordlessly. Mrs. Foster took her purchase and walked back out of the bakery. Erin turned toward the kitchen and saw Vic framed in the doorway, her eyes wide.

"First Mary Lou and now Mrs. Foster… I just don't understand people! Exactly what did we do that was so wrong?"

"I don't know… I mean, I understand the words, but I don't know how we could have done anything any differently. What exactly do they think I was supposed to do? *Not* talk to Terry? Not say anything to the police when I might have a lead?"

"I guess so." Vic gave a wide shrug. "People are all eager for you to solve a mystery until it interferes with their lives. How are you supposed to figure it out? Without ever talking to anyone? How are you supposed to solve it without all of the relevant pieces?"

Erin sprayed the display case and started to polish it with a dry cloth without paying any attention to what she was doing. "I know what Terry would say."

"That you're not supposed to be investigating in the first place," Vic admitted. "But what are we supposed to do? Just ignore it when someone says something? If we didn't tell Terry or the sheriff when we heard something relevant to a case, we would be in trouble for withholding information. Telling him that we've heard something isn't investigating. It's just... helping."

Charley stopped by while Erin and Vic were cleaning up and preparing for the next morning. She swept in like a whirlwind and didn't help them, but perched up on one of the stools to present her plans while they did the work.

"I have some ideas for getting Auntie Clem's involved in some of the community and kids' activities," she told Erin. "We should make the most of the cook-off. Get some promotional mileage out of it."

"I agree, but there isn't a lot of time to prepare anything," Erin said. "If we were going to be in charge of some activity, then we should have started on it already. It's only a couple of weeks away now."

Charley brushed this off with a motion. "There's plenty of time. Kirschoff and his group are taking care of all of the promo already, all we have to do is make sure that we're there when scheduled activities happen. We can hand out water bottles and samples, maybe get some buttons made with the two of you listed as judges, make goodie bags for kids with, like, balloons and small toys and a cookie to go with their ice cream treats. All we have to do is show up and take advantage of the crowds."

Erin sighed. "So you're going to take charge of this? Because I don't have any extra time. We already have to work the staff harder because Vic and I will be involved in the judging and other events.

And I can't be doing a bunch of self-promo when I'm supposed to be there as an official. It just won't sit well with people."

"Yeah, that's fine. Not a problem. I've thrown parties before."

"It isn't exactly a party."

"It's not that different," Charley declared. "And it's the same skills. Coordinating everything, getting supplies, getting everything prepped to go. I'm good at that kind of thing."

Erin didn't say anything. Charley had not shown a lot of organization and initiative in their time as partners. But Erin remembered that her apartment in Moose River had been neat and well-organized. And she had been part of the party scene there, so she probably had plenty of experience getting that kind of thing organized. Maybe Erin just hadn't given her a chance to shine.

"Okay. It's going to have to be your baby, though, you understand? Whether it succeeds or fails will depend on you."

"Great." Charley nodded firmly. "I'm not gonna let you down. What's our budget?"

"I'm not sure." Erin considered. "Why don't you work something up and we'll go over it tomorrow?"

"Great," Charley agreed. She twirled on her chair. "It's best if I'm the one doing it anyway since the moms are not so happy with you right now."

Erin put down the batter she had been pouring into loaf pans and looked at her.

"Well…?" Charley looked back and forth between Erin and Vic and shook her head. "It's the truth. Parents are not so happy when their kids get in trouble with the police."

"That's their fault for breaking the law," Vic said. "Not Erin's for figuring out what was going on."

"I didn't say it was Erin's fault. I said that it was better if I was in charge of kids' activities because she's not in the moms' good books. I didn't say she did anything wrong."

Vic shook her head. She gave Erin a look. "It doesn't matter what anyone says. You did what you were supposed to. If people don't like it, they're just twisting the issues around to satisfy their own consciences."

Erin swallowed and nodded. She picked up the bowl and continued her work. She thought nostalgically of the old days, when she wasn't anchored to anything or anyone and, if things went bad, she could just pick up and run, go somewhere else and start over again. She hadn't realized back then how much freedom she'd had. Now that she was a business owner and a homeowner, she couldn't just run away when there was trouble.

Charley seemed to finally realize that she had made a mistake in saying what she had. She fiddled with her purse for a minute, then changed the topic.

"So… Chef Kirschoff. What's the deal with him?"

"What's the deal?" Erin repeated.

"Yeah. Is he married, got a girlfriend? Anything?"

"Uh, not that I know of," Erin said. She looked at Vic. "You?"

"No, I don't think he has any close relationships right now. Why? You know someone who wants to meet him?"

"Me," Charley said as if it should have been obvious.

Erin looked at her in disbelief. "You're interested in Chef Kirschoff." She thought of Charley's last boyfriend. A mobster. The son of one of the clan leaders. Wild, reckless, unruly, and powerful. How did Charley go from that to a chef?

"He's older than you," Vic pointed out.

"You're one to talk. Willie is what, twice your age?"

"Well…" Vic shrugged. "It doesn't bother us. But it bothers some people. I didn't think you were ready to settle down with someone. Especially someone older."

"He's not ancient. He's still got his hair. He makes good money and is internationally recognized. He travels. And he's got a cute accent."

Erin couldn't quite wrap her mind around this. Of course it was perfectly fine if Charley wanted to pursue a friendship or relationship with Chef Kirschoff. She was an adult, and it was totally up to her. And him. She just couldn't comprehend the jump from Bobby Dixon to Hans Kirschoff.

"I don't think you should jump into anything." Vic surprised Erin with her comment. "I think you should spend some time getting to know him while he's here for the contest. See whether the two of you really are compatible at all."

"Well, of course," Charley agreed. "I wasn't planning to jump into the sack with him."

Erin's face heated. She stared down at her loaf pans as if they were the most interesting things in the world. Vic giggled.

"Why Erin, you're as red as two beets."

Erin focused on getting the rest of the preparations done, ignoring the laughter.

"Why would that make you blush?" Charley demanded. "It's not like you and Officer Piper are only holding hands."

"Officer Piper and I have taken the time to get to know each other."

"And I said that's what I was going to do. Why are you acting like such a prude?"

"I'm not. And I can't help it if I blush."

"Maybe now that you're going to church, you've realized that you're living in sin. I've heard talk around town that the two of you are going to get married."

"We are not. We don't have any plans to get married." Erin didn't think that her face could get any hotter. She must already be scarlet. "And I'm not going to church now. I went to one service with Terry on Christmas Eve. For him. To make him happy."

"So he's pressuring you into going to church? I thought Officer Handsome was perfect in every way."

"He's not perfect," Erin snapped. She pressed her lips together when she realized what she had said. "I mean, he's not pressuring me to go to church. He's never even asked me to once. I volunteered to go with him because I knew that if I wasn't around, that's where he would have been. That's the way he observes Christmas. So I offered to go with him so he wouldn't miss out."

Vic looked at Erin and didn't say anything. Charley shook her head, laughing. "You seem a *little* sensitive about the subject, dear sister." She drew the word little out, exaggerating it.

"I'm not. I'm just answering your question. Terry and I are just fine. And we're not getting married."

Charley tilted her head to one side and shrugged. "*Okay*, if you say so."

"Just leave her alone, Charley," Vic warned. "You've gone far enough."

"Fine."

"You'd better get home and work on that budget," Vic suggested.

"I'll work on it tomorrow. Tonight, I'm going out."

CHAPTER 19

*E*rin looked at the big sedan with a dented fender that pulled up behind Auntie Clem's. Willie was out of town, and she had been expecting Terry to pick her and Vic up. He had volunteered. But the sedan was not Terry's, Erin instantly recognized it as belonging to Beaver. The first time she had seen Rohilda Beaven was when she had rear-ended a drug dealer's car in the middle of Bald Eagle Falls' Main Street. Beaver had claimed that it was an accident at the time, but Erin was quite sure that she had been intentionally provoking Bo Biggles.

Since then, Beaver had become a part of Bald Eagles Falls life when she wasn't on duty. She spent a lot of time in the city with her job with whatever government agency it was she worked for. Erin thought it was the DEA, but it could have been the FBI or another agency. Beaver had never been forthcoming about it.

Beaver had her secrets.

Erin leaned down to look in the window at Beaver. "I was expecting Terry… is he okay?"

"He was feeling a little under the weather, so I told him I'd buzz by and pick you up. Don't worry—I haven't had any accidents recently." She chewed a mouthful of gum, grinning at Erin and Vic.

Erin shook her head. She opened the door behind Beaver and Vic went around to the other side, sitting down in Beaver's passenger seat. The interior of the car smelled strongly of Beaver's usual brand of gum, her deodorant, and a mixture of other smells that Erin associated with her. She clearly spent a lot of time in her car. Driving to wherever her bosses were based to make reports? Sitting on surveillance for hours on end? Making phone inquiries and tracking suspects through social media? Whatever it was Beaver spent her time doing, clearly a lot of it was spent in the car. Erin pulled her seatbelt across her body.

"Terry said he wasn't feeling well?" He wouldn't usually discuss how he felt with anyone other than Erin, and even she had to pry it out of him sometimes.

"It was pretty obvious that he wasn't feeling well. He didn't say so in as many words," Beaver admitted. "But I told him I wanted to pick you up today, since I haven't seen you for a while, and he agreed. That in itself would have told me he's not himself today."

Erin sighed. Beaver had hit the nail on the head. Terry would normally have insisted that he be the one to pick Erin up. He wouldn't want anyone else to take it over. "I hope he's not too bad."

"Did he work today?" Vic inquired.

"Yeah. Morning shift. I prefer he takes afternoons because he's not as likely to stay on for a full shift instead of a half shift. Did he work the full day?" she asked Beaver.

"I don't think so. I was over there mid-afternoon and he was home."

Erin was quiet for the rest of the drive home. She didn't want to discuss Terry too much. Talking about his health, mental or physical, when he wasn't there seemed like a betrayal of confidence. Beaver and Vic were just concerned about how he felt, the same as Erin. They weren't the type who would gossip about him around town. But she still needed to observe some boundaries.

Beaver pulled in front of Erin's house with a slight squeal of tires and a stop that threw them all forward against their seatbelts.

Erin looked up and saw Beaver watching her in the rear-view mirror. Erin shook her head.

"I should tell Officer Piper to keep an eye on you. Reckless driving. You could get a ticket, you know."

Beaver chuckled. "It wouldn't be the first one." She reached over in front of Vic to click open the glovebox, where Erin saw a stack of ragged papers. Were those all traffic tickets, or was Beaver just teasing?

"How are you going to pay all of those?"

"I am not. Any tickets I incur in the course of my job will just disappear." Beaver made a 'vanishing' gesture with her fingers like a magician.

Erin released her seatbelt and got out of the car. "You are a menace."

"Yes, ma'am," Beaver agreed. She got out of the car.

Erin glanced at her as they walked up to the house. She had expected Beaver to drop her at the curb, not to escort her in or stay to visit. Erin didn't want to be rude and tell Beaver that if Terry wasn't feeling well, she shouldn't impose on him. Beaver should have been able to figure that out herself.

The door had been left unlocked. Erin pushed the door open and Beaver followed her into the house.

Terry was leaning his head forward, a cold pack across the back of his head and neck. Erin went to him and touched him on the arm briefly. "Bad today?"

He grunted. "I've had worse."

"Beaver is here."

Terry turned his head to look at their visitor, then returned his head to its previous position and closed his eyes. "What is it, Beaver?"

Beaver sat down on one of the chairs. Erin sat down beside Terry, picking up a noisy Orange Blossom who was trying to get her attention and share all of the details of his day with her. She cuddled him and scratched his ears, but didn't talk to him like she would have if they had been alone. Not because Beaver would have thought that there was anything wrong with it. But it didn't seem very dignified to talk to her cat like a baby in front of a visitor. Other than Vic or Terry, who had heard it plenty of times before.

"I've been hearing some chatter," Beaver began.

"About what?" Erin demanded immediately, the words getting out of her mouth before she'd had a chance to think about them. "Campbell? Theresa?"

Beaver gave Erin a thoughtful look before turning back toward Terry. "I would like to have a better fix on where Theresa Franklin is right now, but that was not what I was talking about."

Terry waited.

"What, then?" Erin prompted. She wanted to get Beaver out of there as quickly as she could to take care of Terry.

"About your latest body."

"My latest body? It's not *my* body!"

"Maybe not, but you have a knack for stumbling across them."

Erin looked for an argument, but couldn't find one. Beaver watched her, chewing her gum slowly. Then she turned her attention back to Terry, though he wasn't looking at her, eyes closed as he iced his neck and head.

"I'm sure lots of people are talking about it," Erin admitted. They came to talk to her at the bakery and they quieted when she walked into a room. They couldn't have been much more obvious. "So that's not news."

"There is no news yet. Not… official news."

"What, then?"

"The initial examination suggests that Ms. Batcombe was dead before she was placed in the freezer."

Erin's eyes went wide and she felt the blood drain out of her face. Terry's arm went around behind her back and pulled her firmly against his side.

"She didn't die in the freezer?" he demanded. "Then, how?"

"A finding hasn't been made yet. I'll hear when it is. But the bottom line is… that body didn't walk into the freezer room on its own."

Erin put her hand down on Terry's leg and squeezed it tightly, trying to anchor herself to him.

"How do they know that? If the postmortem isn't done yet, how would they know she didn't die in there?"

"There are ways of telling when a body has been moved after death. Lividity, for one. You didn't move her, right? According to all of the witness statements, you kept well back after the discovery."

"Yes. I mean, no, I didn't touch her or move her. I stayed back and kept everyone out."

Beaver nodded as if this were what she had expected. Erin had seen enough crime scenes to know to keep back and not touch anything. When she touched things, it just made her interactions with the police during the investigation much more difficult. She wanted to stay below the cops' radar. She didn't want to be treated as a suspect.

Been there, done that.

"How did she die, then?" Terry questioned, not looking up. "No signs of violence?"

"Nothing obvious. But that doesn't mean they won't find anything in the post. Maybe she'd had too much to drink. An allergic reaction. A heart attack. Anything is possible."

"If she had just had an accident or dropped dead… then who would move her?"

"Yeah," Beaver acknowledged. "Exactly. If she didn't die in the freezer, then who moved her into the freezer, and why?"

Erin tried to think of an innocent reason someone might have done that. She couldn't think of anything. If someone had found her dead or had been with her when she died, he should have just called the police or ambulance. There was no innocent reason Erin could think of to move the body.

"Have you heard anything through the grapevine?" Beaver

asked Erin. "From the other judges or officials? Anyone who is entering something into the contest?"

"No. We've had our initial orientation—or started it, anyway—but we haven't had much of a chance to talk and exchange opinions. I just know Vic, and she didn't know any more than I did about Beryl."

"Someone else associated with the contest must have known her."

"Yes… whoever picked her as a judge. Anyone who has lived here long enough to know her or her family. The officials must have been given packages on each of us. Biographies or CV's."

"Did the chef know her?"

"I don't think so. I only know him from the cruise, not because he's from these parts. He didn't say that he was here to see anyone else or had picked out the location because he knew someone here."

"Just you."

Erin's face heated again. She looked over at Terry, but he didn't look up, in the grips of his headache.

"Not just me. Vic too. And Terry and Willie."

"But you're the one he came for. You and he became friends on the cruise, cooked together. Isn't that the history?"

"Yes," Erin agreed reluctantly. She didn't want to think that he had come to Tennessee just for her. He'd had other reasons for picking Whitewater as the location for the contest to be held. He hadn't picked Bald Eagle Falls. If he'd been there just for Erin, he would have picked Bald Eagle Falls, wouldn't he? Maybe he had known Beryl. Maybe they had a history and he'd chosen Whitewater because of her. Erin and Vic had just been a bonus. Erin rubbed the bridge of her nose. She was getting a headache too, worried about being in the middle of another murder investigation.

"Maybe Chef Kirschoff knew Beryl. I don't know."

Beaver nodded slowly, chewing her gum all the time. "You gave a statement to the police in Whitewater?"

"Yes. Of course."

"You can expect that they'll be calling you back."

"I already told them everything I know. Which was next to nothing. I can't help it that I was the one who found her. Don't you think that if I had done something to harm her, I would have stayed away from that cold room? I would have been the last person in the room instead of the first one. It was just a freak accident. A random chance."

"A normal person might have avoided being the first one to open the door. Someone who was thinking and acting logically might have been the last one in instead of the first. But a psychopath might have. An adrenaline junkie would have for sure. There are all kinds of aberrant personalities who would have reveled in being the first in the room and telling the police about it."

"You know me. That's not what I'm like."

"I know more about you than you would probably like," Beaver said. "But what a person appears to be and what they are inside isn't always the same. You have a checkered past. And ever since you moved to Bald Eagle Falls, you've been stumbling into crime scenes." She raised her brows. "*That's* not normal."

Erin's mouth was dry. Her stomach was knotted with anxiety. She counted Beaver as a friend, but the woman had always been an enigma. She liked to make trouble. She liked to cause waves. She was probably just provoking Erin to see if she could get a good reaction. She couldn't *really* think that Erin had anything to do with any of the crime in Bald Eagle Falls or the area. She was just teasing.

"Beaver." Terry lifted the ice pack off of the back of his neck and glared at her. "Leave Erin alone."

Beaver grinned her wide, open-mouthed grin. She was having the time of her life. "I'm just following up on what I heard."

"Leave her be. You know she didn't have anything to do with this."

"Know? No." Beaver stood up slowly. She took a couple of

steps toward the door. "I don't think she did. But I'm not one to jump to conclusions. We'll see where the evidence points."

"All of the cases that Erin has had any involvement in have been solved. She hasn't been guilty of anything. Except maybe asking too many questions and not staying out of an investigation when she's told to. Poor judgment, but nothing criminal."

Beaver nodded, then raised a hand in a wave and left.

Erin shook her head. She was actually shaking. "You know I didn't have anything to do with that woman's death."

"Of course I do." Terry put the ice pack back on his neck, then grimaced. "This is too warm to do any good anymore."

Erin got unsteadily to her feet. "Give that one to me and I'll get another one out."

She swapped the warmed-up ice pack with one from the freezer. She handed it to Terry, thinking of Beryl's body in the freezer as she did so.

eaver had not shared her thoughts or the fact that Beryl's body had been moved with anyone else. Erin didn't have to put up with the questions of curious townspeople speculating about who had moved the body and why. If word got out, she was sure she wouldn't have been able to get a moment's peace and quiet.

So she kept her head down and her ears open. Whatever had happened to Beryl, it was bound to leak out sooner or later. People were always gossiping about police reports in Bald Eagle Falls, even if they didn't know the actual contents themselves. Speculating was fair game. And sometimes, someone knew something they shouldn't and ended up giving himself away.

"Erin." Vic tapped her arm.

Erin reined in her attention. She looked around the bakery, feeling like she had been absent for the previous half hour. What had happened? What had she done? Who had she talked to?

Several of Vic's friends were there. Erin had clearly been blanking them out, focused on her own thoughts and worries.

"Um, sorry? What?"

"Jack is really good with cars."

Erin looked at Vic blankly. "Okay…"

"I wondered if you wanted to go car shopping this weekend. It's the last weekend we have before the contest, and you thought it would be good to have your own car to get around in Whitewater and not have to rely on anyone else's."

"Yeah." Erin had forgotten about that conversation. So much else had been going on that it had completely escaped her mind. "We had talked about that. But I don't think there's enough time now. I haven't done any research. I would need to line up a bunch of different possibilities, and then research each of the cars, and its performance and safety ratings. And then there's financing and negotiating…"

"You don't need to finance. You've got the money in the bank. And I was just saying, Jack is really good with cars. They can help you to find one. Something really good. So you don't have to do all of that research. They can just look at the paper this weekend, and pull a few cars that look good, and they can come with us to look and give it a test drive."

Erin looked at Vic's friends, trying to pick out the one called Jack. "That's a really nice offer, but…"

"Happy to help." Jack said with a smile.

"You must have other things you'd rather be doing this weekend. Aren't you entered in the contest? You'll want to be perfecting your recipe…"

"My recipe is all ready to go. No worries there. Don't you want the help?" Jack was beginning to look a little affronted.

"I just wasn't planning on doing anything that fast. I know we talked about doing it before the contest, but I don't want to rush into anything. And I don't have that much time. We need to get ready for the contest ourselves…"

Vic shook her head. "We don't need to do anything to get ready. We've got a couple of events, but we can work around that."

"Charley has been planning all of this other stuff. I really don't think I can spare the time…"

"You told Charley that she had to be in charge of it herself. She's the one who needs to put the time into it. You gave her your guidance. She can call on you with questions, but you told her she has to be the one taking care of things."

"I know. But you know Charley, she's going to need to be bailed out."

"Not literally this time, I hope."

"That's not funny."

Vic peered at Erin, then decided maybe she had pushed it too far. "Okay, sorry. Didn't mean to hurt your feelings. But I mean… the way that you and Charley originally met…"

"We met because I was looking for her. Not because of… all of that."

Jack was looking back and forth between them. "Well? Does that mean we go ahead and do it? Come on. I'd like to help out. And I need to get my hands greasy. I'm going into automobile withdrawal, here."

Erin sighed. She wasn't going to get out of it by being polite. If she really wanted to tell Jack no, she would have to do so bluntly and risk offending.

"Okay, maybe. Take a look at the paper when it comes out and see if there is anything that looks really good. Midrange, I don't want to pay too much. Not an old beater…" She ignored the way Vic rolled her eyes. She already knew how Vic had felt about her previous car. The one that was no more. "But not something luxury, either. Just… a good 'mom' car, easy to drive, good gas mileage…"

Jack smiled. "Excellent. I'll take a look and let you know. I'm sure I can find you something."

"Maybe. I'm not rushing into it, so if it isn't the right time… I'll just work something out with Terry. He'll let me use his while we're in Whitewater."

~

Erin hadn't heard anything back from Charley about the events and budget that she had approved. She'd expected Charley to be back to her half a dozen times on little things that she wanted Erin's advice or experience on. Not because Charley couldn't be self-sufficient and independent, but because they were partners in the business and Charley wanted to make sure that Erin was fully involved and didn't disapprove of Charley's ideas. It wouldn't look good for them to be on the outs. People would talk and the bakery would lose business.

But Charley had been working away on her own and hadn't gone back to Erin with questions or problems, and that made her nervous, waiting for the other shoe to drop. Sooner or later, Charley would come to Erin with a problem, and the closer it got to the contest date, the more sure Erin was that it would end up derailing everything.

She decided to be proactive and to call Charley and discuss matters with her. If there were any issues, it was best to get them out in the open right away, before they ended up getting blown out of proportion. She tapped Charley's contact picture on the phone and waited for the call to connect.

Charley answered in a couple of rings. "Erin. Hi, how are things coming along?"

"Things are fine on my end, but I don't have a bunch of stuff to plan. How about you? How are your events coming along?"

"Really good. I've been working closely with Chef Kirschoff, and things are really coming together."

"Oh…" That came as a surprise. "Well, that's really good. Chef Kirschoff liked our ideas? He's willing to endorse everything?"

"Yeah. He came up with some really good ways of doing some of them."

"That's great."

"I'm meeting him at lunch today. Why don't you join us, and we can go over anything you're worried about."

Erin felt like she had suddenly been changed from the role of a parent to that of a child. Charley didn't need her to provide any information or advice. Instead, Charley was suggesting that she could bring Erin up to speed and solve any problems she might have. Erin looked around the bakery. Bella was coming on at noon and could help Vic to cover the rush. Erin had left space in her schedule in case she had to rescue Charley, so she had the resources available.

"Yeah, I guess so. That would work fine. Where are you meeting? Chinese?"

"No, the family restaurant. Hans wanted to try it out."

Hans. Charley was calling him by his first name. As if Chef Kirschoff wasn't a world-famous master chef, but just a guy from down the street. Erin gritted her teeth. He had told her to call him Hans. They were friends now. Charley wasn't taking liberties.

"At noon?"

"Yeah. Can you make it?"

Maybe Charley was hoping that Erin wouldn't be able to make it, knowing that they normally had a rush over the lunch hour. "Yes. I can be there."

"Great," Charley responded, sounding surprised. "I'll see you there."

Erin still felt a little guilty leaving Bella and Vic to handle the noon-hour rush, but Vic shooed her away, assuring her that they were up to the task. They certainly didn't need three people to handle a shift that was normally covered by two. Erin would just be underfoot if she stayed to try to help. So she gave herself a stern talking to and got on her way.

She didn't have Terry's truck, so she walked over to the family restaurant. It was only a few blocks, not a hardship, especially in the winter, when the weather was pleasant. It wouldn't have been so easy in the sweltering heat of the summer.

Kirschoff and Charley were at the restaurant already. Erin felt like a third wheel joining them, but she had been invited. Hans stood up to greet her exuberantly, shaking her hand with two hands, then hugging her and bussing both cheeks. He sat back down, smiling widely at her. Charley nodded a greeting, not nearly as effusive.

"Hey, Erin. Glad you could make it."

"Yeah. I'm glad you guys are meeting and sorting things out. That's great."

"Your sister has some excellent ideas," Chef Kirschoff offered. "I'm glad that she got involved."

Erin nodded. And she had to admit he was right. Even without any time to organize anything, Charley had been able to come up with half a dozen ideas that piggybacked off of the already-planned events, good ways to get the name and brand of Auntie Clem's Bakery into the event. And of course, Erin's and Vic's biographies would be published in all of the event materials and read at the beginning of the judging. It would be good publicity for the bakery. She was glad that the contest was still going ahead, even if she felt a little guilty about carrying on as if there hadn't been an untimely death marring the event.

"Did you have any questions? Or have you and Charley already sorted everything out?"

"I think we have most of it covered," Kirschoff said. He patted Charley's hand. "Charley has been very helpful."

The look that Charley returned was more than friendly. She clasped Kirschoff's hand in return, smiling sweetly. "I couldn't have done any of it without Hans."

"And, of course, with the approval of Auntie Clem's Bakery," Kirschoff added, nodding at Erin to include her in all of the accolades.

"Oh, this has all been Charley," Erin said, her face a mask as she tried to keep her smile pinned in place. "Charley was the one who came up with the ideas and has been coordinating everything. All I did was approve the budget and the branding. The broad strokes."

They looked at their menus and discussed Tennessee family

cooking, Erin and Charley interpreting anything obscure on the menu for Chef Kirschoff.

"Charming, just charming," he murmured, reading through it. "I'm glad I made time in my schedule to come here."

"You've never been in Tennessee before?" Charley asked. "You fit right in. I never would have guessed."

Kirschoff laughed heartily. "An old European like me? I don't think so. But thank you anyway! It's too bad that it's only soda pop and ice cream. I've been getting as much local color as I could since I arrived, but there could have been so much more if it had been an actual cook-off instead of a 'cool off.'"

"Some of the ice cream and coke flavors will have a Tennessee twist," Charley offered. "I've heard about some of the creations that are being planned, and you'll still get some classic Tennessee flavors."

Kirschoff nodded. They waved the waitress over and placed their orders.

Erin noticed that when Kirschoff and Charley removed their hands from the top of the table where they had been fully visible, they reconnected underneath the table.

Charley had certainly moved in quickly. It would seem that they were well on their way to a relationship.

Erin couldn't object. After all, she had Terry and wasn't looking for someone else. But she couldn't help feeling a little twinge about Charley stealing her friend. Kirschoff wasn't even Charley's type. She should have just left him alone.

CHAPTER 22

The first big event was the science fair. Erin hadn't been sure what to expect from it. She'd never heard of a science fair being held in connection with a cook-off before. But when she walked into the auditorium of the Whitewater school, she realized that it had been an inspired idea.

The carbon dioxide themed cook-off was a great basis for a science fair. Erin started to walk through the exhibits, seeing projects based around respiration, plants, aquariums, pollution, and of course, food preparation.

The science fair covered the whole range of ages. It wasn't just for the school kids, though a number of the exhibits had obviously been created by children. She saw a baking soda and vinegar volcano ready to be demonstrated. She stopped at another with colorful Pop Rocks on display.

The little girl with round glasses and a long pinafore dress gazed up at her.

"What do Pop Rocks have to do with carbon dioxide?" Erin asked.

The little girl pushed up her glasses with one finger. "Pop Rocks are infused with carbon dioxide at high pressure," she explained, "so it gets trapped inside the candy. When you put Pop

Rocks in your mouth or water, then that's what the fizzing and popping come from. The candy melts, releasing the pockets of carbon dioxide."

"Really!" Erin was amazed. "Who knew! I thought it was just a chemical reaction." She motioned to the baking soda volcano. "That when something in the Pop Rocks gets wet, there's a chemical reaction that makes it pop. I never realized that there was anything trapped inside!"

The little girl smiled proudly. She motioned to the tiny cups with a few Pop Rocks in the bottom of each. "There are free samples if you would like some."

Erin thought it would be rude to refuse them after stopping to talk, so she picked up a cup of purple rocks and spilled them into her mouth. They popped loudly, making her and the girl both laugh.

Erin went on through the various exhibits. She reached the end of the children's displays and studied the more complex adult exhibits. She stopped at some kind of machine with a pressurized tank and twisting tubes that looked like something out of a steampunk story or mad scientist movie.

"What exactly is this?"

The man at the display moved closer to her. He was tall and thin with dark hair and a small mustache. "This is a DIY carbonator," he explained. "I will be using this to make my entry for the contest."

"You can carbonate drinks with this?"

"Of course."

"It's so big! I've seen the little table-top ones that you can buy at the store to use at home. And the big square ones that restaurants use. But I've never seen anything like this."

"It's basically the same thing as the restaurant ones, if you strip off the outer box, it all comes down to the same thing, a way to add carbon dioxide to your flavored syrup. You need a tank and tubes."

Erin nodded. "I guess. This looks really cool, though. And dangerous."

"It's not dangerous. No more so than your barbecue. You turn it on and off. Make sure everything is properly sealed and that it isn't near any heat sources. Nothing is going to happen."

"So, you're registered for the contest?"

"Yes. You're in for a treat."

Erin was surprised that he recognized her as one of the judges, but she supposed she shouldn't be. Her picture and bio were in the literature and the organizers had been making announcements on the TV and radio. They name-dropped whenever they could.

"Well… I'll look forward to it, Mr.…"

He whipped out a business card and handed it to her. "John Slayer," he offered. "Flavorista extraordinaire!"

Erin smiled, taking the card from him. "Very nice to meet you. That's a really interesting machine."

"Thank you! I look forward to tickling your taste buds!"

Erin was glad that the judging was done blind. She would have a tough time judging which sodas and ice creams she liked best if she knew who had made each one.

Erin reached the end of the aisle and noticed a group of parents and youths standing a few yards away, watching her and talking. She tried to ignore the stares, assuming they were looking at one of the exhibits behind her. She recognized some of them as being from Bald Eagle Falls. Occasional customers or families she had met through the Christmas fundraiser at the school. Erin headed over to the water station to get herself a drink, which brought her closer to the little group.

"Got to watch her with the children," someone murmured, loudly enough for Erin to hear even with the noise of the auditorium. "She acts friendly and then takes advantage of them."

Erin's eyes snapped to the speaker, one of the parents from Bald Eagle Falls. The woman, a tired-looking woman in her late thirties, stared back at Erin, making no attempt at hiding the fact that she had noticed Erin's attention.

"I thought she could be trusted," someone else said. "But it turns out she's just looking out for her own interests. And her friends'."

They had to be talking about someone else. It was only coincidence that the tired woman happened to be looking in Erin's direction. Erin would never have done anything to take advantage of a child. Nor was she in the habit of choosing her own interests over those of others. She always tried to respect and help others, especially the little ones.

They were talking about someone else. Probably someone who wasn't even there. Who Erin didn't even know.

"First she says she's an atheist, then she shows up at church," another mother contributed. "I bet she's been lying this whole time, just because she doesn't want to be called out for being a bad Christian."

Erin blinked at this. They couldn't very well be talking about anyone else. Bald Eagle Falls wasn't exactly overflowing with atheists. Not those who would admit it, anyway. And not people who claimed to be atheists and then went to the candlelight service on Christmas Eve.

They could only be talking about her.

Erin froze where she was, trying to figure out what to do. Pretend she hadn't heard them? Defend herself? Try to find some way to explain and make them understand her actions? Let them know that she had heard them, but then ignore them?

They weren't going to understand, no matter how much she tried to explain. They could only understand their own belief system and didn't think that anyone could fall outside it. Anyone who professed otherwise was simply lying.

Erin continued on her way to the water station, out of earshot of the little huddle of parents and youths, and drank the lukewarm water from a paper cup while she thought about it.

She was used to people not understanding her lack of religious beliefs. She got that. People who believed just didn't understand how anyone could not believe. Her attendance at the church service with Terry confused people. It would pass as real life and genuine concerns took over.

The assertion that she would take advantage of the children she was friends with hurt. She would never do anything to harm them.

Mrs. Foster wouldn't let her see Peter anymore because Erin had reported what he had said to the police. Mary Lou was upset with her for mentioning Joshua to Terry, which had resulted in his falling under suspicion and being questioned as part of their investigation. No harm had come to either child. Their parents didn't like falling under police scrutiny, but she had kept the children safe, not vice versa.

"Hi, Erin!" Melissa broke through Erin's dark thoughts, getting into her personal space and smiling at her, her wild dark curls bouncing. "Everything okay?"

Erin took a small step back, giving herself a little more space. "Yeah. Everything is fine," she said, her voice a little wobbly. She looked over at the knot of parents, still talking to each other. About her? Or had they gone on to something else now?

Melissa followed her gaze. She understood immediately. "People will look for any excuse not to make their kids accountable for what they did," she told Erin. "They'd rather blame anyone else than admit that their kids were involved in something illegal, something that hurt a lot of people in Bald Eagle Falls."

"I was trying to keep people safe. To stop the burglaries."

"And you did. You did the right thing, whether all of those people like it or not," Melissa assured her.

"But how could they be mad at me instead of at the people who were breaking the law and hurting others?"

"Because that would mean that they had to take responsibility for what their own kids did."

Erin shook her head. "I got in plenty of trouble as a kid… none of my foster parents ever had any trouble putting the responsibility squarely on my shoulders." Maybe even a bit too much, blaming her for things that she hadn't done or that they themselves had contributed to.

"Well, good for them. That's what they should do. But some parents…" Melissa scowled at the group, "they're always looking for excuses."

They could see that Erin and Melissa were talking about them, though Erin was sure they couldn't hear what was being said. Melissa wasn't exactly covert with her looks.

"How long is this going to go on?"

Melissa shrugged. "I don't know. Some of those kids will get off with probation and community service, but some of them are going to go to prison. I don't imagine that will make people too happy."

Erin broke out in goosebumps. She sipped at her warm water, her skin crawling. How many parents were going to be watching her, waiting for a chance to get back at her for turning the investigation on their children? If their kids went to prison, they weren't likely to forget Erin's part in the arrests.

On TV, when people solved murders or other crimes, there were never any negative consequences. It was always a "happily ever after," with the bad guys being shipped off to jail and the rest of the town happily going about their business. Erin couldn't think of a single mystery series where the person who had helped solve the mystery was ostracized for her part in the arrests.

But she'd known from the beginning that it wasn't a TV show. TV show sleuths never got PTSD from the violence they witnessed, either.

"Just ignore them, Erin," Melissa advised. "Never let people like that bother you. You know you did the right thing."

Erin nodded slowly. "That doesn't make it feel any better, though." She looked at the group. "Maybe I should pull out of judging the competition. I don't really want… the more I'm at the center of attention, the angrier people are going to be about it. And who knows what they might say or do."

"Don't pull out. Don't let people like that dictate your actions."

Erin sighed and looked away. "Does it ever feel like no matter what you do, people aren't going to like it? That there's always going to be a negative consequence no matter how right the decision seems?"

Melissa patted Erin on the back.

CHAPTER 23

*E*rin left the school auditorium with a feeling of relief. She breathed in the cool, crisp air and felt like she had just walked out of prison. She was supposed to be meeting Vic and Willie for lunch, and Terry if he felt well enough and was able to make it. There wasn't much opportunity for Erin to go anywhere but the few Bald Eagle Falls restaurants to eat, so it was nice to have a new place to try out. The Whitewater BBQ joint was supposed to be really good and she was looking forward to trying it out, despite feeling depressed about how some of the people of Bald Eagle Falls now hated her.

She looked around the restaurant and spotted Willie. Not hard to pick out his dark face, stained by the mining and processing of minerals from his mines. He got a lot of looks from people who thought he must be some dirty, homeless guy. But he wasn't. He was hardworking and the processing left a stain on his skin that couldn't be washed out by any amount of scrubbing.

Erin sat down with him. "Hi, Willie."

"Erin." He gave a friendly nod. "How are you this fine day?"

"Oh…" Erin tried not to let her mood show too much. "It's been a bit stressful, but I'm fine."

He studied her for a moment. "I'd hope that something like

this contest would be fun and exciting, but I'm sure there's a lot of stress that goes with it. So much to be done, being in the spotlight, knowing there are deadlines."

"Yeah. All of that," Erin agreed. She didn't tell him about the parents from Bald Eagle Falls. If anyone knew how judgmental people could be there, it was Willie. He always had people looking down at him, commenting on him being lazy, shiftless, and an outsider. Nothing could be further from the truth.

"And then there's finding bodies," Willie continued. "That always puts a crimp in the festivities."

"One body," Erin said firmly. "Just one. And she was…" Erin wasn't sure what she had started off to say. Beryl wasn't anyone Erin knew? She wasn't murdered, had just wandered in there and died on her own? No one seemed to like her very much anyway? Erin let her words die away. "I don't know. I'm trying not to think about it. To let it bother me."

"That's probably a good plan. You don't want to get yourself into something—" He left the sentence as if it were unfinished. Maybe he'd planned to say 'again'?

Erin eyed him, but he looked innocently back at her as if he didn't know what she was thinking.

"Yeah. I'll just leave it to the police," Erin said flatly.

A woman sitting at a nearby table turned and looked at her, maybe overhearing the phrase and wanting to know what excitement was going on, what it was that the police needed to be called about. She looked at Erin for a moment and then smiled.

"You're Erin Price, aren't you? One of the judges?"

"Yes. I am." Erin studied the slim, attractive redhead with freckles across her nose and cheeks. "Are you a contestant?"

"Yes! I'm really excited about the contest. I would tell you all about what I'm making, but I know we're not supposed to talk about it, especially to the judges. But I have this old family recipe that is really fantastic, it is going to blow you away. Really. It's that good."

Erin smiled and nodded politely. "I'm sure it will," she agreed.

"But a lot of people have delicious family recipes. Or new ones. There's a lot of competition."

"Trust me, you'll be seeing this face again." The woman pointed at her own face and drew a circle around it in the air. "I'm Daisy Forsythe."

"It's a pleasure to meet you," Erin told her. She turned her face slightly toward Willie, hoping that Daisy would take the hint and let her continue with her private conversation. Daisy looked at her for another minute, then went back to conversing with the two teen girls at her table.

"You're a celebrity," Willie noted.

Erin glanced around. Vic wasn't there yet, and should have been there ahead of Erin. There was no sign of Terry, but Erin hadn't been sure whether to expect him. She knew that he might not feel like getting into the truck to drive that far, just to have lunch with her. The vibration, noise, and bouncing of the truck tended to aggravate his head. And then there were the crowded conditions and noise of the restaurant. If it were too much for him, he might not be able to make it back home. She slid her phone out to have a look at it and see if either Terry or Vic had texted her. There was a brief message from Vic that she was running late and would be there as soon as she could be.

Erin sighed. "Well, we might as well order. I don't think Terry is going to make it and Vic is running late."

Willie looked at Erin for a moment, then nodded. "All right," he grumbled. "I guess we're on our own."

They motioned for the waitress and placed their orders. Even though Willie hadn't said anything to indicate that he was upset, Erin sensed from his curt manner that he wasn't too happy.

"Sorry neither of the others could make it."

Willie scratched his neck. "At least I've got good company. Officer Piper has a good excuse for not being here. I know he's still having health issues."

"I'm sure Vic has a good reason for being late too."

He shook his head. "She's off with that group of hers. The folks from the boat."

"Still… we don't know what has kept them. There could be a good explanation."

Willie didn't suggest one. Erin had a hard time coming up with one herself. Of course, it was possible that someone's car had broken down. Or someone had fallen ill and had to be taken to the hospital. But other than that, she couldn't really think of a good reason for Vic to be late for their planned lunch. She had known about it ahead of time and should have told her new group of friends that she would need to split at lunchtime.

"She's still coming," Erin pointed out. "She'll be here soon."

Willie raised an eyebrow and didn't argue. Erin knew that like her, Willie didn't particularly like Vic's new friends, or at least the time that she spent with them.

There was no reason Vic couldn't have her own group of friends that she didn't share with either of them, but Erin couldn't help feeling like she had been abandoned when Vic had things to do that didn't involve their little Bald Eagle Falls family.

They had been through so much together, Erin felt unaccountably resentful of Vic having another life.

Vic breezed in half an hour later, not by herself, but surrounded by her giggling, chattering friends. She gave a big wave across the restaurant and she and her friends moved in to join Willie and Erin, dragging tables and chairs over to form a big seating group. She had Nilla, the little white dog with her, and Erin braced for an argument from management telling her that she couldn't bring a dog into the restaurant. But Vic got Nilla settled under the table by her feet, and the waitress pretended not to notice him as she got their drink orders.

"He's been kind of cranky today," Vic said, seeing the direction of Erin's gaze. "I don't know if he's missing Beryl or if we just tired him out, but he has been kind of snappish. Maybe he doesn't like large groups."

Erin bit her lip. "Hey, I thought we were going to…"

"Where's Terry?" Vic asked. "He couldn't make it?"

"No. I guess he's not feeling up to it. I thought you were going to ditch us too."

"I wouldn't do that! We just got held up. Things took longer than we expected." Vic looked around at the others. "Do you guys want actual meals? I'm not hungry after everything else we've had. I thought maybe just share some appetizers?"

"Or desserts," Melanie suggested, her white teeth gleaming against her dark complexion. "I wouldn't mind something sweet."

"Mmm, not for me." Vic shook her head. "I've got sugary drinks and desserts coming up in a week." She looked at Erin. "I should probably watch my calories until then."

"And deep-fried appetizers are better?" Melanie countered.

"Well…" Vic opened the menu she had grabbed as they walked in and scanned the appetizers. "There are a few things that wouldn't be too bad. Bruschetta. Veggies with dip. What do you guys want?"

There was some discussion and, eventually, they settled on a couple of appetizers to share. They continued to chatter among themselves, not involving Erin and Willie in the conversation, which centered around the places they had already visited and any other sightseeing that was still on their lists. When their appetizers arrived, they quieted, giving their attention to the food.

"Oh, Erin," Jack touched Erin's arm. "I know we didn't find anything for you before this weekend, but I found some car listings in the city that you might be interested in looking at today or tomorrow. Some pretty good opportunities. Do you want to have a look at them together?"

Erin shook her head. "I have a lot of things to get done this weekend. I don't think I'll have the time."

"You shouldn't let them slide. I think we could put you in a car that you'd be really happy with."

"We?"

Jack laughed. "I sound like a car salesman, don't I? Sorry! I get in the habit of talking that way to clients. I don't mean to presume!"

"I don't think I have the time to do anything until the contest is over. Really. It's going to keep me really busy, and I don't want my attention to be divided with another responsibility."

"Vic can find the time to go out with us, and you both have the same job, don't you?" Jack challenged.

Erin closed her eyes and took a deep breath. She opened them and looked at Vic, signaling for her to deal with it. For a moment, Vic didn't say anything, raising an eyebrow at Erin to see if she would answer herself. When Erin didn't, Vic finally spoke up.

"Erin does have other responsibilities too. She's the owner of the bakery, so even though she's away, there is still work that needs to be done and things that need to be managed. And Terry, her partner, he's still suffering from a head injury. So there's that." She paused, waiting to see if Erin would fill anything else in. Because obviously, those things were not taking up a lot of Erin's time. She just didn't want to go car shopping with Jack.

"I thought that other woman was the owner of the bakery?" Melanie put in.

Erin looked at her. "Who?" Her thoughts went immediately to Beryl. As far as she knew, Beryl Batcombe did not own a bakery. Still, Erin's mind flashed back to the death of Angela Plaint, the former owner of The Bake Shoppe, which would have been Erin's competition, if Angela hadn't been killed or if Charley had decided to go ahead with her plan to run The Bake Shoppe herself. For some reason, Beryl's and Angela's deaths became intertwined in her mind.

But Beryl's death had been an accident and she wasn't a bakery owner.

"We saw Charley earlier," Vic explained, seeing Erin's look of confusion. "That's who she means."

"Oh. Yes, Charley and I are partners in Auntie Clem's Bakery."

"And she's the one getting all cozy with Chef Kirschoff, right?" Melanie persisted. "She's taking care of all of the activities associated with the competition."

Getting cozy with Kirschoff? Erin flashed a look at Vic, who gave a shrug. "They were looking pretty… friendly," she admitted.

"I told Charley not to get involved with him!"

Clayton raised an eyebrow at Erin, interested.

"Why not?" Melanie put in. "What does it matter who he is interested in? As long as it's not a contest entrant, it doesn't make any difference. You have a man, don't you?"

"Who says she can only have one?" Jack challenged.

Erin felt her eyes widen. She shook her head. "Yes, I have a… partner already. And I'm not looking for another one. But the two of them… Chef Kirschoff isn't Charley's type. Charley will just end up getting bored with him, breaking up and hurting his feelings. I don't want her to… upset him. Mess up his life."

"You've got a good opinion of your co-owner." Melanie shook her head. "Everybody gets jammed up sometimes. We'll all end up in relationships that don't work out. If she's happy with him and he's happy with her, then just leave it alone and see what works out. Unless," she gave a nod in Jack's direction, "you already have an understanding with Chef Kirschoff."

"Or unless he has one with someone else," Clayton contributed.

"No. It isn't like that." Erin took a drink, trying to hide her embarrassment. "I just don't think it's a good idea."

Melanie shrugged. "Then let them make their mistakes. That's the way life goes."

CHAPTER 24

$\mathcal{E}$rin had been planning to spend most of the afternoon relaxing, despite her claim that she was far too busy for car shopping.

And maybe she shouldn't have lied and made out that she couldn't spend any time car shopping that weekend. Maybe it was the universe getting back at her for breaking the rules. Though Erin didn't believe in karma or in universal rules.

She was walking from the restaurant to the hotel to have a nap or spend some time just browsing the web for new recipes or spending some time on social media. She didn't see Deputy Coleman until he was right in front of her. They stopped just a few feet away from each other, Coleman holding his hand up in a tentative signal to stop.

"What? Oh, Deputy Coleman. Sorry, I was off in my own little world. Can I… help you with something?"

She knew better than to ask a cop that. She really did.

"Well, I was actually hoping for the chance to have a further conversation with you. Do you have some time now to come talk to me?"

"Uh… I was just going back to my hotel…"

"I figured I'd probably find you here this weekend, attending to more business with our little contest."

"Yeah. There's lots to be done for a contest like this." Which wasn't quite true, because Erin wasn't actually taking care of any of the organizational details as she implied. She had a few commitments, but mostly the contest organizers and sponsors just wanted her to be seen around town and for her to actually participate in the judging the week after that.

"So is there any chance I could take you away from it for a while? It won't be all afternoon this time."

Erin's mind went back to the tedious questioning in the glass room. She hated being in that fish tank, with everyone looking in at her, watching to see if she would break and admit to... whatever they might think she had done.

"I really don't think I'm up to it. I mean... I could spend a few minutes with you here, at my hotel, but I don't think I have the time to get to the police station."

Coleman studied her with a hint of amusement in his eyes. So maybe he saw right through her attempts to put him off and understood how much she had hated being questioned in the middle of the brightly-lit tank.

"Yes, if you could spare a few minutes, that would be very helpful," he agreed.

Erin wished she hadn't made the offer. She wished that Terry had made it to lunch and was with her. He would be better at turning Coleman down. She wasn't doing a very good job of it.

They walked together the last block and a half to the hotel. They found a table in the bar and grill on the main floor and ordered a round of hot drinks; coffee for Coleman and tea for Erin.

"Never been much of a tea-drinker myself," Coleman confessed when their drinks were brought to the table.

"I really wasn't before I came here. Except I did learn a lot about tea when I stayed here with my aunt."

"Here?"

"In Bald Eagle Falls. My Aunt Clementine owned a tea room, and she looked after me a few times while she was working there, so I learned a lot about the teas she sold."

"How old were you?"

"Just little. I was eight when I… left."

Coleman sipped his coffee. "I have to have my caffeine."

"I'm the opposite. I'm used to getting up very early in the morning to have bread baked before we open. If I had caffeine in the afternoon, I'd never be able to sleep."

He nodded. "So what brought you back to God's country if you left when you were eight?"

"I inherited my aunt's tea shop. Except I reopened it as a bakery. Auntie Clem's."

He nodded. They had talked about her ownership of Auntie Clem's Bakery during their last interview. "That was lucky, then."

"Some luck. Some hard work."

"I don't doubt it," Coleman agreed.

Erin looked around restlessly. "So what did you want to talk to me about? I told you everything I could the first time."

"There have been developments. I was hoping that you might be able to give me a hand with some of the smaller points."

"I can't imagine what I could help you with. I told you everything I know."

"The first thing that came to light was that Ms. Batcombe did not die in that freezer."

Luckily, Erin was already aware of this, so it didn't take her off guard. "So I heard. But you know I wasn't the one who put her there. I have a dozen witnesses who know that I wasn't dragging a dead body when I went into the freezer. People might have noticed that."

Coleman cracked a smile. "I would think that if you had anything to do with it, you would have put her there much earlier."

"And then decided to lead everyone to the body? I can't imagine why I would do something like that."

"We've seen a lot of crazy things. You've heard of criminals returning to the scene of a crime. It's never a smart thing to do, yet people do. They're drawn back there."

"I didn't drag her in there."

"No. I don't imagine you did. What time was it when you saw her the night before?"

"Oh… that's a good question." Erin thought back. "It must have been something like nine o'clock. Really late for me. I was wiped out. No way I could concentrate on all of the speeches. So I went out for a short walk, a bit of fresh air."

"Are you a smoker?"

"No."

"So you went outside for…?"

"Just for the fresh air, like I said. Get out of the stuffy conference room and cool off, clear my head."

"Which door did you use?"

Erin took a moment to orient herself within the hotel and pointed. "Just out the front lobby doors. Other people were coming and going. People must have seen me. Other than Beryl, I mean. There must have been other attendees who saw me go out and end up talking to Beryl." She thought about it. "Though… we were right against the side of the hotel, leaning up against the wall… so nobody inside would have been able to see us. But someone coming up to the hotel, they could have."

"Not a lot of people arriving around that time. The hotel was mostly filled with people there for the orientation meetings. And they were all in the conference room when you went out for your breath of fresh air."

"I suppose."

"So it was around nine o'clock when you spoke to Ms. Batcombe."

"That would be my guess, yes. I don't think I actually looked at the time, so that's not one hundred percent."

"And did you see her after that?"

"No."

"When you separated, did she go her own direction? Back to her car?"

"No. She was still there smoking. I didn't see her after that. Until I found her in the freezer."

"So you were smoking outside."

"No, Beryl was smoking outside. I wasn't. And I didn't enjoy her second-hand smoke, so I didn't spend long out there."

"What did the two of you talk about? The contest?"

"Yeah. It was the only thing we had in common, so that's what we talked about."

"She was another of the judges."

"Right."

"How many of the judges do you know?"

"Just me and Vic. I've seen or met the others now, but I still don't *know* them. Just been introduced."

"Did you and Ms. Batcombe argue?"

"Argue?" Erin knew she was stalling and that he would recognize it, but she needed time to arrange her thoughts. "No, not really. She expressed some opinions… and I didn't agree… so I left. I didn't stay to discuss it with her."

"What opinions?"

"Just opinions about the contest and my friends. I didn't like it, so…"

"What do you know about her history?"

"Nothing. I told you, I don't know her."

"You've read the bios of the other judges. And I'm sure you must have followed the bits that made it to the paper after she died."

"Yes. But that's just… dry facts, really."

"You didn't think she belonged at the conference? That she wasn't qualified to judge?"

"What? I never said that."

"You didn't have a very good opinion of her."

"Well…" Erin felt like she was being backed into a corner. She couldn't afford to get on Coleman's bad side.

There was no reason for him to consider her a suspect. She hadn't known Beryl Batcombe. That was the truth.

"I didn't have any opinion of her before that night. And my opinion that night was just... She was a bad-tempered, close-minded woman, not someone I wanted to get to know."

"And since then?"

"What?"

"Has anything you have learned since then changed your opinion of her?"

Erin hesitated. "Not for the better. No."

"The press coverage of her has not been very complimentary."

Erin had read most of what had been written about Beryl. What was she supposed to do? Ignore it? She took a sip of her tea, shrugging with one shoulder.

"You were not the last one to see Ms. Batcombe," Coleman advised.

Erin was relieved to hear it. She didn't want to be the last one. To be a suspect because not only had she found the body but because no one had seen Beryl between the time that Erin saw her smoking and the time she found the body. That would be a bad situation. She let out her breath. "Good."

He continued to watch her impassively, giving nothing away.

"Someone saw her in her car shortly after that. She was... ill."

"Oh." So maybe it was natural causes. Erin didn't know how that would translate to someone dragging the body into the freezer. Who would find a person who had died of natural causes and decide to put her in the freezer instead of calling the police or ambulance? She looked at Coleman. "Who saw her? How did they know she was sick? They must have talked...?"

"No. She was leaning out of her car door, vomiting."

"Oh."

"They assumed she'd had too much to drink."

"Right... well, maybe... but she wasn't drunk when I saw her. Not that I could tell. She wasn't slurring or unsteady." Erin pictured Beryl in her mind, lighting a cigarette with a steady hand. She had been leaning against the building, so there wasn't any staggering or obviously drunk behavior. "So maybe… she had a drink or two after I saw her? And then she went somewhere… did she have a car accident? Because she had been drinking?"

"No. It doesn't appear the car was in an accident."

"You found it, then? Was it parked near the restaurant?"

He raised an eyebrow. "Why?"

"I don't know… I was just trying to picture it all. She left the hotel, she was sick… If someone thought she'd been drinking, did they stop her? Did she get out at the restaurant and… wander in there? She was sick, and she got disoriented, fell asleep there…"

"I told you she didn't die in the freezer."

"Right… well, did she die in the restaurant, and someone put her in the freezer to… I don't know… hide the evidence that anything had happened there, or to preserve the body, or…"

He watched her, waiting to see what else she came up with. Erin shrugged. "I really don't know. I don't understand why someone would move the body."

"Maybe the reason will come to light when we have gathered more information."

"If she didn't die in a car accident, and didn't die in the freezer, then what happened? Was it natural? Did someone… hurt her?"

"That's under investigation at the moment. And as I'm sure you've been told before, the police don't share what information they have with civilians. I'm investigating this case, not you."

So he had gotten around to checking her background and knew that she had been involved in murder investigations before. But he didn't know that she had done her best to stay out of them.

Usually.

Mostly.

It wasn't her fault that she had been dragged into investigations in the first place.

"I'm not investigating it. I'm in the middle of a cook-off competition. You're the one who tracked me down."

Coleman had the good grace to shrug, admitting that part was true.

"I don't see how much help I can be to you. I really don't know anything. Like I said, I just talked to Beryl for a minute. I don't know her, and I don't know what happened to her after I went back inside. Just because I was the first one to walk into that freezer, that doesn't mean I had anything to do with it."

"No, ma'am," Coleman agreed. "It was important to get your feedback that she didn't seem drunk, though. That tells me that maybe there's something more we need to look for. We still don't have all of the pieces to this puzzle."

Erin was encouraged by this. Maybe he didn't consider her a suspect. She was one of the last people to see Beryl before she died, so her window on what had happened was important.

CHAPTER 25

*E*rin was finally able to retreat to her room. It had been a frustrating day. Everywhere she went, it seemed like people were criticizing her or being unsupportive. Her mind was spinning with everything she'd had to deal with, and trying to sort out what she had learned from Coleman. Even though she wasn't investigating Beryl's death—she had plenty of other work to do— she wanted to sit down and start writing up some lists. Everything she knew about it, down to the smallest details. The things that Coleman had said that had disturbed her. She also wanted to get down her random thoughts about the bakery and possible ways to deal with the issue of Charley having a relationship with Chef Kirschoff—one option would have to be just minding her own business. But she wanted to do something about it.

She swiped her card to unlock the hotel room door and threw her heavy purse down on the bed. She kicked off her shoes and flopped down. It felt wonderful to just be by herself on the cool bedspread and not have any more obligations.

Her phone vibrated. Erin dug it out of her purse and checked the screen. She didn't want to talk to anyone and hoped that it was just an alarm for an event she had decided not to go to or a message saying that the whole competition had been called off, and not anyone she had to talk to.

It was a text from Terry.

Erin flipped over and straightened out so that she was lying comfortably on her back with the pillow under her head. She tapped the screen and called Terry back.

"Erin, I'm sorry." He apologized without even saying hello. His voice was hoarse. "I wasn't feeling very well and I just now got myself together enough to even send you a message."

"It's okay. Did you take something? Do you need to see someone? You sound pretty bad and I'm worried about not being there to take care of you."

"I don't need anyone to take care of me. I'll just go back to sleep. It will be better tomorrow."

"Have you had anything to eat?"

"No. Too nauseated."

"I thought the headaches were getting better. Aren't they supposed to be going away by now?"

"The doctors said they might last for a few months..." Terry trailed off.

Erin knew that there was also the possibility that the headaches would never go away completely. She had thought that by now, he would be back on his feet, working the same shifts as he had in the old days, getting around town with K9 by his side and taking care of all of the little problems in Bald Eagle Falls. She had not expected that she would still be worrying about him. That he would still be unable to work full time. That the stupid headaches would still be coming almost daily.

"I know." She sighed. "Have you taken a pill?" He still hadn't answered that question.

"They don't help."

"I notice a difference when you take them. It doesn't seem to get quite as bad, and you're able to sleep better and recover faster."

"I think you see what you want to see."

"Then you should talk to the doctor about getting something stronger."

"I don't want something that is going to knock me out or make me too impaired to work." His voice was brittle. It wasn't the first time they'd had this conversation.

"But you can't work if the headaches are bad either. You can recover faster and get back to work sooner if you take them."

"Fine. I'll take one."

She didn't know whether he would or not. He might intend to and then forget by the time they got off the phone. Or he might not have any intention of taking one. Since she wasn't there to see, she wouldn't know the difference.

"Do you want to talk for a bit, or is it too bad?"

She gave him a few moments to consider, not interrupting his thought process. She heard him shift around.

"I can't do anything else. We might as well talk for a bit."

"Okay. Maybe it will distract you."

"Maybe."

Erin fished around for something to discuss with him. Nothing personal. Nothing more about his headaches or how long it was going to take him to recover. And similarly, nothing about her problems, like the dreams that she was still having. She had thought more than once before that she would sleep better alone. If she and Terry weren't both in the house, restless and fighting their demons, then she might be able to get to sleep faster and not be woken up in the night so many times. But sleeping away from him in the hotel in Whitewater had not been restful. She tossed and turned, jumped at every noise she heard in the hotel. The pipes in the walls, footsteps in the halls, the whir of the elevator, people talking or shouting in their own rooms. It was like trying to sleep in a beehive of activity.

"I talked to Deputy Coleman again today."

"Oh? What did he have to say? I don't want you talking to him, Erin. You shouldn't be talking to him without a lawyer or someone else there to protect your interests. Who knows what ideas he might get in his head about you being involved in this woman's death."

"He doesn't—"

"It's not like it hasn't happened before. You can't be too careful. You don't know what he's thinking, even if he's treating you like a confidante instead of a suspect. Some of these guys are really good at getting people to trust them and think that they're best of friends."

"It's not like that. He's not buddy-buddy. He just had some more questions about when I saw Beryl."

"You've already given him a statement. I wouldn't talk to him about anything else. Tell him to talk to your lawyer."

"I don't have a lawyer."

"Get one. I can give you some names. I'm serious, Erin. I don't want to get a call from Vic telling me that you've been thrown in jail."

"I'm not going to get thrown in jail. Everything is fine. I'm done talking with him, I'm back in my room. Just relaxing and talking to you to blow off the stresses of the day."

He was quiet for a minute. "Yeah. Okay. Sorry for being paranoid. It's just... I know how these things can look. Did you find anything out from him? Anything that hasn't been in the news?"

Erin filled him in on what she knew, which wasn't a whole lot. But the fact that Beryl hadn't died of hypothermia in the cold room was important. As was her being sick between her discussion with Erin and her untimely death.

"Do you think she could have been poisoned?" Erin suggested. "The witness thought that maybe she was drunk, but I don't think there was enough time between me talking to her and her... death... for her to get drunk. Maybe someone gave her something... either before I talked to her, and she just hadn't had a chance to react to it yet, or right after we talked?"

"I suppose," Terry said slowly. "You don't know who she might have seen or what she might have had to eat or drink during that time."

"No. Who knows who might have given her something. From what the papers have said… other people didn't like her much better than I did."

"She doesn't sound like a very likable person. And usually, the papers go out of their way to portray a sympathetic victim. You don't want people to jump in and say, 'I would have killed her myself if I'd had the chance.'"

Erin giggled. "I haven't heard anyone say that yet, but they haven't been too complimentary."

"It all reminds me a little bit about when you first came to Bald Eagle Falls."

Erin immediately understood the connection. She'd already been thinking it herself. "Angela Plaint?"

"Yes. While she was alive, people wouldn't say a bad word about her. But after she was gone, and we were questioning suspects or witnesses… the ugly stuff started to come to light. The Baptist ladies would still defend her, say that she just had rough edges, or had dealt with a lot in her life with her husband and son disappearing and her daughter committing suicide. It wasn't like she had things easy. But other people go through a lot of trials in life and still manage not to act like… Angela Plaint."

Erin shook her head, thinking about all that they had discovered about Angela Plaint and her family's secrets. Most of her problems had been of her own making. Despite being a church-going woman her whole life, she had not been the epitome of Christian behavior.

"I wonder what secrets Beryl had. I haven't heard much about her family, have you? I wonder if Coleman has talked to them." She thought about the Plaint boys and the havoc they had caused.

"Haven't really seen anything about any. I don't think she was ever married. Her family has been in Tennessee for generations, so she probably has plenty of cousins and other kin in Whitewater and the surrounding areas. But I don't think there's any immediate family. Her parents have passed."

"She didn't have anything to do with that, did she?"

"Well… I hope not. Maybe something for Coleman to look at." His voice grew firm. "Coleman, not you. Don't you go asking anyone questions about it."

"I'm not. I'm hibernating in my hotel room. I've decided I don't like being around people."

He gave a chuckle. Not quite his old laugh. Weak and cut short. She imagined his wince as he realized that laughing, like everything else, hurt his head. "Sounds like you've had a hard day."

"Between parents from Bald Eagle Falls, and Vic and her friends, Charley and Chef Kirschoff, and being harassed about this woman I don't even know dying, I'm about ready to poison someone myself. Whoever crosses my path next. I'm not going to be picky about it."

"Oh—I was trying not to forget when you were talking about someone poisoning her—Doc dropped off a report from the lab about Orange Blossom."

Erin took in a sharp breath of air. She needed to know everything she could about what had made her cat sick. But on the other hand, she didn't want to hear it. The vet figured that he probably got into some household poison, even though Erin had been unable to find any spills or toothmarks on anything that Orange Blossom shouldn't have been into. She wanted to know what had made him sick, but she was going to be devastated if it were something that she had given to him or let him get into through her own negligence.

She blew out her breath slowly, trying to relax her body. "Okay. Did you look at it? What does it say?"

There was the rattling of paper. Terry didn't say whether he had already looked at it when it had arrived, or whether this was the first time he saw the contents.

"Okay. It says…" Terry sighed. "They found an alkaloid in his system. Probably holly."

"Holly?"

"Yes. You have to be careful of those Christmas plants. A lot of them are poisonous to pets."

"But… I didn't have any holly."

"Then how did he get it?"

"He couldn't have gotten it from the house. Does it grow around here? Could someone have… tracked it in on their boots or something?"

"I'm pretty sure it grows in these parts. Are you sure you didn't have any… in a wreath, or mistletoe decoration or something like that?"

"No. I only had one wreath, and that was from Adele. There was no holly in it. I know what holly looks like. It has these plasticky, spiky leaves and red berries. I didn't have any."

"Maybe there is something else that has that compound in it. Something that we did have around."

"But I didn't. I didn't have anything like that around. I know that Orange Blossom or Marshmallow could get into any plants. I wouldn't have anything in the house without checking first to make sure that it wasn't toxic."

Terry didn't say anything. Erin shook her head, thinking it through.

"But that means… it wasn't an accident. Blossom was intentionally poisoned."

One of the Bald Eagle Falls burglars, one of the Grinches, had poisoned her baby.

 $\mathcal{E}$ rin had been up for a few hours when there was a light knock on her door. She looked over at it, wondering who would be up already. It was still pretty early in the morning for non-bakers. People who actually slept until after the sun came up. It was too early to be housekeeping. And she wasn't sure she wanted to talk with anyone who was associated with the contest.

She went to the door and looked out the peephole. It was difficult to make anything out. She eventually opened the door, unable to make out who it was through the fisheye lens.

"Oh! Joshua." Erin smiled and took the chain off the door. "What are you doing here?" She opened the door wide and motioned for him to join her.

"I'm covering the competition."

Erin frowned, trying to make sense of what he was saying. "What do you mean, covering it?"

Joshua pulled a notepad out of his pocket and turned to a fresh page. He retrieved a pen from another pocket and held them up, poised to write. "I got an extra credit assignment. To report on the cooking competition. For English Language Arts."

"Oh, I see. Well, good for you." Erin smiled.

Joshua hadn't been doing very well in school. Erin knew that

Mary Lou had been worried about him. After Campbell, her older son, had dropped out, she had done everything within her power to make sure that Joshua stayed in school, even though she knew that she couldn't do anything if he decided that he too was done with school. An extra credit assignment would help to bring his marks up. And even more important than that, he was getting out there and making an effort to do something, instead of just hiding at home and not socializing or doing any extra-curricular activities. It was better for his mental health if he got out and did things.

"Have a seat," Erin pointed toward the single chair in the room, pushed in at the table that doubled as a writing table and entertainment center. Erin sat on the bed. "So, tell me about the assignment. What do you need to do?"

"Cover everything. Get as many human interest stories as I can and hand them in to my teacher. She's going to see if she can get some of them published in the paper if they are good enough. Just… being like a real reporter. Looking for the scoop."

"At an ice cream contest, there should be plenty of scoops." Erin laughed.

"Oh, you did not just say that. I'm going to have to put in my article that you tell really bad jokes!"

"You're only supposed to write the truth."

"That would be the truth."

"What have you reported on so far? I guess there's not much you can report on until the actual competition begins."

"No way. There's plenty to report on. The science fair yesterday and today, that's good human interest stuff. Talking to people, reporting on what they are making and what interesting things I can find out about them. And, of course…"

She knew what he was going to say before he said it. Of course.

"Beryl Batcombe."

"Right." Erin looked for a way to avoid the conversation. "What else? You should do a spotlight on Vic, she's really young to be judging a competition like this. And Charley has piggybacked on a bunch of different activities to promote Auntie Clem's. She's really outdone herself. She should get some publicity for that."

Joshua wrote down a couple of notes. "Yeah, those are good ideas. But they're not going to beat out a body showing up in the freezer."

"I'm sure that they'll be able to explain everything before long. It's probably nothing more mysterious than…" Erin cast about for an example. "A heart attack. Or some other preexisting condition. It's probably nothing very interesting at all."

"If it was a heart attack, then who moved the body?" Joshua challenged.

So he already knew that part.

"I don't know. I can show you where the police station is. Maybe they'll give you a statement. A quote you can use in your story."

"Something other than 'no comment'? I doubt it."

"You don't know unless you ask. The policeman in charge over there is Deputy Coleman. Maybe if you took him out for coffee, he'd give you a hand."

Joshua wrote this down, but was not dissuaded from his plan to interview Erin. "You were the one to find the body, Miss Erin. Even if you don't know anything about what happened, just finding the body is interesting. People will want to know what that's like. What you saw and felt. It's perfect."

"No… it's not interesting. It's not a news story. It's… it's somebody's life. Someone who probably had family and friends who cared about her. She's not just a headline in the paper."

"But it wouldn't be very respectful to ignore her death and go on as if nothing had happened," Joshua pointed out. "We should be talking about it, not ignoring it."

He had a point there. Erin kept expecting the contest organizers to make a bigger deal of it. To cancel the contest. To make a statement about how important Beryl had been to the contest and how she would be missed. To name something after her. As it was, they had stayed quiet on the whole subject. Erin knew they were rounding up another judge so that they couldn't end up with a tied vote, but other than that, they had simply gone on as if Beryl had decided not to judge the contest after all. As if she were still at home living out her life.

"You could look at her obituary, track down some of her family, see what they had to say about her. There must be someone who has positive things to say about her."

Joshua raised his brows in a query. Erin realized that she had put her foot right in her mouth. She had vowed not to say anything bad about Beryl to Joshua. And 'everybody hated her' was not the thing that Erin wanted to see on the front page of the paper.

"I mean. There are a lot of people who loved her," Erin amended. "I'm sure there will be a lot of people at her funeral if they hold one… she must have family around here."

Joshua nodded. "Yeah. I don't think I'll have any difficulty finding people to talk about her." He leaned the chair back an inch, making it squeal loudly. "But what I'm interested in right now is hearing about finding her body."

"You said you want to be respectful of her."

"Yes."

"Then writing about her body being discovered isn't really something that—"

"I'll do a sidebar about what a wonderful woman she was and all of her charitable activities," Joshua said dryly. "But what people want to read about is what happened to her. How she was found in the freezer."

"We really don't know what happened, though. That part of the story is still a mystery."

"Mysteries are good. Keep people coming back for more. Keep them talking about it."

Erin shook her head. Joshua cocked his head to the side.

"Do you want me to fail my assignment?"

"No. I just don't think that what your teacher wanted was for you to focus on an accident. That's not the real story. She wanted you to report on the contest. I can give you some literature, talk about what's going on this weekend, and everything that is going to happen as we ramp up to the contest next weekend…"

"I heard," Joshua said slowly, "that they are investigating Ms. Batcombe's death as a murder."

urder?

Erin's jaw dropped.

She shook her head. "It was an accident," she asserted. "Who would want to kill her?"

But she remembered how she and Terry had compared Beryl's personality with that of Angela Plaint's. And there had been no lack of suspects for Angela Plaint's murder.

"It wasn't what it looked like," Joshua pointed out. "It sounded in the first few reports like she had just wandered into this freezer or got caught in it somehow. But from what I hear, her body was moved there. After she was dead."

Erin didn't know who he had heard it from, but she had already heard it from a couple of different sources. People were clearly talking about it. If Joshua knew about it, then it wasn't just limited to law enforcement anymore.

"Yes… I heard that."

"Then it has to be murder. Who would move the body otherwise?"

"I don't know. I'm still trying to figure it out. Why would someone murder her and move the body? Why not just leave her where she was? That doesn't make any sense, either."

"Maybe they were hoping it would look like an accident. The police would think she was just drunk or disoriented or got stuck."

"I don't know… I suppose it's as good a reason as any. But I don't like to think that… it was deliberate. I was hoping to avoid any more nightmares…"

Joshua nodded sympathetically and wrote something in the notebook. What? That Erin was having nightmares? She didn't exactly want that spread all over Tennessee.

"So why don't you tell me about it?" he urged. "How you happened to be the one to find the body? What you thought when you first saw it. And maybe… any ideas you might have on who the culprit is."

Erin sighed. "I don't really want to be the feature story in the newspaper."

"Then give me another direction to investigate. Point me in the direction of the person you think did it." His eyes sparkled.

"I don't want you getting involved in chasing after a murderer. Nothing that is going to put you in harm's way. Does your mother know that you're here?" Erin hadn't even thought of Mary Lou yet. Mary Lou did not want her to have anything to do with Joshua.

"I told her I was going to talk to you. I told her it was for extra credit, so I can get my English grade up."

"And she said it was okay?"

"She wasn't happy about it. But she wants me to do something other than sitting at home all the time moping around. And she wants me to start paying attention to my academics so that I have somewhere to go with my life."

"I don't want a story to be focused on me and all of my feelings. And… I'm not going to encourage you to investigate it on your own. That's a really bad idea. Remember when you guys wanted to go into the city to help to prove that Campbell wasn't guilty? Just how did that turn out?"

Joshua's expression turned serious. "I'm going to be careful.

I'm not going to go chasing after dangerous people. I just want… something to put in my story. A hook that will make it unique."

Erin's thoughts went sideways, from Beryl to Orange Blossom. Had they both been poisoned? If they had, then who had poisoned Beryl? And what about Orange Blossom? Someone would have to have been in her house to give the poison to Blossom. She didn't let him run wild outside. He was an indoor cat. She wanted him to be safe.

"Erin?" Joshua prompted. "It must have been quite a shock to walk into that room and see Batcombe's body there."

"Yes… it was. I certainly wasn't expecting it."

"What did you think? Did you know it was murder right away? Or did you think it was an accident?"

Erin cast her mind back. The shock tended to erase a lot of the other, more logical thoughts. What had she thought?

"I just… I saw her body there… and I guess at first I thought she had just gotten there ahead of us and was waiting for us… or she was asleep… she was supposed to be with our tour group, so I was sort of mad that she had gone on ahead of us."

Joshua nodded encouragingly. "How long did it take you to realize that she was actually dead?"

"It all happens in an instant. It isn't like you're having a conversation with yourself and you can articulate it all… I was mad at her and I realized she was dead all at once, in a split-second."

"Uh-huh." Joshua was scribbling some notes. "Did you scream?"

"No."

"Did anyone?" he persisted hopefully.

"No, I don't think so. Not that I remember." She thought back, but it wasn't all crystal clear. She had kept everyone out of the room, making sure that no one could contaminate the scene, but her mind had been skipping around, trying to avoid looking at Beryl or speculating on what had happened.

An accident. Just an accident.

But it wasn't. Even though she had been shocked when Joshua had said that it was a murder, she had known all along. She had known that Beryl hadn't gone from smoking at the hotel to sitting quietly in the freezer until she died.

She had known that the vitriolic woman must have had enemies. If Erin felt so strongly about her after five minutes, then she could only imagine how much Beryl had alienated the people who had known her for longer.

"Who do you think did it?" Joshua asked. "How did everyone else react?"

Erin thought back. Vic had been behind her, bottlenecked in the doorway so she couldn't get in to see.

No one in the contest group had seen the body except for Erin. Vic had kept everyone else back. There had been protests, but no one was really that intent on getting into the freezer. It was just a freezer, not that exciting. When they realized that there had been a medical emergency, the protests had died away and people had only been curious to catch a glimpse of what had happened.

The police came. The doctor came. Then Coleman.

Vic had been white-faced when she realized what Erin had found. She certainly hadn't known anything ahead of time. Not that Erin would ever have suspected Vic of killing Beryl anyway. If Vic had been in a fight with Beryl, it would have been a knock-down, drag-out, public fight. Vic knew what she was doing and Beryl would not have looked calm and serene, her skin unmarked.

Chef Kirschoff had been on the tour; jolly, making jokes, acting like he was enthralled with Sherry the guide's long and detailed descriptions. He'd probably written most of the patter himself. No one had tried to stop Erin from opening the freezer door. While it was true that their attention should have been on Sherry, at least a few of them were bored and looking for something else to occupy their attention and, if someone had dumped Beryl's body in there, their eyes would surely have been on the door rather than on Sherry.

Had anyone been paying more attention to her than they

should have? She didn't think anyone had been watching her, but she hadn't checked to see.

"I don't know who would have a reason to hurt Beryl. I don't remember anyone acting suspiciously when I opened the freezer… if it was someone in that group—" Erin suppressed a shudder, "—then he or she is a good actor."

Joshua nodded. "Who was there?"

Erin shrugged. "Most of the people associated with organizing the contest. Me and Vic, Chef Kirschoff, the guide, other judges, sponsors, people involved in the administrative stuff. So that everyone would know what to do when it was time for the competition."

"The names of the judges are all up on the website. Can you give me the names of anyone else who was there?"

Erin shook her head. "I really don't even know anyone. Contact the organizers. I don't know if they'll give you anything."

"I thought Vic would be here with you. You guys aren't sharing a room?"

"Well, officially we are, but Willie has been in town this weekend, so they have been off on their own and I have the room to myself." Erin thought of the little white dog and wondered how Vic and Willie were handling the new family member. She smiled.

"Do you think she would talk to me?" Joshua asked.

"I don't know. That's up to her."

There was a knock at the door. Erin looked toward it and frowned. She wasn't expecting anyone else, and it was still too early to be housekeeping. Her mind jumped immediately to Vic, since they had just been discussing her.

"Vicky?" she called out without getting up from the bed.

There was no answering call. Erin pushed herself up and went to the door. Maybe a message had been left for her at the front desk. Or there was a plumbing problem.

She looked through the peephole, but there was no one there. Erin waited, but nobody moved into view. She opened the door and looked around. No one was there. She looked back at Joshua.

"Someone did knock on my door, didn't they? It wasn't the next room...?"

"Well, could have been, I guess. It sounded like your door, but it could have just been a loud knock for next door."

Erin looked both directions down the hall, but there was nothing to see. She couldn't hear any conversations going on in the rooms next to hers. And she'd been able to hear voices through the walls the previous night. All night long.

Just as she was closing the door, her eyes caught on a folded note on the carpet. She bent down and picked it up.

"I guess someone left a message for me."

She shut the door and turned back toward Joshua. He looked at his phone. "I guess I should leave you alone. Thanks for everything…"

"Sorry I didn't give you very much. But like I said, I didn't know Beryl. And there wasn't really anything to me finding her… I just saw her there… and told Vic to call for help. I wish everyone wouldn't make such a big deal of it being me."

Joshua nodded as he stood up. "Well, if you didn't have a history, maybe people wouldn't. But this is… an awful lot like what happened to Angela Plaint." He looked apologetic. "Maybe just on the surface, but is anyone looking at whether she had an allergic reaction? And who might have been interested in…" he shrugged, looking uncomfortable, "getting her out of the way?"

"You'll have to ask Deputy Coleman. I'm not getting involved."

Joshua rolled his eyes. Did that mean that he didn't believe her? Or that he thought that she should help? Or that Coleman would never find the culprit or would never talk to him? Joshua said goodbye and she saw him out.

As Erin turned back to her room, her phone started ringing. It was buried in her purse somewhere and it rang a few times before she managed to dig it out. She saw Vic's profile picture on the screen. She picked up.

"Hi, Vic."

"Erin, did you hear?"

"Hear what?"

"Are you in your room?"

"Yes."

"Stay there, I'll come over."

Erin held the phone more tightly. "Is everything okay? What happened?" She thought immediately of Terry. Had something happened to him? Had he done something stupid, harming himself or making a mistake due to the pain and brain fog?

"Just stay there. I'll be right over."

Erin stayed put as she was told. Vic and Willie had taken another room in the hotel, on a different floor because the contest participants had taken a large block of rooms on the floor Erin was on. Erin heard the elevator approaching. She opened her door and stood, waiting for the doors to open. They parted and Vic hurried down the hallway toward her, Willie lagging behind.

"Now, don't get worked up," she warned. "We don't know anything yet."

"You know something!" Erin said. "What's this all about? What happened? It's not Terry?"

"Terry?" Vic looked at her blankly. "No, this isn't anything to do with Terry."

Erin let out a sigh of relief, her legs buckling so that she had to catch herself on the doorframe. Vic took her arm. Willie picked up his pace and took Erin's other arm. They walked her back into her hotel room to where she could sit down on the bed.

"What is it?" Erin demanded, pulling away from them. "What happened?"

"There was an accident. We don't know very many details yet."

Erin was still thinking of Terry, even though Vic had said it wasn't anything to do with him. Had he gotten behind the wheel when he was too medicated to drive? Or was seeing double because of his head? She always worried that he was going to do too much. That he wouldn't be able to accurately judge what he could manage.

"Hans and Charley were unloading some of the supplies and equipment for next week, staging them in preparation for set-up."

"Hans and Charley."

"Yes. And we don't know all of the details, but there was some kind of explosion."

Erin blinked at her. "A bomb?"

"I highly doubt it was a bomb," Willie told her. "They have pressurized canisters of CO_2. My guess is that one of them was faulty. A flaw in the canister…"

"Oh." She thought of the big carbonation machine at the

science fair. It had looked dangerous. Was it something like that? Erin took in long, slow breaths, trying to sort out what this meant to her. She didn't know whether to be more worried about Charley, her half-sister and partner in the business, or Chef Kirschoff.

Of course, she should be more concerned about Charley. But despite their blood relationship, Erin had a hard time feeling close to Charley. The two of them had little in common. Charley was hard-headed and wanted to do things her own way.

With Chef Kirschoff, on the other hand, she had an instant connection. Their love of baking and his interest in her specialized knowledge had sparked a deep friendship that had persisted after their chance meeting on the Alaskan cruise.

"I'm sure they're both fine," Vic reassured Erin. "There was an emergency crew, and they were taken to the hospital for treatment. No one has said that they were badly hurt. There is police tape around the area where it happened, so no one can get close, but no one is saying that there were serious injuries."

"They don't take people to the hospital for no reason."

"After an explosion, they would want to take you to the hospital even if you got out of it without a scratch," Willie interjected. "Trust me."

"So, you think that they're both okay."

Vic and Willie nodded. Erin looked around the room. "Who did you hear about it from?"

"Willie went out for coffee."

"*Good* coffee," Willie intoned.

"For good coffee," Vic repeated with a weak laugh. "And he saw the police tape and the emergency vehicles and the crowd gathering."

Willie nodded his agreement.

"But you were there after it happened. You didn't see them."

"That's right. They had already been taken away."

"Has anyone tried to call them?" Erin grabbed her phone and tapped it. She looked for Chef Kirschoff's number.

"We tried both of them. Neither is answering."

"Their phones were probably put somewhere else, with their personal effects." Willie scratched the back of his neck. "They don't like patients trying to call and text in the middle of treatment."

"So you think they were injured. That they're in surgery."

"Not necessarily. They might just be doing a neurological assessment to make sure that there isn't any concussion. Or they could be sitting around bored in a waiting room, but they aren't allowed to have their phones turned on. You know how hospitals are."

Erin shifted around, anxious, wanting to get up and do something. "We should go see them. Go to the hospital so we can find out how they are."

"We'll hear as soon as there is any news. Some of the other contest people are already on their way." Vic looked at the time on her phone. "Probably there already, just waiting for news."

"They'll shut down the contest," Erin told them with certainty. "We might as well go home because it's not going to happen now. They'll shut it down after this."

"They didn't shut it down when Beryl died."

"But they will now. That's two accidents. People will think that the contest is cursed."

"Accidents…?" Willie raised his brows at Erin. "What makes you think that they were accidents?"

$\mathcal{E}$rin looked at Willie's earnest expression, then at Vic. She dropped her gaze to her hands. She knew that Beryl hadn't walked into that freezer under her own power.

But Charley and Chef Kirschoff? That was an accident. A defective canister, that was what Willie had said.

"Okay… a death and an accident," she amended. "I thought that they would cancel the competition after Beryl's death, but they didn't. But an explosion? That's going to scare people off. They're not going to want to take part in the competition. Not if they think that the equipment is faulty."

Willie nodded. "I suspect so. You can't expect people to want to participate in a contest under those conditions. It's something that's fun to do, but no one wants to risk their life to participate."

"It's too bad. Chef Kirschoff is going to be really disappointed. He put a lot of work into this. He really believes in it."

"He should just be grateful that he's walking away from it alive," Vic drawled. "He could be deader than a lobster in butter sauce."

Erin looked at her, mouth dropping open. She was shocked and amused at the expression at the same time and didn't know whether to laugh or cry. She ended up doing a little of both, trying to catch her breath while Vic gave her a hug and patted her on the back.

"I'm sorry, I'm sorry. I didn't mean to upset you. I've got foot-in-mouth disease. It's okay, Erin. It's going to be okay."

Erin gasped and giggled and tried to wipe at the tears streaming out of her eyes. "I don't—know—why I'm—"

"You're a little bit hysterical," Willie said, stepping back from her a little as if it might be contagious. Or maybe, like many men, he just didn't know what to do when a woman started to cry, and planned to flee the scene. Not that he hadn't seen Erin cry before. "You've had a shock."

Vic rubbed Erin's back. "It's okay. We shouldn't have sprung everything on you so fast, and then me saying something so insensitive…"

"It's okay," Erin gasped. She hiccuped. "Oh—I hate it—when I get—hiccups!" She tried to avoid hiccuping and sniffling at the same time. She looked around for tissues and, not finding any, staggered into the bathroom. She shut the door to give herself some privacy and space to recover without everyone looking at her like she was broken. She blew her nose, washed her face with cold water, and did her best to stop the hiccups. She held her breath while trying to count as high as she could, had a drink, and sat down on the toilet with her head between her knees. The last one might only work for fainting but, by that time, the hiccups were making her head spin, so maybe it would work for both.

Vic knocked on the door. "Are you going to be okay, Erin?"

"I'm good now. Why don't you guys go have breakfast? I just need some time."

"We can wait for you."

"No, go eat. I want to be alone."

"You shouldn't be alone after something like this." Vic's voice was muted as she turned away from the door to talk to Willie. "Should she? You shouldn't leave someone alone when they're hysterical."

"She's quieted down," Willie assured her. "If she says she needs some space, then give her some space."

"Fine. Okay." Vic pressed her face against the door again to talk to Erin. "Do you want us to bring you up some breakfast when we're done? You'll need something to eat too."

"Sure. Just grab me a muffin or something." Erin wasn't hungry, her stomach feeling a bit sick after all of the hiccuping and sniffling. She hated crying and hated the way that it made her feel sick for hours afterward. Some people said they felt better after a good cry, but Erin was always headachy and sick to her stomach. And embarrassed at having been so emotional in front of someone else. She wished Terry were there. He would make her feel better.

"We'll be back after breakfast, then," Vic promised. "I'm sorry, again. I really didn't mean to upset you."

"It's just the news of the accident." Erin blew her nose. "That's all. I'll be okay. I'll be better when I've had a chance to talk to both of them. But it's fine. Really."

By the time Vic and Willie returned from breakfast, Erin had most of her things packed. Vic handed Erin a blueberry muffin and looked around, frowning. She had the dog with her, and Nilla snuffled around the room investigating everything.

"What's going on? You're packing?" Vic asked.

"I'm going home. They're going to cancel the competition, so there's no point in staying around here. I need to see Terry. I'll need to take care of things at the bakery, especially if Charley is… under the weather."

"They haven't announced that they are canceling the competition."

"It doesn't matter. They will. They have to."

"You may be right, Erin," Willie admitted. "But you should

probably wait for the announcement. If you just disappear, people are going to be worried."

"I'm not disappearing. I'm going home. I'll leave a message at the front desk. I'll call the organizers and let them know. But I'm not going to stay around."

Erin continued to pack her bags. Vic and Willie stood watching her and Nilla.

"Are you running away because you're afraid?" Willie asked after some time.

Erin turned and looked at him. "I'm not running away. I'm going home. That's completely different."

She had run away enough times to know the difference. She was going home to Terry and her animals. And her bakery. Where people didn't get into accidents or die.

Usually.

Not recently, anyway.

"Are you going to come back if they say the contest is going ahead?" Vic questioned.

"I don't know."

Willie picked up a piece of paper from the multipurpose table. "Is this something important?" He unfolded it with a flick and glanced down at it as he handed it to Erin.

Erin grasped the note, but Willie didn't let it go. Erin tugged harder, frowning. Willie stared at it, then turned his eyes to Erin's face as he finally let go. Erin looked at the paper, trying to remember where it had come from.

"Is someone threatening you? Is that why you're leaving?"

Erin looked at Willie.

Vic gave a laugh of disbelief. "What?"

Erin read the note.

Go home unless you want to be next.

"Oh." Her heart thudded so hard in her chest that it hurt. "I didn't even see that before."

"You didn't see it?" Willie repeated. "It was right here on your table. You're packing your bags. Of course you saw it."

"No, I didn't. I was just… someone left it at my door. I had just picked it up when Vic called, and said to stay put, so I knew something bad had happened. I don't even remember putting it down."

"Who left it at your door?" Vic was beside Erin, looking at the note, her mouth open. "I can't believe someone would…"

"I don't know. When I looked out the peephole, there was no one there. The note was just on the floor. I thought it was going to be you at the door, but when I looked out, there was no one there. Then I saw the note on the floor… I suppose someone might have dropped it there by mistake. It might not have even been intended for me."

"You need to call the police, Erin," Vic told her seriously.

"No. I just want to go home. What does it matter? The note said to go home, I'm going home anyway, so it doesn't make any difference. Whoever left it there will think that I'm doing what they said to do, and everything will be fine."

"You could be in danger."

"Not if I go home."

"There's no guarantee of that."

"It says to go home."

"They might just want to get you away from the hotel or away from the rest of the group. Somewhere you're more isolated."

"In my house? With a burglar alarm and a cop and a police dog?"

"They might not know that part."

"Even if they don't, I'll still be safe."

"Vic is right." Willie put in his bit. "You need to report this to the authorities."

"Can I just tell the hotel or the contest organizers? Does it have to be the police?"

"You already know the answer to that. Why don't you want to go to the police?"

Vic gave Willie a look that said he should have known the answer to that question.

"I've already had to talk to the police twice. They think I had something to do with Beryl's death. I don't want to have to talk to them again. To Deputy Coleman. I just want to go home, and this will all be over."

CHAPTER 30

*B*ut she knew she would end up having to go to the police station. No matter how many arguments she had against it, Willie and Vic were right. She needed to let the authorities know what was going on. So she got her whining done and then agreed to let Willie drive her to the station.

"But I don't want you to stay there or go in with me. Just drop me off."

"You'll need a ride when you're done."

"I'll call you. Or I'll walk back here. It's not that far. Nothing in Whitewater is very far."

"I don't mind coming in with you, Erin. I'd like to help."

"No. I'll deal with it myself."

In the end, he agreed to do as Erin asked.

There was a different police officer at the front desk from the one who had been there the last time Erin had been in. So Sommers didn't have to work every shift at reception. It was good that she had someone else to take that duty now and then. Erin imagined it wasn't much fun to be dealing with complaints all day long. Erin sometimes got sick of standing behind the counter at the bakery, and people were much happier to be getting chocolate muffins than citations.

The male officer on the desk this time was Williams. He looked at Erin for a moment as if trying to place her, then nodded. "Miss… Price, isn't it?"

"Yes."

"How can we serve you today?"

"I need to file a report about a threatening note that I got."

"Oh?"

Erin slid it across the counter to him, under the big window. Williams touched it with a fingertip to reposition it. It didn't take long to read.

"Is that it?"

"Yes. That's it."

"Have you received any other threats?"

"No."

"Do you know who it's from?"

"No."

"How was it sent to you? Mail? In person?"

"It was left on the floor outside my hotel room. Someone knocked on my door, and then left it there for me."

"And you don't have any idea who."

"No."

"Why would someone be threatening you? Why do they want you to go home?"

"I don't know. I guess they don't want the competition to go ahead."

His gaze sharpened. "This is about the competition?"

"Well, that's the only reason I'm in town, so I assume so. I figured that with everything that is going on… Beryl's death and now this explosion today… someone is trying to get the competition shut down."

"How do you know about the explosion?" he asked suspiciously. He had a thin mustache over his lip, and he scratched it now, looking at Erin as if she might be there to attack him.

"Doesn't everybody in town know about the explosion by

now?" Erin challenged. "Anyone who didn't hear or see it has at least been told about it by now."

"Did you see it?"

"No. Vic came and told me."

He looked at her for a moment longer, then back down at the note again, weighing what he should do.

"Don't you think you should tell Deputy Coleman?" Erin suggested. "He'll want to know about it, won't he?"

Williams chewed his lip. "Suppose so." But he didn't make any move to call or go find Coleman. Erin looked through the glass guard into the squad room, looking for Coleman. But he didn't appear to be in the cubicles or in the glassed-in interrogation room. He might have been in an office that actually had walls and a door.

"Is he in?"

"He's out on an investigation at the moment."

"Well, I'll just leave that here with you. I'm going back to Bald Eagle Falls."

"You're leaving?" He raised his eyebrows.

"Yes. I decided to leave before I got that. And the note didn't exactly encourage me to stay."

"No, I would guess not."

"So I'll just leave you that."

"You'll need to file a report."

Erin rolled her eyes. "Then please get me the form. I don't want to be standing around waiting all day. I want to go back to my own house and… everyone."

"Does that mean you won't be judging the competition?"

"Do you think the contest is going to go ahead?" she asked.

"Well…" He scratched his mustache again as he considered. "I just don't know about that. Folks are pretty excited about holding it. And the grand prize… that ain't nothing to sneeze at."

"No," Erin agreed. "It isn't. But are people willing to risk their lives for it? I'm not."

She'd had enough 'accidents.' She wasn't about to tempt fate by meeting another head-on. Back in Bald Eagle Falls, she would be safe. She could put the contest behind her and go on with her life. The way it had been before Chef Kirschoff had come to town.

"Do you know how Charley and Chef Kirschoff are? I haven't heard anything and… well, Charley is my sister and Hans is my friend. I'd like to know how they are."

"We will be making an official statement later today."

"Come on. You're not going to tell me whether my sister is alive or dead?"

His eyebrows went way up. "Your sister is alive," he said. "No one ever said otherwise."

"Well, that's something, anyway. Is she okay? Is she badly injured? No one could say how badly either of them was injured. I assume since they were both rushed to the city hospital… that it wasn't just minor scrapes and bruises. Is it… critical? Do you know?"

He shifted uncomfortably. He knew he wasn't supposed to be releasing that information to members of the public. But Erin wasn't the public. She was Charley's sister.

"You don't share the same last name as your sister?"

"No. We had different fathers and she was adopted. That doesn't make her any less my sister."

"I just don't think… maybe when Deputy Coleman gets in, he could give you a call. I'm really not supposed to talk about it."

"So she's okay?" Erin scrutinized Williams's face for any tells. If Charley was in bad shape, she would have expected to see something in his expression that would tell her that. A certain gravitas or blankness. But he didn't seem bothered by her statement that Charley was okay. So she must be.

"And Chef Kirschoff? If he's badly injured, then the contest will be off for sure."

Again, no flicker of worry. And he wanted the contest to go on. Maybe he or a friend or family member was entering something into the contest, hoping to win the grand prize. He showed no sign of being concerned that Chef Kirschoff was too badly injured to continue with the competition.

"Okay." Erin breathed out. "So, where's the form I need to fill out?"

Williams rifled through files under the counter to find the right form for Erin, and indicated the portions she should fill out.

~

By the afternoon, word of the explosion had spread beyond Whitewater's boundaries, all the way back to Bald Eagle Falls. Several calls had come to Erin's phone, but she looked at the caller ID's and ignored them. Until she saw Terry's number. That one, she wanted to take.

"Terry. Hi!"

"Are you okay, Erin? Is everything all right?"

"I'm fine. Did you hear about the accident? About Chef Kirschoff and Charley?"

"Yes. They hadn't released names, and I couldn't find out… I'm glad it wasn't you or Vic. Is Charley okay?"

"As far as I know. They haven't released an official statement yet. But from what I've been able to discern, I think her injuries were minor."

"You're not at the hospital?"

"No. I don't have a car. Willie said that he would drive me back to Bald Eagle Falls later today; I'm coming home."

"No. I mean, I'm glad that you're coming home. But don't wait for Willie to drive you back here. I'll come pick you up, and we can go to the hospital."

Erin's heart warmed at his offer. "Are you sure? I don't know how you're feeling. That's going to be a long drive and bouncing around bothers your head."

"I'm sure. I will head out right away. If I'm too tired when I pick you up, you can drive."

"I can drive your truck?" He didn't like letting anyone else driving his truck. Erin knew it was a sacrifice.

"If I'm not feeling well," Terry said sternly. "And right now, I'm doing pretty good, so don't count your chickens."

"I won't. Thank you, Terry. I really appreciate it."

"I'm not going to keep you from seeing your sister and making sure everyone is okay. If you were the one who was hurt, do you think anything could stop me from coming to you?"

Her heart swelled again. A lump in Erin's throat that was making it difficult for her to talk. She swallowed hard.

"No," she agreed.

"Nothing," he reiterated.

Even though Terry wasn't using his police cruiser, he got there faster than he should have. Erin supposed that if he were pulled over, he could probably still talk himself out of a ticket by virtue of being a policeman. Who would argue with a fellow cop on his way to an emergency, even if he didn't happen to have a light bar?

He called Erin as he approached the hotel, so she was outside waiting for him when he arrived. Erin climbed up into the cab of the truck and greeted Terry with a kiss.

"Thank you again for coming to get me. And for taking me to the hospital."

"You're welcome." He kissed her again, then held her face with his palms cupped over her cheeks, looking into her eyes. "How are you?"

"I'm okay."

K9 stuck his head over the seat from the back and tried to lick Erin's face. She squealed and pulled back.

"What's going on with this competition?" Terry put the truck into gear. Erin pulled her seatbelt on. "I don't understand what's going on. Is it just a coincidence?"

"It could be."

He glanced over at her. "Do you really think that?"

"Well… no. I think… I don't know what to think. I don't want to think about it at all, to tell the truth. Beryl's death looked like it was just an accident… but it wasn't. And this thing with Charley… I want to hear what happened. The police aren't telling anybody anything. I think they'll probably make some kind of release tonight, a statement that they're looking into it and there is no indication of foul play. Something like that."

"Unless there is."

"Right. Although… would they say that there was? Or would they just pretend that there wasn't?"

"The police department won't usually lie to the newspaper. It causes trust issues. So if they thought there was foul play but they didn't want the public to know that yet, they would just say it was still under active investigation. They wouldn't say that there was not foul play, and they wouldn't say that there was."

Erin nodded. Maybe Charley would tell her that they had made a stupid mistake, or that they had recognized that the canister was defective. Maybe it had been dropped or they could see a flaw in the metal. Or Chef Kirschoff would be able to tell them something. He must know something about CO2 canisters. He would have had to learn about how to use and handle them for the contest. He would have had some kind of safety training, wouldn't he?

"You don't think it is too bad, do you? What did you hear?"

"I didn't hear anything official." Terry's tone was apologetic. "They won't be releasing anything until all of the proper authorities have been notified and family notifications made. They don't want families finding out on the news."

"But I am family."

"Yes… but not legally. Her next of kin would be her adoptive parents."

"Next of kin?" Erin echoed. *Why would they need next of kin? Unless…*

"No, don't go there," Terry warned. "I'm not saying that she is dead or dying. Just that when they make family notifications, they will go to the spouse first, and then to parents, and then look more broadly if there is no spouse or parents. They won't be looking for a non-legal half-sister, unless Charley asks them to call you."

"Oh." Erin considered this. "Okay. I know they're probably just fine. Word would have gotten around if they were horribly injured or killed. But I'm just scared that when I get there... I'll find out..."

"I'll be with you. You won't be in this alone. And like you say, I'm sure it will be just fine."

"Yeah. Thanks."

Erin watched out the window as Terry drove, letting the conversation fall away. They didn't need to keep talking. They would just keep going over the same stuff over and over again.

CHAPTER 31

Finally, they were at the hospital. Erin struggled not to appear impatient as Terry found parking and paid for it. Why did hospital parking always have to be so tedious? It should have just been free. And there should have been a lot more of it. People had to go visit their family and friends. It was a necessity, not a luxury. They should have been able to visit without having to deal with all of the problems associated with finding a legitimate spot, dealing with broken or antiquated machines, and having to scrounge for the correct amount of money or make the machines accept credit cards when they were in a grumpy mood.

Then there was the issue of finding someone who could tell them where to find Charley and Kirschoff. Everything was just so overly complicated.

It was going to be more difficult to get in to see Kirschoff, but Erin was finally able to talk a nurse receptionist into believing that she was Charley's sister and was therefore allowed to see her.

Erin breathed a sigh of relief when they entered Charley's room and found her sitting up, playing with the TV remote, a crease between her eyebrows.

"Charley! Are you okay? How are you?"

"Erin! And Terry." Her eyes dropped to K9 at Terry's side.

"And… the furry one. I'm okay. Really, everything is fine. I want to go, but they keep saying that I have a *confession* and I can't drive. I said I could get a cab, but they say they want to watch me. To make sure that…" Charley trailed off, unsure how to finish the sentence. She poked at buttons on the remote impatiently. "I can't make this thing work!"

"You probably have to pay extra for TV," Terry suggested. "Did you pay for one?"

"I don't know. They just stuck me in this room and told me that I have to stay here until I confess." She frowned. "Is that right?"

"Pretty close," Terry said smoothly. "Why don't I go ask the nurse about the TV, and you can visit with Erin for now?" He took the remote out of Charley's hand and put it on the side table.

Charley looked again at Erin. "So you finally made it."

"I got here as soon as I could. I needed a ride, and I had to deal with some police stuff, and then getting here and finding out where you were…"

"Oh." Charley nodded her understanding. "Well, that makes sense, I guess. Can you drive me home, then? I want to get out of here."

"We probably can, after we talk to the doctor and make sure. If they want you here under observation…"

"I'm sure it would be fine."

"We'll just check to be sure." Erin sat down on the chair beside Charley's bed. "I'm glad to see that you're okay. I was worried that you might have been hurt a lot worse than you are."

"I'm really okay."

"And Chef Kirschoff—Hans? How is he?"

"Last I saw him, he seemed okay." Charley looked around as if she expected him to be nearby. "Where did he go?"

"I don't know where his room is. I was hoping you'd know, because the hospital doesn't want to give us any information. We're not family, they can't give us private health information and all that. What a pain in the neck it is."

Charley nodded vaguely.

"Can you tell me what happened?" Erin asked. "All that I've heard is that one of the CO2 canisters exploded. That sounds really scary. I was afraid that you'd be… all cut up. I thought of a bomb." She felt like a new parent counting fingers and toes, as she studied Charley to make sure that everything was intact. But Charley seemed to be fine, other than a little confusion. Hopefully, her concussion was mild and wouldn't continue to cause problems like Terry's head injury.

"I was helping Hans with getting everything staged for next week. Everything we can. Because next week, things will be pretty crazy, and we'll have to go from one place to another without any time to fiddle around. There will be lots of volunteers helping out, but most of the work has to be done ahead of time."

Erin nodded. That all made sense.

"There are lots of canisters. They need enough for all of the entries. Hans had a bunch in the truck, and we were taking them into the restaurant to be stored there until the contest started."

"Uh-huh."

"And then… I don't know. Hans put several of them down at a time, and there was a clank, you know, from them banging together, and then… boom! It sounded like a thunderclap. I thought… like you say, a bomb went off. We were both knocked around. I'm not sure, it's kind of patchy, what happened between the explosion and getting here… My ears were ringing. My throat hurt. My head was throbbing. Like I'd been out in the sun for too long."

"And Hans? He didn't look like he was hurt too badly?"

"I don't know. I don't think so. We were both… we could both get up. We walked to the ambulance, they didn't have to bring the gurneys out…"

"Was there a fire? Shrapnel?"

"*Shrapnel,*" Charley repeated. "I was trying to remember that word! It just wouldn't come. I kept thinking Sharpie, but that's a kind of dog."

Erin suppressed a smile. "So there wasn't any? You didn't get any shrapnel injuries?"

She hadn't been able to spot any bandages on Charley's body, but she was partially covered by her hospital johnny and a sheet.

"No... I don't think so. There was a big blast..." Charley's eyes were unfocused. "There was... there was a hole in the wall. Like a big, gaping hole, and there were clouds of dust. I think it was dust, from the drywall..." She shook her head. "Half of the kitchen was gone."

There was a tight knot in Erin's stomach as she thought about it. She had been so relieved to see that Charley was all in one piece that she had assumed it had just been a little bang, and that everyone had overreacted.

"But you were okay. And Hans. He was okay."

Charley's eyes were distant for a minute. The silence drew out. She finally shook her head. "They said we were lucky. They said we could have been badly hurt or killed."

The knot in Erin's stomach tightened. Was it just an accident? Chef Kirschoff had dropped one of the canisters or put it down too hard? One of them was defective and being jarred had caused just enough damage for it to break open and the pressurized contents to cause the damage?

"You must have been really scared."

"Not really. I think... I was too shocked to be scared. The ambulance came right away. We didn't have to wait for long."

"That's good. I'm glad someone was there to help you out right away."

Charley nodded. She picked up the remote control from the table next to her and pointed it at the TV. Nothing happened. "I can't figure out what's wrong with this thing."

Erin turned to look at the doorway. She could hear Terry talking to the nurse at the central nursing station. Trying to get more details or to get them to turn on Charley's TV so she could watch something. Charley continued to press buttons on the remote and, eventually, Terry returned.

"They'll turn it on. But it takes time."

"Thanks. That will probably help her to stay calm."

Charley looked up. "Who are you talking about?"

"About you. Getting the TV turned on for you. So you won't be so bored."

"Oh." Charley nodded her head in agreement and pressed a few more buttons on the remote. "I thought maybe you were talking about Batcombe."

Erin looked at Terry.

"What about Beryl Batcombe?" she asked Charley eventually.

"Where is she? Did you hear what happened?"

"Uh… what did you hear?" Erin didn't want Charley to be upset if she didn't remember that Beryl was dead. And she wanted to know if Charley might have some insight that Erin didn't. She had been working closely with Chef Kirschoff. He might have said something to her about Beryl. Being one of the organizers of the event, Kirschoff would have to know more about Beryl than Erin or any of the other people who were only incidental to it.

"She was found in the freezer!" Charley said in a low, secretive tone. She looked around, eyeing Terry.

"He already knows," Erin assured her.

"What was she doing in the freezer?" Charley hissed. "She wasn't supposed to be in there."

"No. I'm not sure why she was put in there. Maybe when we find out why she was put there… we'll have a better idea of who put her there."

"Who put her there," Charley echoed.

"Yeah. She didn't get there herself, you know." Or maybe Charley didn't know that. Or didn't remember it.

"I was asking Hans about her. Did you know that they… knew each other before?"

"Oh. Is that how she got to be a judge for the competition? Because they already knew each other?"

Charley nodded. "They knew each other a loooong time ago." Charley blinked at Erin a couple of times.

"A long time ago. Okay. Well, it was nice of him to remember and to ask her to be a judge, wasn't it?"

"She was… what's the word?" Charley murmured.

"I don't know. I only met her for a few minutes."

"What was she, then? What did you think of her?"

"I don't know what you're looking for. She had… opinions," Erin said delicately.

"Yeah, yeah," Charley nodded seriously. "That's right. Opinions. And recipes."

Erin nodded, suppressing a laugh. "But she wasn't one of the contestants, she was going to be one of the judges. Was she a cook? Is that how Chef Kirschoff knew her?"

"She always had new recipes. Always something new to try. Everybody knew."

"She must have been a good cook."

"That's not the word though." Charley shook her head slowly. "I think… hmm… do you know what it is?"

"No. What word are you looking for? Can you use it in a sentence, and maybe I can think of what word it is."

"Aspirations?" Charley asked, looking up. She searched her concussed memory for the bit of information she was looking for. "Like Caesar. Not the salad."

Erin tried to think of a word that Charley might be mixing up with aspirations. Inspiration? Aspirate? What did any of it have to do with Caesar salad?

"Is it something you put into a Caesar salad? An ingredient?"

"Not that kind of Caesar."

"The drink?"

"No. No, no, no. You're not getting it. Not cooking. Though he was shish kabobbed."

"Who was?"

"Caesar."

It was Terry who spoke up. Of all of them, the one who was having the most serious problems with his brain and proper recall.

"Julius Caesar? He was stabbed," he said as an aside to Erin. "I think that's where the shish kabobbed comes into it. If not… I'm not sure what she means."

"Julius Caesar." Charley nodded. "Stabbed in the back. He was."

"Yes," Terry agreed. "Why are you bringing Julius Caesar up? What does he have to do with anything? He didn't have anything to do with Beryl Batcombe. If there is a connection…. I have no idea what it is."

Had Terry been looking into Beryl Batcombe's background? Had he been investigating quietly, even though he wasn't with her and wasn't on the Whitewater police force?

"Aspirations." Charley sighed. "He had aspirations."

"He sure did."

"And Batcombe. She did too. Hans said."

"Aspirations to do what?"

Charley shook her head, unsure of the answer. She put her hands in the air, lifting them up to one level, and then another level higher. "Aspirations."

Terry looked at Erin and shrugged. Despite Charley's assertion that she was fine, there were clearly still a few issues there. And what about Kirschoff? Would he be able to answer any questions? Would he remember the explosion and what had happened before and after it?

Charley shook her head, letting her breath out hard in exasperation. "You know how it is when a word is right on the tip of your tongue, and you know everything about it, but you can't quite get it…?"

"Yes, that's really frustrating," Erin agreed.

"I wish I could remember the word. It just… won't come."

"It will probably come back later," Terry offered. "Once you relax and stop trying to think of it. That's how it always is."

"But I don't want to lose it… I want to remember what I'm talking about."

"I'll remind you later," Erin said. "You were talking about Beryl, and you were trying to remember a word that you connect with her. Chef Kirschoff said that she is... that she had...?"

Charley didn't respond to the prompts. She just shook her head in frustration. "I can see it. I know what it means. I just can't remember it."

"I'll remind you later. When you're feeling a bit better. You'll remember."

"I hope so." Charley sank back into her pillow. "You remind me."

CHAPTER 32

They decided that bringing Charley home from the hospital wasn't a good idea. She was still experiencing confusion and lapses of memory and attention, and the doctors wanted to keep an eye on her for a little longer. A day or two. Then they could be more sure that she was completely stable. Or as stable as Charley could be.

"We'll come back and see you again soon," Erin promised. "And we'll try to find out how Chef Kirschoff is."

"I want to go home," Charley repeated.

"I know. I just don't think you're ready yet. We'll listen to the doctors and, hopefully… you'll recover quickly. It's good that you don't have any physical injuries. You'll heal fast."

After leaving Charley's room, they stopped at the nursing station again and tried to get more information on Chef Kirschoff.

"I'm afraid I can't give you any information," the nurse said, shaking her head. "There are privacy issues. Maybe you can get in touch with his family, and they'll fill you in on what you need to know."

"I don't know anything about his family. They're not from around here. They're going to need someone local to deal with the hospital…"

"If you can get in touch with his family, they'll let you know how you can help. They can appoint you his representative. But until that happens…"

"Could you talk to him? Ask him if he wants to see us?"

She looked up and down the hallway. "I'd like to help you. I really would. But we have very strict rules that we're required to follow. Mr. Kirschoff will have to fill out a form with the names of people that he gives us permission to talk to. I can't do anything else."

"We're good friends. He asked me to be one of the judges for his contest. You've heard about the competition that they're running in Whitewater, right? That's his thing. And he asked me…"

"That doesn't mean he wants any medical information shared with you."

"Erin, I'm just going to go for a little walk around the unit," Terry told her.

Erin shook her head in irritation. He could have jumped in, shown his badge, demanded information. Chances were, they still wouldn't have gotten anywhere, but he could have at least tried. He left her to talk to the nurse, K9 heeling close to his side.

"What about Charley? They came in together, she's asking how he is. You could tell her, right?"

"No, ma'am." The nurse's voice was getting more stern and impatient.

Erin couldn't blame her for being irritated. But at the same time, she couldn't let it go. Maybe there was nothing more she could do, but she wasn't going to leave until she was sure she had done everything she could…

When Terry finished looping around the unit, he raised an eyebrow at Erin and jerked his head to the side slightly. Erin stood staring at him for a moment, unsure what he wanted. She gave up on the nurse and walked over to him. Terry put his hand on her arm and, without saying anything, guided her down the hall. Erin wasn't sure what he was up to. He pointed to the name panel beside one of the doors. Erin glanced at it. Kirschoff.

She rolled her eyes and shook her head. "He was here all along? Why couldn't she just tell us that?"

"I suspect they shouldn't even have the names by the door. After you?"

Erin preceded him into the room. There was a man in the bed nearest the door that she didn't know. But when she went past him and around the curtain, she saw Kirschoff.

He was lying in the bed, eyes closed, apparently asleep. Erin wasn't sure if she should try to wake him up or just be satisfied that she had seen him and that, like Charley, he seemed to have been relatively unscathed by the explosion. He had a bandage across part of his forehead and temple, but all body parts seemed to be accounted for. For an explosion that had blown a hole right through the wall, the two people standing close by seemed to have been miraculously preserved.

Terry came up behind Erin and, while she looked at Kirschoff, put an arm around her waist and gave her a little squeeze.

"He looks all right."

"Yeah. He does."

"We should probably let him sleep. We can stop in again tomorrow and see them both."

"Okay."

She spent a few more breaths looking at Kirschoff, then nodded and started for the door. Terry followed her out. They didn't say anything as they passed the nursing station.

As they stood waiting for the elevator, Erin tried to relax all of her muscles. "Thank you for finding him. That really helped."

"Glad it helped. I knew it was important for you to see Kirschoff."

Despite all of his help, his voice held a bit of a bite when he said Kirschoff's name. Erin glanced over at him.

"I just wanted to make sure he was okay."

"Yes."

"If it was one of your friends, you would have wanted to see too."

"Yes."

Erin wished she knew what to say to him. Was he seriously upset about her wanting to see Kirschoff? Was he jealous?

"If it was you, I wouldn't just let you sleep and come back tomorrow."

He looked at her.

"I would stay beside you," Erin said. "I wouldn't leave even if they tried to kick me out. I'd be right beside you."

Maybe he remembered how she had been with him after he had been injured. She'd been there with him until he had been released. Sometimes she would let Vic or Willie sit with him while she went to eat, but mostly, they had to bring her food, because she wouldn't leave him to go down to the hospital cafeteria.

Terry reached around her again to pull her against him. "Yeah."

"I hope they were able to reach his family so they know what happened. I wouldn't want him to be all alone here."

"I'm sure they have. Charley said they were both awake and mobile after the explosion, so he would have been able to tell them who to call for him."

"If he has anyone. I don't even know if he has any family."

"Then he could give them the name of a friend. If he didn't have them call you, then he must have had them call someone."

"I suppose."

CHAPTER 33

*I*t felt to Erin like she had been away from Bald Eagle Falls for a long time. Much as it had felt to return there after the cruise. She was glad to be home, away from the turmoil in Whitewater.

The news out of Whitewater Junction was pretty low-key. The police made a statement that the explosion was under investigation and that the injured parties were in stable condition. Erin waited for a release from the contest organizers saying that they were calling everything off, but it didn't come. She was checking her computer again when the doorbell rang.

She got up to answer it but then heard Terry open the door and speak to the caller. He didn't call her to say that it was someone who wanted her, so Erin sank back down to her seat. She would check her email to see if she had missed anything from the contest, and then she would go see who had come to the door. It clearly wasn't for her, or Terry would have called her.

There it was in her mailbox, finally. An email from the contest to all of the judges, volunteers, and participants. Erin skimmed down the page, then returned to the top, confused.

It wasn't a statement that the contest was being shut down,

but an assurance that they were still going ahead. The venue would change slightly, but they had already secured another restaurant and were sourcing replacement materials for anything they had lost in the explosion. The email expressed sympathy for Charley and Chef Kirschoff and said that Kirschoff would still be able to spearhead the contest preparations.

Erin shook her head in disbelief. What would it take for them to actually shut the competition down? Didn't they realize that either the two incidents were related or the contest was cursed? Not that Erin believed in curses.

But it couldn't just be a coincidence. First, one of the judges killed under mysterious circumstances, and then one of the organizers nearly died in an explosion? They had to be related.

The note that Erin had received clinched it.

There was no way that someone was threatening her after two random accidents. There were so many other accidents that could occur if she went back to Whitewater to judge the contest. She had recovered physically from the last attempt on her life, but she didn't much feel like putting it on the line again.

She trashed the email, wishing that she could do something more dramatic, like actually crumpling it up and throwing it in the garbage in real life. And then lighting it on fire. But there was no point in printing it out just so she could throw it away.

She closed the lid to her computer and walked out to the living room.

Beaver sat across from Terry, who was on the couch with K9 at his feet. Beaver had one ankle resting across the other knee, legs wide, taking up lots of space. Beaver always seemed to take up the maximum space possible. Erin wondered whether it was because, as a woman in a profession that was dominated by men, she needed to physically show her coworkers that she deserved just as much attention and respect as anyone else. Or maybe it was just Beaver's nature. She was no shrinking violet.

"Erin!" Beaver cracked her gum. "Good to see you back here.

I'm sure Terry's glad to get you back from Whitewater. I wouldn't want *my* partner out there, fending for herself."

Erin shrugged. "I just… couldn't justify staying out there with everything that is going on. I was sure that they would cancel the competition."

"Are they going to?"

"I just got an email. They're going ahead."

Terry frowned. "What are you going to do?"

"I don't know. They have other judges. It's not just me. So maybe if I duck out… They should still be able to go ahead using the other judges. In fact, if I drop out, they've lost two judges, and they're back down to an odd number. So no tied votes."

"What about Vic?"

"I don't know what she'll do. But if enough of us quit, they're going to have to cancel."

"If she stays with it, will you?"

Erin shook her head. "I just don't know. I have a few days… I'll have to make a decision. I just don't know what it will be."

"Fair enough," Beaver allowed. "It's wise not to jump to a snap decision."

Erin shrugged. She sat down with Terry. She didn't know if Beaver had shown up to have a discussion about law enforcement, but she didn't feel like staying by herself in front of the computer. She wanted to be around others. Terry put his arm around her, making no objection.

"How has Mary Lou been toward you?" Beaver asked.

Erin was startled at her bluntness. She shouldn't be surprised by anything Beaver did, especially not being blunt. That was Beaver.

"I haven't seen her. She hasn't come by the bakery. I was hoping that… she would have forgiven me by now. But…"

Beaver nodded. She chewed her gum. "I didn't think she would be quite so stubborn either," she admitted. "I was hoping that once she'd had a chance to cool off, she would see…"

"I can understand her being upset," Erin said. "I mean, I

did… mention Joshua's name to the police. That was… I don't know. I guess if I was put in that position again, I would probably do exactly the same thing. I didn't do it to get Joshua in trouble, I just wanted to find out who was behind the burglaries."

Beaver grunted her agreement.

"And as far as the stuff that happened when Campbell was in jail… I didn't… I didn't really have anything to do with that. I was trying to talk the others out of it. I told them what they were doing was dangerous."

"But they went ahead. And so did you."

Erin nodded. "I wanted to keep them out of trouble. But I guess Mary Lou didn't see it that way. She thought I should have done something else. I don't know what. I don't think it would have done any good for me to have called her. Maybe we could have stopped Joshua from going that time, but it wouldn't have stopped him from trying to clear Campbell's name. The next time, it might have been without any backup."

"Teenagers don't always have the best judgment. Joshua's got a pretty good head on his shoulders. But where Cam is concerned…"

"His heart overruled his head."

"Yes. The boys were very close before Cam left home. They looked after each other. At first, I thought that was just Cam looking after Josh, but I think a fair amount was going the other direction. Josh reining big brother in. Keeping track of him. Making sure Cam didn't go off and do something stupid. Cam may have been older, bigger and stronger, but Josh is more careful. He thinks things through."

"I saw him in Whitewater. He is doing a report on the contest for his English class. Or reports. They're hoping to publish something in the paper."

"You saw him…?"

"He came to see me. Wanted to interview me, because I'm one of the judges and because of… well… Beryl. Finding her. You know."

Beaver chewed her gum, considering this. "How much interest does he have in Batcombe's death?"

"I think it interested him more than the contest. I told him I didn't really know anything and didn't want to talk to him about it, but he was pretty persistent. Of course. It makes perfect sense that he would be more interested in a… death than in ice cream and coke."

Beaver nodded vigorously. "Of course. Far more interesting reporting on a human popsicle."

"Eww."

They all laughed.

Erin leaned her head on Terry's shoulder, thinking about Mary Lou and Beaver. "I didn't think you cared what anyone thinks of you. You just do what's right for you."

"Well…" Beaver chewed thoughtfully, shifting her wad of gum from one side to the other. "I don't let it affect the choices I make. I'll do what I need to do. Or what I want to. But that doesn't mean that I'm not disappointed if I get cross-threaded with someone. A good decent person, like Mary Lou or you."

"Me?"

"I can't guarantee I'm not going to do anything that will upset you. Something that would threaten our friendship." Beaver sighed and stared up at the ceiling. "I hope that day doesn't come, but I can't guarantee it. I do tend to… rub people the wrong way."

"Oh." Erin shrugged. "I was pretty ticked when you and Terry didn't tell me about the safe house and forced me to be a part of all *that*. But I got over it."

"Yeah. Some people, like Mary Lou, it's not that easy. She doesn't like to let it go."

"But she wouldn't do anything about it," Erin hastened to put in. "She might tell you off and avoid you, but she would never… poison your cornflakes or anything like that."

Beaver laughed loudly. "I can just see Mary Lou doing that."

"It's funny because she would never do anything like that. She's the person that Angela Plaint probably hurt the most, other than her own family, but Mary Lou didn't do anything to hurt her. And when Roger… did what he did, Mary Lou was horrified. She would never say that was okay. She holds herself to certain standards."

Beaver's eyes were far away. She chewed and tapped rhythmically on her knee, deep in thought.

$\mathcal{E}$rin went into Auntie Clem's Bakery even though she had arranged for her other employees to cover all of the shifts while she and Vic were involved in the competition. Erin hadn't gone as far as to cancel those arrangements, even though she didn't plan to go back to Whitewater, but she needed to lose herself in some baking. There was nothing like working batters and doughs and pulling something delicious out of the ovens. It was therapeutic, and she missed it on the days she didn't go in, no matter how tired she got when she was working. Often enough, if she didn't have to go to Auntie Clem's, she could be found baking something in her own kitchen. It had become such a part of who she was.

"Hi, Erin!" Bella greeted enthusiastically. "I wasn't expecting to see you today! You just couldn't stay away, could you?"

Erin shook her head. "You know me!"

"Everything is on track, but if you wanted to get started on some banana muffins, I wouldn't argue."

"Sounds good," Erin agreed. She put on her hat and apron and started to pull out the bowls and ingredients she would need.

Gwen, one of the girls that Bella went to school with, was also on shift. Bella took a peek out front to make sure that things were not too busy for Gwen, then started on washing up the pans in the sink.

"So, what are you doing back in Bald Eagle Falls?" Bella asked. "I thought you were going to stay in Whitewater until the competition was over."

"I was, but I'm concerned about everything that's happening. I thought… I expected them to cancel the contest after the explosion. For them to just go ahead like nothing had happened…"

"I thought it was a little strange too," Bella agreed. "But I guess they've already sunk a lot of time and money into the contest, and they would lose out if it didn't go ahead now."

"I suppose so," Erin agreed. "I figured that with Chef Kirschoff being put out of commission, they wouldn't be able to do anything."

"He's a big part of it, isn't he?" Bella asked.

"Yes. Definitely. When he first came and asked Vic and me if we would be judges, I thought it was just some small contest, and that he got involved because someone wanted to use his name. This famous chef, you know. Good publicity. I didn't realize that he pretty much floated the whole thing. His idea, he drummed up the sponsors, picked the judges personally, all of that."

"Really? I didn't know that. So is he directing it all from his hospital bed or what?"

"He called me this morning. And yes… he's been driving the doctors and nurses crazy trying to run a three-ring circus over the phone while he's supposed to be resting and recovering." Erin smiled. She'd been able to hear the complaints in the background, with Kirschoff's ebullient voice booming over everyone else.

Bella giggled. "Well, good for him, I guess. He's really lucky that he wasn't killed in that explosion."

Erin carefully measured flour into the bowl. "He says they have to completely replace the CO2 bottles. Send them all back and have them replaced with new ones. So that they can be sure that there aren't any more defective ones. Big expense."

"Yeah, I got an email about that. I'm glad. I didn't know if I wanted to go ahead with my contest entry. I didn't want to have to worry about whether the canister I was using was okay or not."

"I thought you were making ice cream." Erin was pretty sure that Bella would be using dry ice for that, not a CO2 bottle.

Bella looked at her sideways. "I might have changed my entry."

"Oh, okay. Well, that's good, actually, because I won't know which entry is yours."

"Exactly. I don't want you giving me the grand prize just because you think I'm a great employee."

Erin laughed. "That could happen."

"See? I don't want to put you in that position."

Erin thought about going back to Whitewater to judge the contest. She didn't want to, but she also didn't want to let down the competition officials. And Vic. And all of the contestants like Bella, who had put the work into developing new recipes for the contest.

"Are you okay?" Bella looked at Erin.

"Yes, I'm fine. I'm just worried about the competition. We don't want any more accidents."

"Do you think that's what they are? Just accidents?"

"I don't know how Beryl's death could have been an accident, but the explosion... I don't think someone did that on purpose, do you? Charley and Chef Kirschoff could have been killed. It's amazing that they got out of there without any serious injuries."

Bella didn't say anything, scrubbing the pans thoroughly. Erin watched the beaters whirl the batter around and around in the bowl. Bella didn't point out that they'd been confronted with people with murderous intentions in the past. It wasn't as far-fetched as it might sound. And that was exactly why Erin didn't want to be put in that situation again.

"What did Chef Kirschoff say when you told him you don't want to go back?"

"Well... I didn't tell him. I let the other organizers know, but I didn't want to upset Chef Kirschoff while he was recovering… he could have a heart attack or a stroke."

Erin peeled bananas and worked on mashing them into a chunky slop. "He said that they are tightening up security measures. Maybe he doesn't think that anyone is trying to kill him or to sabotage the competition, but he's taking precautions."

"That's good. So you don't need to worry about keeping safe. He'll make sure that everyone is protected."

Erin nodded in agreement. Chef Kirschoff was taking the situation seriously. She wished he had canceled the contest, but the next best thing was that there would be security guards and a police presence. There would be ambulances and paramedics in the parking lot.

What could go wrong?

CHAPTER 35

Happily, both Chef Kirschoff and Charley had been released from the hospital, cleared to return to their regular activities. Both had minor after-effects from the explosion, but they were expected to recover quickly and were allowed to do whatever they felt up to.

Erin invited them both over for dinner. That way, they didn't have to worry about getting up the energy to make their own meal or go out, and could still have a nourishing home-cooked meal. Erin was feeling a little at a loss without having to go to the bakery every day. Cooking gave her something to do.

The animals had all been given their treats and were out from underfoot. Erin, Terry, Charley, and Chef Kirschoff sat around the table to partake.

"This looks great, Erin." Charley looked over the dishes on the table. It wasn't anything fancy, just some noodle casserole, garlic bread, and salad, but it was good food. "The stuff that they serve you at the hospital…" She shook her head. "It shouldn't really be called food. I'm sure it passes all of the nutritional requirements, but so do vitamin pills."

Chef Kirschoff nodded vigorously. Erin had been a little nervous about feeding him. Charley was young and she was Erin's sister. Erin didn't feel like she had to impress Charley with her cooking skills. That wasn't going to change if she didn't think Erin's cooking was up to snuff. But serving a world-famous chef was another story. Terry had told her to just make what she normally would; Kirschoff wouldn't be expecting a gourmet meal. Erin knew Terry was right, but she was still anxious about it.

"It smells delicious," Kirschoff agreed. "This is just what we need. Good, home-cooked comfort food."

Erin nodded, relieved. "I hope you like it."

"Your casserole is fine," Terry assured her. "They would be crazy not to like it."

She shrugged and started passing dishes around for everyone to dish up. They ate a few bites, made the appropriate noises, and the conversation turned to the topic on everyone's mind—the contest.

"Are you sure you should still run it?" Erin asked. "You're not worried about any more trouble? And you can get everything done, even though you had to take a couple of days off in the hospital?"

"Yes. I'm sure it will be just fine," Kirschoff assured her. "We are taking all of the necessary precautions. And I can't afford to lose a judge, Erin. You have to be there."

Terry gave Erin a stern look that told her to stand her ground and not let Kirschoff push her into participating. She gave him a brief nod.

"I'm just worried that... I don't know. That this was all targeted. Someone wants to shut the contest down."

"No one wants to shut the contest down. This is the best thing that's happened to this region in years. It's bringing in a capital injection that the area is badly in need of. It's giving people some-thing to do, to be happy about, to draw closer together and bond as neighbors. It isn't just a cooking contest," he said gravely. "It's so much more than that."

Erin shrugged and nodded. She knew it was all of those things, but she was afraid that it was going to crater and all of the people Kirschoff was trying to help were going to end up getting hurt and being angry and bitter about it.

"It's just ice cream and cola," Terry pointed out. "Let's not forget that. It's great to have all of those lofty goals, but we need to stay realistic about it. It's a fun time, good entertainment, sugary food, not the United Nations."

"Not the United Nations," Kirschoff repeated, laughing. Erin had been afraid that he would be offended by Terry's words, but he took them with good grace. "Ah. It's too bad that Beryl will not get a chance to see it. She had the vision."

There was a moment of silence while everyone considered this. Erin ate a couple of bites of casserole.

"Did you know her well?"

"Yes, yes, she was a good friend." Kirschoff used a crust of bread to soak up some of the sauce from the casserole.

"You'd known her for a long time? I wondered how she had been picked as a judge."

"Well, you are right. It was my choice. A perk of being in charge is that you can give all the good positions to your friends. Repay people for supporting you through the years."

"Where did you know Beryl from?"

She couldn't imagine that they had known each other through school or work. And Kirschoff had said that he hadn't been to Tennessee before.

Kirschoff cleared his throat a couple of times. "Years ago, she was very interested in food and cooking, had some old family recipes that she wanted to make into a book. Thought about opening a restaurant. Some mutual connections put us in touch with each other. Beryl was a very… persistent woman. She generally got what she wanted, sooner or later."

"Ambitious!" Charley said suddenly.

Everyone looked at her. Kirschoff pursed his lips. "Well… yes."

"That's the word I was trying to think of! Oh, it's been stuck in my brain for two days! I'm so glad to finally shake it loose!"

"Ambitious." Erin remembered how Charley had been struggling to find the word when they had visited. "What's the connection to Caesar?"

Kirschoff cleared his throat and quoted:

"The noble Brutus
Hath told you Caesar was ambitious:
If it were so, it was a grievous fault,
And grievously hath Caesar answer'd it.
Here, under leave of Brutus and the rest–
For Brutus is an honorable man;
So are they all, all honorable men–"

"Wow." It sounded vaguely familiar to Erin, but she certainly didn't have any long passages of Shakespeare memorized as Kirschoff did.

"Yes! That's it. That's what I was trying to remember." Charley slapped the table. "That's why Brutus said he murdered Caesar, who was supposed to be his best friend, almost a father to him. But he did it because Caesar was too ambitious."

And Charley had said that Beryl was ambitious. Kirschoff had verified it with the little that he had said. Had Beryl's ambition led to her death as well? Had she stepped on too many toes in her quest to get what she wanted?

And what was it she wanted? To judge the contest? To publish her recipes? Open a restaurant?

They were all quiet for a while.

"So did she ever open a restaurant?" Terry asked. "Did she ever do any of those things she wanted to?"

"She published her recipes through a small local printer. Sold a few copies in tourist shops, but it didn't make the big hit she hoped it would. And no... she never opened that restaurant. But if she'd lived, I wouldn't doubt that she would have, sooner or later."

"Ambitious," Charley repeated, savoring the word. Now that she remembered it, she wasn't going to let herself forget.

Kirschoff's pocket started to trill. He jumped and clutched at it. He pulled his phone out and fumbled to silence it. "I'm so sorry. How rude of me. I thought it was on silent."

Looking at the screen, he frowned.

"I hate to do this, but I need to take this. It will only be a minute."

"Sure," Erin said. "Grab one of the bedrooms if you need some privacy."

He only walked out into the living room and took the call there. The normally effusive Chef Kirschoff was unusually quiet, his voice pitched low and his back turned to them. Erin attempted to carry on a conversation while he was on the phone so that they wouldn't be eavesdropping on his conversation. It was only natural to be curious and listen in on what he was saying.

Kirschoff was longer than one minute but, eventually, he returned to the kitchen and sat down. He wasn't smiling. His brows were drawn down thoughtfully, so that he was almost scowling. Erin touched his arm as he sat back down.

"Is everything okay?"

His eyes flicked over each of them. He scratched his chin, mouth turned down in a frown.

"I have a contact who promised to get me any new information from the medical examiner's office."

Terry raised his brows. He would want to know who the contact was, but he kept quiet for the moment and waited to see what Kirschoff would volunteer.

"About Beryl?" Charley asked, leaning toward Kirschoff. She put her hand on Kirschoff's other arm. Erin withdrew her own hand, slightly embarrassed. It looked strange if they were both pawing at Kirschoff's arm, trying to comfort him. Charley was the one who was interested in a relationship with him, he was her territory more than Erin's.

No one else seemed to notice Erin's embarrassment. Terry and

Charley were both watching Kirschoff's face intently. Erin too was interested in hearing what his friend in the medical examiner's office had passed on about Beryl's autopsy. It was a little grim for dinner conversation, but she couldn't exactly tell him to wait until they were finished eating to bring up postmortem results.

Kirschoff picked at the food on his plate, but no longer looked interested in it. He looked troubled. "The cause of death was apparently carbon dioxide toxicity."

"Carbon dioxide? That can kill you?" Charley shook her head. "There's carbon dioxide in the air we breathe all the time, isn't there? That's what we exhale."

"Apparently, it can kill you if you get too much of it," Kirschoff said slowly. "It is not common, and it is very hard to find in an autopsy, but I guess when it was suggested that Beryl might have been poisoned—the police said something about her acting intoxicated—the medical examiner connected our cook-off theme with some of the indications in the postmortem, and... he was able to confirm that the air in her lungs was much too high in CO2." Kirschoff looked at them. "How could that be?"

"Didn't he have any suggestions?"

"I know people sometimes use compressed gasses to get high, or to change their voices, like helium... but how would... why would she be breathing CO2?"

"It must have gotten into her car from her exhaust system," Charley suggested. "I've heard of that before. If there is a leak in the system and it is feeding carbon dioxide into the car, that can kill you."

"That's carbon monoxide," Terry corrected. "Fires, exhaust, things like that can cause carbon monoxide poisoning. But carbon dioxide? Have you ever heard of that before?" he asked Kirschoff.

"Yes. Yes, all of the training that we needed to take for this project. Carbon dioxide is toxic, so we have to get instruction about how you could get it... signs and symptoms... what to do..."

Erin nodded. "So what did they say? People must get it accidentally if you had to have safety training. So maybe it was just an accident."

"There have been cases where theaters or other venues have had carbon dioxide leaks in the tubing for their carbonation machines. People start getting dizzy or faint… throwing up… you have to be aware of the danger. Get them inspected regularly. Recognize the symptoms when you see them." Talking about it seemed to have galvanized him. He spoke more fluidly, remembering what he had learned. "There are guidelines for transporting dry ice, because that's another time when you can end up with too much in the air. If you have a bunch of dry ice in an enclosed area."

"You probably have to cover it tightly," Erin suggested.

"No. If you seal it, the container could explode." He touched the bandage on his temple, then lowered his hand again. "And then there are cases when someone has done something stupid like dump a load of dry ice into a swimming pool, asphyxiating a bunch of people at once."

Erin tried to reconcile any of these methods of poisoning with what had happened with Beryl. Coleman had said that she had been in her car. She had leaned out of it, throwing up, and the witness had thought that she was drunk. Maybe she wasn't drunk, but was being poisoned by carbon dioxide in her car.

"Would Beryl have been transporting dry ice?"

"No. We won't be using dry ice until the weekend. It would have been too early to be transporting and storing it. It would all be gone by the time we were ready to use it."

"But she could have been doing it for some other reason… maybe she had a recipe she wanted to try out. Or some kind of… experiment for the science fair. Anything…?"

"She was a judge. She couldn't participate in the contest or the science fair."

"You said she had a bunch of family recipes, though. Maybe she was experimenting just for her own entertainment. She wanted to prove to herself that she could make… better ice cream than the people who were entering the contest." Erin floundered for a more reasonable explanation. Did Beryl seem like the kind of person who would be experimenting with dry ice for fun? She hadn't seemed to Erin to be the fun-loving kind.

Kirschoff was shaking his head. "None of that sounds plausible. I can't imagine how she would have gotten exposed to that much carbon dioxide."

"Well then, it's simple, isn't it?" Charley asked, looking at Terry. "It was deliberate. She was poisoned."

"Murder?" Kirschoff protested. He pushed his plate away from himself firmly. "No. It couldn't be. No."

"Why else would someone move her body and put it in the freezer?" Terry asked. "They were trying to cover up the cause of death. They figured if she was found in the freezer, we would just assume that she froze to death."

"That's what I thought when I saw her," Erin agreed. "I just assumed… until they said that she'd been moved."

"And clearly, whoever did it didn't think that the police would be able to tell that she had been moved. Or that the medical examiner would be able to tell that she had been exposed to that concentration of carbon dioxide."

They all sat in silence, thinking about what that meant.

"So she was murdered," Charley said.

Erin looked for a way that Beryl could have been accidentally poisoned, but the methods that Kirschoff suggested didn't seem to fit. Beryl wouldn't have been transporting a large amount of dry ice. She hadn't been sitting in a theater or restaurant with a carbon dioxide leak. And if it had been an accident in a restaurant, they would have called for the paramedics to see if she could be revived. It would have been all over the news.

It had to be murder. And the murderer had next moved to an exploding gas canister, something that could have killed multiple people. Whoever wanted to stop the contest was desperate. They were willing to see a lot of people die.

CHAPTER 36

Despite Erin's resolution not to judge the contest, Kirschoff was able to wear her down and convince her that notwithstanding all that had happened so far, she and the others involved with the contest would be perfectly safe. He expounded upon all of the security measures they would have in place.

Once Erin broke down and agreed to go back to Whitewater and follow through on the contract she had signed, she got one more security measure. Terry would not let her go back on her own. He would return with her and stay with her at all times. She kept the hotel room and Vic had already booked another room with Willie and Nilla. If Willie were not staying over for the full time, Terry would pay Vic's hotel bill for the remainder of the time. She could have a room all to herself. But Erin suspected that once Willie caught wind of the possible danger to the judges, he too would decide to stick around and make sure Vic was safe.

In a couple more days, they were back in Whitewater, ramping up for the actual contest.

Vic came up to Erin's room with Nilla and they introduced the dogs. Erin expected that the little dog would be cowering behind Vic's legs upon being faced with the much larger German shepherd, but instead, Nilla appeared to be the aggressor, barreling in to sniff K9 thoroughly, circling around him. K9 stood there, shoulders rounded a little as he looked down at the little white dog, shifting his feet as Nilla poked his nose in awkward places. He sniffed Nilla curiously and looked at Terry.

"Sorry, bud," Terry chuckled. "Good boy. You're being very patient."

K9's big tail swept back and forth slowly. Eventually, he lay down, tired of the little dog's antics. Nilla investigated the rest of the hotel room, then returned to K9 and snuggled close to him.

Terry supervised the dogs while they talked. Erin told Vic about how Terry would be staying with her, and that maybe Willie should stick around to provide extra security for Vic as well.

"I don't need anyone guarding me," Vic protested. "I'm perfectly capable of looking after myself!" She patted her concealed holster, eyes blazing. "Willie can go back to Bald Eagle Falls if he wants. I don't need him to look after me."

Erin looked over at Terry, but he was watching K9, carefully avoiding their discussion.

The last time they had gone in somewhere expecting Vic to be able to protect herself with her gun—the last couple of times, in fact—Erin and Vic had ended up being held at gunpoint. Vic's gun hadn't even come out until it was too late. There had been no shoot-outs; someone had gotten the drop on them and they had been unable to do anything about it.

"It never hurts to have one more person on your side," Erin said tactfully.

Vic glared at her, but finally nodded. "Yeah. As long as you don't think I'm some helpless woman that needs a man to protect her."

"I never said that."

"I can take care of myself."

"I know. It's just that this time, we have some psycho out there who could be targeting us because we're involved with the contest.

And that's… not a position we want to be in. We don't want… this person… to be able to get to us easily."

Terry looked over at them suddenly, his face full of tension. His quick movement made Erin jump and the anxiety in his face was so pronounced it actually made her look back toward the door to see if someone had snuck in behind them.

"Terry….?"

Terry looked at Erin, apparently not seeing her panic, and his gaze slid past her to Vic. "What about… Theresa?"

Vic rolled her eyes. "What about Theresa? She got the drop on you too, if you remember. I wasn't exactly helpless. We rescued you, not the other way around."

He shook this off with a toss of his head like a dog. "That's not what I mean. I mean… she's still out there." He blinked at them. "What if this is Theresa?"

"What?"

"What if the person who is sabotaging the contest, trying to get it shut down, is Theresa."

The color drained from Vic's face. "No. It couldn't be. It's too dangerous for her to show her face around here. She wouldn't come back looking for trouble when she might get caught. She's too wily."

"If she heard that you were judging it, you and Erin, she could decide to do something about it. Figure she could get at you if she was careful."

"But she hasn't been careful. Whoever it is hasn't been careful. If it was Theresa trying to get at me, then why would she kill off Beryl? Why would she cause the explosion that could have killed Charley and Hans? That wouldn't make any sense. She would stay under cover until she could target me."

They all sat there, looking at each other and trying to calculate just how crazy Theresa was. She had attacked them all before. She'd had all of them under her control. She'd nearly killed Terry and Detective Jack Ward. She'd killed Bo Biggles. The police figured she was responsible for the death of her parents and a number of hits for the Jackson clan. She wasn't called Crazy Theresa for nothing.

She might go after Vic or Erin, or even Terry or Willie, but there was no motive for her to kill Beryl. It wasn't like Theresa could have mistaken Beryl for Erin or Vic. There would be no reason for her to kill Kirschoff or Charley or to shut down the contest.

Erin was pretty sure that there was no way it could be Theresa. Pretty sure.

~

Erin was jumpy being back in Whitewater.

Everything would be fine. She now had plenty of security. And Vic was armed, though Erin wasn't sure how much good Vic's gun would be if someone managed to make it past the rest of the layers of security. It would probably mean that someone had managed to sneak through the security and got the drop on them. Or that it was someone close to them that they would never have suspected. Or maybe that the security had been faced with overwhelming force. In the first two cases, Vic probably wouldn't even get her gun out until it was too late and, in the last, a single handgun wasn't going to do much good against such power.

They just had to hope that whoever was behind the incidents was finished or would be too cautious to attack again because of the increased security.

During the opening ceremonies for the contest, Erin was all eyes, continually checking the wings of the stage to make sure that no one was sneaking up on them, searching the crowd for anyone menacing or any sign of weapons, unable to concentrate on what Chef Kirschoff and the sponsors had to say. Vic had to nudge her when they were expected to get up and acknowledge the applause as their names were called.

More speeches. No apparent threats. Everything went as

smoothly as if they had been planning for this for two years instead of just a few weeks.

More applause.

Unexpected fireworks. Erin nearly jumped out of her seat. She clutched at Vic's arm and looked around, thinking they were being attacked from all sides. Vic put her hand over Erin's, trying to calm her. Lots of *oohing* and *aahing* and thrilled gasps from the crowd as, for the next twenty minutes, the fireworks kept going on in a dazzling display overhead.

The fireworks were followed by a social event with sponsors and contestants. Not a full dinner, but drinks and hors d'oeuvres. Erin was glad to get away from the open-air amphitheater. It felt safer inside the ballroom at the hotel.

"You okay?" Vic asked, patting Erin on the shoulder as they were able to rejoin the men.

"Yeah. Just a little jumpy."

"Well, Terry's here." Vic looked around and pointed at the doors. "And there's plenty of security. Nothing is going to happen in here."

Erin nodded her agreement. If she could just make her body believe that too. Terry gave her a hug, holding her close.

"You want to dance?" he suggested, nodding to the dance floor. Erin hadn't been planning to, but she hadn't been able to do much that could be considered romantic with Terry lately, so she agreed.

"Sure. Sounds good."

Terry had K9 *stay* close by. He sat watching them, ears pricked up curiously. It was a slow song, so she didn't have to worry about Terry bouncing around too much and aggravating his head. It felt good, holding each other close and pretending that everything was normal again. That nothing had ever happened to put their lives or relationship at risk—just a normal couple in love, enjoying time together slow-dancing.

When the song ended and they left the dance floor, however, Terry seemed a little unsteady. It was hard for Erin to put her finger on anything. It just seemed like he was moving more slowly than he should, his reactions just a bit off. The lights started to flash as a faster number started. Terry's hand went up to his forehead.

"You're not feeling well," Erin guessed.

He tried to shrug it off. "I'm fine."

"I don't think you are. Is the music bothering you?"

He sighed. "The music. The lights. The fireworks. I have to admit… they made me a bit jumpy too. Nothing like loud bangs and the smell of gunpowder to get a policeman's adrenaline going."

"Do you want to knock off for the night? Head back to the hotel room?"

"You still need to circulate and make nice."

"I can circulate for a little while and then come up. I'm safe while I'm here, and Willie can walk me up."

Terry shook his head. "No, really… I said that I would stay here and look after you."

"I was mostly worried about being outside or going around town by myself. But here, it's all secure. I'll be all right." Even though Erin was still nervous and jumpy, she didn't want Terry staying there if his head was bothering him. If he didn't take care of himself, he would be out of commission for several days. Which wasn't what either of them wanted.

"I don't know. Are you sure?"

"Why don't you go over and talk with Willie, see what he thinks."

Even though Terry had never fully trusted Willie, he did trust Willie's opinion on security matters. Whatever his personal opinion, Willie was the first one Terry would go to for things like search and rescue or Willie's other areas of expertise.

"Okay. You stay here. Don't get into any trouble."

Erin wasn't sure what trouble she was going to get into at the event. She wasn't going to leave the ballroom or even have any alcohol. Terry called K9 to heel and left her to talk to Willie.

Erin smiled at people, shook hands, and tried to remember names to go with all of the faces. Crowds were not her thing, but she had signed up for it when she had agreed to help Chef Kirschoff out with the judging. The judges were expected to schmooze with the contestants, town council members, sponsors, and anyone else who might bring in more business and good publicity.

Everything was pretty much a blur. Smile, shake hands, say nice things about the contest and looking forward to trying out all of the great entries. Move on to the next person and repeat.

"Hey, Erin," a large hand clapped over Erin's arm, nearly sending her through the roof. She yelped and pulled back, but the offender didn't even seem to notice. "Hey, how's it going? Good party!"

"Yes." She pulled back from him, trying to get perspective.

Norman. She remembered the name, but where did she know him from? Was he one of the sponsors or the competitors? She smiled politely, waiting for him to fill her in on the details.

"I'm really glad that they decided to go ahead with the competition," Norman said. "I'll bet you are too."

"Well… I wasn't too sure about that."

"But all of the exposure that you're getting, and the honorarium. You wouldn't want to miss out on that."

"I don't want to get in the middle of something that might be dangerous, either."

"Oh, come on…" He gave her a knowing look. "You say that you don't want to be involved, but I remember what happened on the ship." He tapped the side of his nose.

He was one of Vic's friends. That's how she knew him. He was one of the contestants.

"I didn't want to get in the middle of that either… it just happened. I never… I don't want to put myself or anyone around me at risk."

"But you don't think there really is any risk, do you? I mean, what's going to happen? It's a cooking contest!"

"You know what happened to Beryl."

He made a *pfff* noise and waved her comment away. "Beryl? That was just an accident. And if it wasn't… well, I can think of a lot of people who wanted her out of the contest."

"It wasn't just an accident." She didn't tell him it was CO2 poisoning or murder, but if it wasn't an accident, then he had to know that it had been intentional and targeted.

"I think it was. The police here, this podunk little town, they're just making up drama. Probably the first death they've had to investigate in twenty years. They're making the best of it."

Erin shook her head. Not only was she irritated at him for arguing, but she didn't like him talking about Whitewater that way and, by association, any little town in the area, like Bald Eagle Falls. "Sorry, I have to go see someone…" she told Norman, and headed across the floor to a knot of people.

He followed her, talking the whole time as if she wanted to hear him instead of leaving him behind.

"Beryl. Everyone wanted her out. The only reason she was selected as a judge was that she was Kirschoff's old flame. So he gave in to her badgering and let her be a judge."

Erin stopped and stared at him. Was that how people thought of her too? Because she was friends with Kirschoff, he had been persuaded to put her on the judges' panel? She hadn't approached him, he had approached her and asked her to be on it. And they had never been lovers, just cooking friends, enjoying the exchange of recipes and tips and whipping up a couple of creations together.

"You didn't know that?" Norman laughed loudly. "I suppose he told you that you were the only one. You didn't know that he was involved with Beryl?"

"I don't know anything about it," Erin said icily. "His affairs are his own business. It doesn't have anything to do with me."

"I bet you would have liked to have stabbed her! Am I right? Acting like she owns Kirschoff, when he's out dogging around with everyone else?"

"I don't know what you're talking about. I haven't seen him

since we were on the cruise. We didn't have any kind of relationship then or now. I don't know anything about who is… friendly with him."

"Yeah. Did he tell you he's married, too?" His braying laughter rang out again. People turned to stare.

Erin swallowed. Had Chef Kirschoff ever mentioned that he had a wife? Or even implied it? Charley had her sights set on him, and that didn't seem to matter at all to Kirschoff. He was happy to play along.

She could bet that Charley had no idea he had a wife.

"I wouldn't know anything about that."

"Well, he is," Norman asserted. "You just ask him."

Vic appeared at Norman's side, looking at him like she wasn't sure what was up with him. "Norman? What's going on?"

"I was just telling your friend here about Beryl Batcombe and Chef Kirschoff." He raised and lowered thick eyebrows in a Groucho Marx leer.

"Beryl and Hans?" Vic shook her head and took a step back. "No way. Who told you that?"

"I saw the two of them together myself, heard them arguing."

"How much have you had to drink tonight?" Vic arched her eyebrows.

"I'm not drunk. Okay, maybe I'm a little bit buzzed, but that's all. Hardly had anything yet."

"Well, maybe you'd better cut it off there. I wouldn't want you to put your foot in your mouth and say something that you can't take back later."

"It's true. I haven't told you anything that isn't true."

"But maybe you'd better call it a night. You get buzzed like this, and your judgment is off."

He rolled his eyes at Vic and stalked away. Not out of the ballroom, but toward the bar and more people he could share his theories with.

"Thanks," Erin told Vic. "I was having problems getting away from him."

"He should not be spreading rumors like that around. He should know better. And maybe he does when he's sober."

"Did Terry talk to Willie?"

Vic nodded and looked around. She spotted her boyfriend across the ballroom and gave him a little wave. "Yeah. They talked. I think he convinced Terry that he could manage to keep us both safe and sent him up to his room to sleep. I don't want his head getting too bad."

"Yeah. Me either. It seemed like it could be the beginning of a big one. I'll just stay down here for a few more minutes, then I'll go up and make sure he's taken his medication and gone to bed."

Vic nodded. She took another look at Norman. "Sorry about him. I don't know what he's going on about."

"He says... that Beryl and Chef Kirschoff were—uh—together. And that Kirschoff is married...?"

"Yeah, I think I heard that."

"He's married? But he and Charley..."

Vic shrugged uncomfortably. "I don't know. Maybe he told her. Maybe they have an open relationship. Or they're separated."

Somehow, Erin couldn't picture that. "She certainly doesn't sound like a very nice woman."

"His wife?"

"Beryl."

"Yeah, well, that's exactly what you told me, isn't it? You said that she was bad news before she died. She really wound you up that night."

Erin gave her a sideways look. "Just don't go spreading that around. I don't want Coleman hearing that I had a motive to murder her."

"I know you didn't. I won't say anything." Vic patted Erin on the arm. "Every time I hear something about her, it seems like there's someone else who would have liked to have gotten her out of the way."

"That's what Norman was just saying. But he... put Chef

Kirschoff at the top of his list. Hans would never do anything like that! He's not a violent man."

"We don't really know him well enough to know what kind of a man he is," Vic pointed out. "So we've had dinner together a couple of times and had a few meetings and conversations. That doesn't mean that we know him. Not like you would need to know someone in order to say that."

"Can you see him hurting anyone? Getting violent?"

"Whether I can or not, that doesn't mean anything. Getting violent…? I've seen some videos of him blowing his top in the kitchen. Believe me, he was not a meek and mild-mannered little chef."

"A commercial kitchen can be high-stress." Erin knew that wasn't an excuse. She just didn't want to hear what Vic had to say. She sighed. "Don't tell me that he could actually be a suspect."

"We don't know," Vic said. "You know how hard it can be to tell whether someone could actually kill someone else or not."

Erin, unfortunately, had learned this. It was one of the reasons she hadn't wanted to go back to the competition.

CHAPTER 37

*E*rin had already been in the ballroom for longer than she had wanted to. Each time she approached a competitor, Beryl and the explosion were the topic of conversation. All kinds of speculations were tossed around about who or what kind of person could have killed her. Erin really didn't want to hear any more guesses.

"Would you mind walking me upstairs now?" she asked Willie. "It's not a big deal. I could just go up on my own. But... I did tell Terry that I wouldn't walk around on my own."

"Of course," Willie agreed. "He asked me and I said I would walk you up."

Vic tagged along so that she wouldn't be on her own either.

"I'm sorry about this," Erin apologized. "Acting as security guard probably wasn't the way you planned on spending your weekend."

"I'm happy to do it," Willie assured her. "Other work can wait. I'd rather know the two of you are safe."

"There probably isn't any real danger. But..."

"One person is dead and two others ended up in the hospital. In my books, that's enough reason to be cautious."

"I suppose. I just feel a little silly about it."

Willie shook his head. "No worries."

He walked Erin to her door. Erin swiped the key card and let herself in. The lights were on, so she suspected Terry hadn't gone to sleep like he had said he would. She rolled her eyes and prepared herself to patiently coax him into doing what he needed to do for his health.

"He's not sleeping?" Willie asked.

"I don't think so."

"Do you want me to stick around?"

"No, we're good for the night."

Erin took a step into the hotel room, then heard Terry in the bathroom being sick. She stopped where she was.

It was possible that a migraine had made him sick to his stomach. Sometimes that happened, but it was rare for him. But she again heard Coleman telling her about Beryl throwing up before she had died. One of the symptoms of carbon dioxide poisoning.

She looked over her shoulder at Willie. He had also heard and hadn't turned around to leave. "Hang on…"

"Yeah."

K9 lay outside the bathroom, looking concerned. Erin tapped on the door. "Terry?" She opened it and peeked in.

"Sick," Terry muttered. "Be out in a few minutes."

"Terry, is it your head? Is it because of a migraine?"

He shook his head uncertainly. "Really wobbly on my feet. Room is spinning. And then my stomach…"

Erin looked at him, hunched over the toilet, her stomach in a tight, sick knot. She looked at Willie once more, and Vic behind him, straining to see past and find out what was going on.

"Do you have a headache too?"

"Some… not like usual."

Erin sniffed the air. But she knew that CO2 was odorless. There would be no way for her to sniff it out if there were a higher-than-normal concentration of CO2 in the room. All she could smell was vomit and sweat.

"I think we should take you to the hospital."

"No. I'll be fine."

"I'm worried, Terry. Beryl was poisoned with CO2. She was throwing up. If someone is trying to kill the judges or the contest, they could have poisoned the air in the room…"

"I wasn't feeling well before I came up here. That's why I came up," he reminded her.

That was true. Was it something else, then? Could someone have poisoned food or drink that was being served in the ballroom? If so, they could have dozens of sick people on their hands before long.

"I really think… we need to make sure this isn't another 'accident' related to the competition."

"I'll just go to bed once… I'm done."

Erin looked at Willie. "What do you think?"

"I think there have already been too many accidents in the course of this competition. He's probably fine." Willie pressed his lips together in a thin, straight line. "But I wouldn't want to bet anyone's life on it."

"Willie agrees," Erin told Terry. "Grab the garbage can and let's get you out of here in case there is carbon dioxide."

Terry rested his head on his arm, leaning on the edge of the toilet. "Erin… I'm not up to it."

"We'll help you. You can't stay here."

He was ready to argue, but Erin dug in her heels.

"I'm not letting you tell me no. So you can waste your time arguing, or you can come," she told him as firmly as she could. She hated arguments and really hoped that he wouldn't fight her on it. It would just make him sicker and weaker.

"Okay," Terry agreed. "Give me a minute to get my strength…"

Erin pulled her phone out and took a look at the time. "One minute. I don't know how long it takes someone to be poisoned by breathing too much CO2, so I'm not leaving it any longer than that."

"Mmm. A little less literal…?"

"No." Erin kept her eyes on the clock.

After another pause, Terry reached for the garbage can and tried to push himself to his feet. It took a couple of tries. He was much more unsteady than he had been down in the ballroom. There was a pain in Erin's chest and she tried to keep herself from panicking. It wouldn't help anyone for her to flip out. She pushed the door open the rest of the way and slid an arm around Terry, trying to stabilize him and help to support his weight.

Once she got him out of the bathroom, Willie inserted himself on the other side and helped to steady the garbage can Terry was carrying. "There you go. Let's go."

"I don't want to go to the hospital," Terry said. "Can we just… get another room?"

"No. I want to be close to the hospital in case you get any worse."

K9 followed. They let the hotel room door shut behind them. It was slow going to get Terry down to Willie's truck and to get him settled into a seat.

"Thanks. I'm going to be fine now," Terry assured them. "Really. I'm feeling better in the fresh air."

The rest of them piled into the truck. Erin sat next to Terry and tried not to stare at him. They only made it a couple of blocks before Terry started throwing up again. The pungent acid smell made Erin gag. It was a good thing she was sitting the closest to the garbage can, because she might end up needing it as well. She'd always been super sensitive to smells.

"Uh oh." Vic buzzed down her window and motioned for Willie to do the same. "We'll try to get you lots of fresh air."

Erin inched her face closer to the open window, gulping the chilly, sweet air as if she were drinking it.

"I'd be fine in another hotel room," Terry muttered.

And maybe he would have been. Or if they went home or booked a hotel in one of the nearby towns where nobody knew where they were to follow them and poison them again.

But she didn't know how much CO_2 he might have in his

system already, and if they had to do something special to clear it out, or if he just needed to replace it with clean air. She couldn't stop thinking about Beryl dying so quickly after throwing up. She hadn't had anyone to take care of her. But Terry did, and Erin was not going to let anything happen to him on her watch.

"Do you remember when you were poisoned and I had to rush you to the hospital?" Willie asked Erin. She suspected he was trying to distract her and get her thinking about something other than whether Terry was going to die from how much CO2 he'd inhaled already.

"I don't remember much about it," she said. "You went really fast. I was kind of confused as to what was going on."

"Yes, you were," he agreed.

"And you were singing, weren't you?" Erin shook her head. "Did I ever thank you for how quickly you got me to the hospital for treatment?"

"You did. I'm glad I managed to get you there in time."

"Me too," Terry agreed, still hanging his head in the garbage can, breathing shallowly. "But I don't think this is CO2 poisoning. Just… a bug, maybe. I could just sleep it off…"

"Then you can sleep it off at the hospital," Erin advised. "I just need to know that you'll have medical care if… something goes wrong."

"Just a bug," Terry repeated.

"If is it carbon dioxide, then how did it get in the room?" Vic asked. "How does that work? I know you could get it from a malfunctioning furnace."

"That's carbon monoxide," Terry said into the can.

"Chef Kirschoff says it happens with carbonation machines with bad tubes, or from dry ice," Erin told Vic.

"But there wasn't any carbonation machine or dry ice in the hotel room."

"No. But… someone could have leaked it there earlier in the day when we weren't around… maybe just opened up the valve on one of those canisters. That would work, wouldn't it?"

"Sure," Willie nodded. "I don't know how fast after that it would dissipate."

"I guess maybe we should have looked around for anything weird before we left the hotel room. I didn't think about finding a CO2 source, just getting him out of there."

"I'm sure that was the right thing to do," Willie assured her. "You have to worry about safety first, investigating later. If there is a CO2 canister in the room, it will be there when we get back."

"No, it won't. Whoever put it there will take it back out. If they could get in without being detected once, they can get in a second time when they realize they've failed."

"True."

"Maybe we should call that policeman," Vic suggested. "He could investigate before they have a chance to remove the evidence. Don't you think?"

"No…I really don't want to talk to him again. He's going to have questions…"

"That's his job. You wouldn't be a suspect, just a witness."

"That's what they told me the first time. But I sure felt like a suspect."

"What did he say about the threatening note?"

Erin breathed out in a hiss. "Oh, boy."

Terry raised his head slightly to look at her. His face shone with a layer of sweat. His hair was gathering into little peaks from the moisture. "Threatening note?"

Vic's eyes widened. She mouthed, "You didn't tell him?"

Erin just closed her eyes.

"What threatening note?" Terry demanded.

None of them said anything at first. Willie finally spoke up. "Erin received a threatening note before she went back to Bald Eagle Falls. Telling her to get out of the contest. Or else."

"Why didn't you tell me this?"

"I… meant to. It didn't come up. There was so much else going on, with Charley and Chef Kirschoff. And… everything."

"You should have told me. You don't hide something like that, Erin. If we're a partnership, a team, then…" he trailed off.

She didn't want him thinking that they weren't.

"It isn't that. It's just like I said. Too much going on. I didn't really… take it that seriously. And… I didn't want to worry you. You have enough to worry about these days."

"You still tell me. I want to know. It's a lot more stressful thinking that you're trying to do everything alone and not sharing with me."

"I suppose."

"You didn't take it seriously?"

"No… Yes and no… I was planning to go back to Bald Eagle Falls anyway, so it didn't really make any difference."

"And *did* you report it?"

"Yes. I went in and reported it. But I don't think they took it too seriously either."

"With one person already dead and two injured? They certainly should have."

"But it could have just been a hoax. Someone unrelated to Beryl's death. I don't know. I didn't want to take it seriously either. I just wanted… to get home to you."

They were quiet.

Terry wasn't able to continue the discussion. He was soon retching again, though there wasn't anything but stringy yellow acid left in his stomach. Erin looked away, trying to ignore it and keep her own stomach under control.

They reached the hospital without any mishaps. Erin helped get Terry checked in and his garbage can was swapped for a basin. He sat in the waiting area for a doctor to be freed up to deal with him. When a nurse finally called him to a curtained area to hear his story and give him a preliminary check, she noted he was dehydrated and started an IV.

"We'll take good care of you," she promised. "Probably just a stomach bug."

"That's what I said," Terry agreed.

And they were all happy to believe that, until the other cases started to roll in.

Erin had been kicked out of Terry's curtained cubicle while the doctor examined him. It was Vic who first saw Melanie come in, hunched over, carrying a bowl. Her lips were dry and cracked. She looked miserable. Vic looked at Erin and then hurried over to Melanie.

"Hey, Mel, are you okay?"

"Sick," Melanie groaned. "I don't know, maybe just the flu, but it feels too…"

"Do you think it could be something else?"

"Maybe." Melanie positioned herself in the line for the triage nurse. "Food poisoning, maybe?"

Vic patted her on the back and murmured some encouraging words, then returned to Erin's side. "I think you should place that call to the policeman."

It *was* weird that the two of them both got sick at about the same time. Erin tried to find an explanation. It could be something completely innocent. Someone carrying a virus had been in contact with both of them. Something that they had eaten in the ballroom. The flashing lights and pounding beat of the music. Different things could affect people.

But they had to be careful in case it was poisoning. Erin

couldn't just ignore that because of her own reluctance to talk to the police.

"Okay. I will." They weren't supposed to have phones turned on in the emergency room, so she went out the doors to sit in the patio area that everyone used for smoking, even though there were signs with big lettering warning people that it was against the by-laws to smoke there. Erin shivered. She found Coleman's contact information and tapped it.

She was hoping that Coleman wouldn't answer. He'd be busy with something else. But even if he were busy, she still needed to report her suspicions to someone official. Maybe, like with the written threat, they would brush it off.

CHAPTER 39

$\mathcal{B}$y the time Coleman was convinced that there was something for him to look into, there were three more people from the contest in the emergency room. And they just kept coming.

A policeman showed up, not Coleman himself, and confirmed that they were looking into it. They had shut down the event in the ballroom and taped off all of the food serving and preparation areas. The hotel was doing a room-to-room check and checking participants off a checklist to ensure that no one was non-responsive in their hotel room or unaccounted for.

"Must be food poisoning," Deputy Wake said with authority. "Shrimp or something that was being served at the event. Seafood and egg dishes can wreak havoc if they're not properly prepared and stored."

Erin nodded and scratched K9's ears. He was restless sitting with her when he was used to always being with Terry.

As a baker, she didn't have to worry as much about food poisoning, but she did have breakfast muffins with bacon in them and used eggs and milk in the kitchen. Surfaces had to be kept clean and everything washed thoroughly so that uncooked egg didn't come into contact with prepared food. But a catering business should have been knowledgeable about all of the necessary precautions and should have been able to prevent the spread of any pathogen.

"This is pretty crazy. I've had what might have been food poisoning before, but I've never seen anything like this."

"Probably negligence," Wake said with a vigorous nod. "I bet the catering company gets their butts sued. And probably the event coordinators too."

"It's not their fault."

"They're cooks, they should know well enough what precautions need to be followed."

Erin hadn't considered that. She could see his point, but Chef Kirschoff couldn't have been involved in every little detail. Surely no one expected that he would be inspecting kitchens and taking the holding temperature of the dishes the catering company had prepared. He would be relying on them to know what they were doing.

"How is Chef Kirschoff? I haven't seen him here." Erin looked around, in case he had shown up since she had been talking to Wake.

"Sounds like he's got it, but not badly enough to be hospitalized yet. They'll be keeping an eye on everyone to make sure they are okay."

Erin looked at the time on her phone. Terry was finally sleeping peacefully. She wanted to be by his side when he woke up again, but with the amount of time he'd spent throwing up, she figured that wouldn't be for a few more hours. In the meantime, she wanted to know what was going on with the competition and whether they were going to cancel it or not.

"Are you shutting down the contest?"

He barked out a laugh. "I don't have the authority to do that."

"I mean… the police department. Or the Town Council. Is anyone going to say that there have been enough problems with it, it needs to be closed down?"

"I don't think anyone but the organizers or sponsors can do that. It isn't really up to the PD or Town Council."

"The Town Council could withdraw their permits."

"You'd have to talk to someone there. I don't know. But I get the feeling that people are more interested in going ahead than in shutting it down. They've worked so hard to get this far, they're not going to let some psycho with an agenda get it shut down."

"Who would want to shut it down so badly?" Erin mused. "I mean, it's not like it's political, supporting some kind of controversial charity. It's just a fun contest. A chance at a prize."

"Maybe someone trying to eliminate their competitors. Make them too sick to enter anything."

"But the first victim was a judge, not an entrant. And Charley is a competitor, but Chef Kirschoff is an organizer. I can't figure out who would have a motive to harm all three. And then... everyone who's sick now."

"Maybe it's a smokescreen. Not everyone was being targeted. Some of them were to throw us off. Especially the food poisoning." Wake made a motion to include all the victims in the waiting room. "That could just be intended to throw us off the trail. Or only one person was actually being targeted, and the rest are collateral damage."

If that were true, then the mind behind all of the incidents was very disturbed—someone who didn't care who got in his way.

When Terry was released from the hospital, they all went back to the hotel. Willie dropped them off to gas up the truck. Terry was still looking tired and drawn, so Erin had him sit on one of the cushy lobby chairs with K9 and she and Vic went to the front desk to inquire about whether their rooms were available or whether the police had sealed them off for their investigation. Vic put down a couple of bags of groceries she had picked up while they had been waiting for Terry to be released.

"Everything is just as it was, Miss Price," the young woman at the desk assured Erin. "The police did ask to have a look at it, but they didn't find anything wrong. Of course, there were many more people who were affected by then, so we knew it wasn't was localized to your room."

"Right, of course," Erin agreed. She leaned forward, keeping her voice low. "Have they made any progress on figuring out what happened? Was the food contaminated? Was it food poisoning? Was it tampered with?"

The woman looked back and forth. "We're not supposed to say anything about it, I'm sorry."

"I think the hotel owes it to their guests to let them know what they have found out and what they are going to do to keep it from happening in the future. We still have other events scheduled. No one wants to get sick from going to them."

"I'm sure there will not be a repeat at any of the other events. We have identified the problems and they have been taken care of."

"What was it, then?"

"I don't know all of the details."

"I'm one of the judges and I'm a cook. I want to know if it is going to be safe for me to go forward. I want to know where the problem was."

The hotel worker hesitated. "I don't know…"

"Was food not prepared properly? Stored properly? Was something put into it?"

"It was the storage," she said finally. "There was something wrong with the thermostats or the temperature sensors. I don't know all of the details, but I guess it means that they were not kept cold enough."

Erin nodded. "Who had access to the fridges?"

"The police are investigating. I'm sure the cooks have given them all of the information they need to investigate it. We won't be using our own fridges for the remainder of the activities. We will be outsourcing, and there will be monitoring and extra security." The woman shook her head. "It's a nightmare, I'll tell you that. They're worried we're going to end up with a loss from this competition instead of a profit. When the hotel is hosting all of the guests! It should have been a great money-maker."

Erin nodded sympathetically. "Well, who knows, maybe it will still turn out all right."

$\mathcal{E}$rin beckoned to Terry. He got up and joined them. Erin watched as Vic picked up her groceries once again.

"Do you want some help with that?"

"Oh, I'm okay. You go ahead and get Terry settled."

"Terry will be fine." Erin looked at him, and he nodded. "This looks like a two-person job."

"I can manage."

They all walked to the elevator. "Where's your keycard?" Erin asked Vic. "You're going to have to put everything down to find it and get it out."

"Uh… in my wallet…" Vic bounced her handbag with her hip. "In there."

Erin hit the buttons for her floor and Vic's and unzipped Vic's little bag. She pulled out Vic's wallet and managed to find the room key. When the elevator stopped, she got out on Vic's floor and nodded to Terry. "I'll see you in a minute."

"Sure."

Erin followed Vic to her hotel room and slid the card key into the reader. The indicator light turned green, and she turned the handle and pushed it open for Vic. She followed Vic in.

"There you are. I'll just put the key—" Erin cut herself off.

Vic looked around the room in dismay. "What happened? Someone broke into my room!"

Everything was in disarray. Pillows and blankets strewn on the floor, clothes everywhere, the lamp knocked over, clock hanging off of the bedside table by its electrical cord.

"What were they looking for?" Erin breathed. She tried to imagine what someone might think Vic had. Valuables? Some evidence that was related to Beryl's death? Did they confuse Vic's room with Erin's and think that they were tossing her room?

There was a growling and yipping sound from the bathroom. They both turned toward it at once.

"Nilla!" Vic opened the door and saw that the bathroom was in a similar state, with a yellow puddle in the corner. She smacked her forehead. "Oh no!"

"You left him here by himself?" Erin asked.

"I thought he'd be okay for a couple of hours. And then... when everything happened with Terry, I didn't even think about him being locked up here by himself..."

"Well..." Erin started picking up the clothes strewn across the floor. "At least he found things to do to keep himself entertained!"

Back in their room, Erin brought up the competition once more time. They had discussed it at length at the hospital, but Erin could see just by looking at him that Terry was still feeling pretty rough.

"Are you sure you still want to go ahead with this? I feel bad that I'm causing all of this trouble and that you got sick because of my thing. You don't want to just go back to Bald Eagle Falls?"

"I already told you no. I'm not going back without you."

"And I could quit and go back with you."

"This is supposed to be good publicity for your bakery. It's going to be negative publicity if you back out now, right before the contest. You've worked hard to make this happen. I'm not going to back down because some psycho is trying to sabotage the thing." He gave her a hard stare. "Tennesseans are tough. You just try pushing us and see what happens. We just push back harder. People might have been willing to close down the contest after Batcombe's death. But after everything that's happened? Hell, no. We're not letting someone push us around."

Erin chuckled and shook her head. "That's crazy."

But she'd seen the same reaction from others. Fold in the face of danger? Run from the threat? No way. Each misfortune just seemed to make people more determined to keep the contest going. There was no way people were going to back out after the food poisoning incident. They would stand strong and show everyone the stuff they were made of.

"It may be crazy," Terry agreed. "I know I should be telling you to just stay out of it and be safe. How many times have I told you that? But this guy—whoever he is—has my blood up now. I want to see this thing through."

"Okay. So I guess as long as the contest goes ahead, so do we."

He nodded firmly. "That's right."

Terry was still short on sleep. He soon drifted off as Erin did some work on her computer.

Well, *some* work.

Some mindless entertainment, reading social media, and following rabbit trails. The internet offered unlimited possibilities for letting her mind wander.

Erin read through each of the social media posts that she came across about the contest. And of course, about the bad luck that had plagued it since Beryl was found dead in a commercial freezer.

But Beryl hadn't died there. The news stories didn't follow up on that detail. They made it sound like an accident. Erin read through the articles, comparing them to see who had the most recent details and who was just reposting what had happened days before.

One of the local sites had more details on Beryl than the rest. Not about her being dead before she was put in the freezer, but her biographical information. Most of the sites just copied what was written in the contest promotional bio, or some of the later stories used phrases from her obituary. But the Tattler did not.

Beryl Batcombe, author of the controversial book, *Recipes from Mawmaw's Kitchen, Traditional Tennessean Cookery...*

Erin frowned. She recalled that Chef Kirschoff had told her that Beryl's cookbook had not done as well as she had expected it to. But how could a cookbook be controversial? She couldn't think of what could be less controversial than a collection of recipes.

She tapped the name of the book into her search bar. The article that Erin had been reading did not pop up, but several older articles did. Written, Erin assumed, soon after it had been published. She clicked on the first one and scanned the page.

Beryl had been accused of stealing other people's recipes and then passing them off as her own (or her mawmaw's.) Always a difficult allegation to prove, since many different people could have similar recipes. Sometimes basic recipes that had been passed down for generations and may have originated from the back of a tub of Crisco. She knew from her own business research that lists of ingredients could not be copyrighted, only the narrative instructions.

But it would seem that Beryl hadn't bothered to put the directions in her own words, and more than one person had spoken up to say that she had stolen their family recipes and was pretending that they were from her fictional grandma.

Well, Erin supposed she did have a grandma—two of them, plus more in each previous generation—but it would appear that none of them had passed down her collection of recipes to her.

She got out her notepad and made a few notes. Had Beryl been planning to open her dream restaurant on the back of the contest? It seemed just like her to use the competition as the publicity and leverage she needed to get a leg up with her new restaurant.

She was ambitious.

Maybe that was why she had been in the freezer. Maybe she had been hoping to get the Buttermilk Biscuits restaurant shut down and to take over the location for herself, and had ended up getting stuck there.

But that wasn't what had happened, because she hadn't died in the restaurant.

Not in the freezer, anyway. Had the police figured out where she had been killed? Had she died inside the restaurant and her killer had dragged her into the freezer to get her out of sight? Or had she died in her car? Had it been parked in the restaurant parking lot?

Erin stared thoughtfully at her notes.

CHAPTER 41

Terry was still asleep when Erin decided to call Chef Kirschoff. She didn't want to wake Terry up but, after waiting for a while, she decided she couldn't wait. She would have to take the chance. If he were deeply asleep, her call wouldn't wake him, and if he were only in a light sleep cycle, he would probably want her to wake him up anyway.

She dialed Kirschoff's number. He might not be up yet either. The police officer she had talked to had said that he only ended up with a mild case of food poisoning, but it could have gotten worse over time. He might be trying to catch up on his sleep, just like Terry.

The phone rang a few times and then it was answered. "Hans here."

"Uh, Hans. Chef Kirschoff. It's Erin."

"Erin," his voice was warm. "How are you? Don't tell me that you got this beastly food poisoning, please!"

"No. I managed not to get it, but Terry got a pretty good case. One of the first ones. We spent the night at the hospital."

"Oh, how awful. Tell him how sorry I am. It seems like we can't catch a break for this contest. Every time we think we have put all of the bad luck behind us, something else comes up."

"It's not just bad luck."

"I know that… but you don't think that the food poisoning is related, do you? That wasn't intentional. Just an equipment malfunction."

"Have the police identified whether it was a malfunction or tampering?"

"Tampering? Who would tamper with the fridges? Why would anyone *want* to give people food poisoning?"

"Why would anyone want to kill Beryl? Or you or Charley?"

"No one tried to kill us," Kirschoff grumbled. "That was just… there's no proof that anyone tampered with the canister that blew up. That was just a coincidence. There's nothing to tie it to Beryl's death."

"Except that she was killed with carbon dioxide, and it was a carbon dioxide canister that exploded."

"That was just… coincidence. Everything is connected with carbon dioxide right now. That's the whole theme of the cook-off. Wherever you go, you're going to run into something to do with carbon dioxide."

Erin had to admit that was true.

The only incident that they knew for sure was not an accident was Beryl's death. And not knowing exactly how she had been poisoned, they couldn't prove that it was murder and not just some bizarre happenstance, like the people who had dumped dry ice into their swimming pool and ended up poisoning their party guests. Her death could have been accidental and the moving of her body… Erin couldn't think of an explanation for that.

"Anyway, that isn't exactly why I was calling you."

"Oh, I am sorry. I have distracted you."

"No, that's okay. I was actually wondering whether you know where I could get a copy of Beryl's cookbook."

"Her cookbook? I don't know if it is in any of the stores anymore. It didn't sell, so they've probably all been returned to the publisher."

"But somebody in town must have bought it. Did you? The

library or Chamber of Commerce? Or maybe she has family members that have a copy?"

She thought about the revelation that Kirschoff had a family. But it was not the right time to bring it up. He would not want to talk to her about that and she wouldn't get a lead on the cookbook.

"No, no family. I don't know if the library would have a copy. Maybe they pick up publications by local authors," Kirschoff said doubtfully.

"How about you? Do you have a copy? I only need to borrow it, I would give it back to you."

"I don't think I have a copy… certainly not here. It would be at home, if I do."

"Oh, okay. I'll check around town. Someone must have a copy or two."

"Yes, I would think someone would."

"So… you knew, Beryl, right?"

"Yes. We already talked about that. At your house."

"Right. I just wondered… I guess she must have contacted you and told you that she wanted to be one of the judges. You said that she was persistent. That she would get what she wanted."

"Yes…?"

"She reached out to you, then? It wasn't like with me and Vic where you just dropped in on us and asked us if we would be judges?"

He cleared his throat. "I don't know who started the conversation…"

That sounded like an evasion. He didn't know whether she had brought it up or whether he had? Did they talk to each other all the time? Or had it been a call out of the blue? Beryl looking for a way to advance.

"Anyway… it doesn't matter who started the conversation. I just wondered if she had told you why she wanted to be one of the judges. Did you guys talk about that?"

There was silence from Kirschoff. Maybe he thought she was

trying to trap him somehow. But if he were just interested in promoting the contest, and she had just wanted to be a judge, then what was there to hide?

Nothing, right?

"I mean, Vic and I agreed that it would be good publicity for Auntie Clem's. A good way for us to get the bakery out there in the public eyes. And because I like ice cream."

Kirschoff laughed. "It was the same for Beryl, I'm sure. She wanted the publicity. And she liked ice cream." He chuckled to himself.

"She wanted the publicity? Because of her book?"

"Well… maybe it would have helped her book sales…"

"Why did she want publicity then? Was she…"

She hoped that he would fill in the blanks. It was hard for her to guess what Beryl might have been thinking. Some people just liked to be in the limelight.

"Was she what?" Kirschoff prompted unhelpfully.

"I just thought maybe… she was trying to get publicity for the restaurant she wanted to open. Maybe she was doing a financing and figured if people saw her judging the contest… they would have more trust in her…?"

"Maybe."

She hadn't expected him to spill all of Beryl's plans, but it would be nice if he'd at least jump in with a few of the details.

"Was she going to open her restaurant?"

"I don't know… it was in the early stages. She needed a location, the financing, all of the beginning steps. She needed a plan."

"So was it just a dream? Or did she figure that with the contest, she could make it a reality?"

"I don't know, Erin. Maybe a bit of both."

Erin gave an exasperated sigh. "So you guys were just talking… and she said she would like to be a judge, and you said 'okay, sure,' and that was it? That seems… unlikely. How did she even know you were going to be running a contest? And why did you decide on Whitewater as the location, if not because of Beryl?"

"I really don't think you need to pry into it, Erin. It's just one of those things. We don't know what happened to Beryl. We'll probably never know. It will be one of those cold cases on TV."

"You know a lot more than you are saying."

"Beryl was an old friend."

"A lover."

There were a few seconds of dead silence. "Who told you that?" Kirschoff eventually asked.

"A lot of people talking about Beryl. More than one person must know that the two of you were in a relationship."

"You make it sound sordid. It was nothing like that. Just… two friends… enjoying each other's company."

"Even though you were married to someone else."

"I travel a lot. I am away from my family for long periods of time."

"So you do have a family. And you're carrying on with Beryl and with Charley and who else?"

"I told you, you don't understand. It wasn't like that."

Erin was silent in response this time. She waited. Chef Kirschoff didn't say anything for a long time.

He had been such a nice man. She had enjoyed cooking with him. He had been so warm and real, so comforting to work with. Someone who understood what it was like to adapt his food to different diets so that everyone could enjoy it.

It was like Vic with her LGBT friends from the cruise. They shared certain experiences with each other that Erin would never have. Erin had enjoyed experiences with Chef Kirschoff that were different from what she had with her other friends. A shared base of experiences that made her feel like she really knew him.

When, in fact, she had not even known that he was married.

"Erin. When I am home with my wife… I am with her. She has all of my attention. Everything that I can give. We are good friends and very close. But when I am traveling, it is different. She isn't there. I can talk to her on the phone, but I can't… reach out and touch her. And I am a person who needs… I need the physical presence."

"That's a cop-out for cheating."

"You can't judge someone else's relationship by your own standards. Every relationship is different. The relationship I have with my wife works… and it has enough room in it for me to… have other friends."

Erin snorted in disgust. "Okay. Whatever works for you. But you'd better make sure that Charley knows you have a family. Or I'll tell her. And she won't like it coming from me."

Kirschoff's long sigh carried down the phone line. "Fine. Yes, Erin. I will tell her. You leave it to me to do it my own way."

"I'm not waiting for long. So don't wait until the contest is over. Give her a chance to make an informed decision."

"When I leave here, she will be staying and I will be going away. Why does anything have to change? There is a natural breaking point."

"No. I'm not letting you play around until it's time to leave town, and then just disappear without explaining."

That wouldn't be fair to Charley. She deserved to know before she went any further in the relationship just exactly what the parameters were. Maybe she wouldn't care that he already had a commitment with someone else.

But Erin would have. So she felt it was her responsibility to let Charley know.

When she got off the phone, Terry rolled over and looked at her. Erin's face got warm.

"How long have you been awake?"

"Long enough." He smiled and didn't say anything about her being a good or bad sister. Or about investigating something that was none of her business. Maybe he knew it was pointless to try to rein her in. It had never worked before, so what was the point in trying?

"How are you feeling? You look a lot better."

"Yeah." He stretched. "I'm feeling pretty decent right now. I don't know whether it is the IV from the hospital or something else, but I actually feel human again."

He didn't say that he felt better than he had in months, but there was something about him. The way he was holding himself. The warm smile. The little hint of a dimple in one cheek. He seemed like the old Terry for once.

CHAPTER 42

The day that Erin had been waiting for and dreading had finally arrived. Lots of fanfare and flags. Crowds of people who had come to watch the competition and to hopefully get some tasty samples themselves.

The day dawned bright and clear. The first day was the contest for the carbonated drinks. The second day would be ice cream. And then things would go back to normal again. Or settle at a new normal. Maybe things would be better than they had been, with some new customers for Auntie Clem's Bakery. Maybe things had been permanently changed and Erin would lose Chef Kirschoff as a friend. She hated to think they would never see each other or cook together after the contest. But if he was the kind of guy who traveled all over the world with a girl in every port… was that really the sort of person she wanted to be associated with?

But the anticipation was finally over.

During the morning, they had watched both live and recorded video of contestants working in various commercial kitchens that the contest had rented. They were not allowed to know who had made what beverages, since the judging was a blind taste-test rather than contestants being judged on their skill or professional demeanor in the kitchen. The audience was told the background stories of a number of the contestants, but the judges were not privy to that information. Viewers might have their favorites, but the judges would not hear any of the inspiring or gut-wrenching back stories until after the judging was complete.

The judging was to take place in the high school auditorium. There were tiered benches along one wall, and the judge's table was on a stage that also functioned as a separate, smaller gym. Erin felt nervous having to sit in front of the crowd of people and cameras. It was even more nerve-racking than she had anticipated.

She looked for the people she knew. Vic was at the judging table with her. Terry stood near the front of the gym with K9 at his side. She could see Willie out in the hallway through one of the gym doors. He had Nilla with him, and Erin assumed that he wasn't allowed to enter as long as he had the dog with him. K9 was different, being a police dog.

Vic hadn't managed to find anyone else who would look after the dog during the judging, and she wasn't going to leave him alone in the hotel room again. Erin smiled, remembering the chaos the little whirlwind had wreaked in the small room.

Erin sat down at the long table with the other judges. Each beverage was brought to them in a tiny glass flute. They could drink it down, or taste it and spit, or some combination. In the first round, each judge would give each of the entries a numeric score out of ten. The scores would all be added together, and entries with the top twelve scores would go on to the second round, where they would have a series of "face offs" where each drink would be paired with another. The judges would vote on which of the two drinks would go on to the next round, and so on until they had a first, second, and third place.

That was the portion for which they had to have an odd number of judges so that they could not be deadlocked as to which of the pairs would move into the next round. Erin looked at the newest recruited judge with curiosity.

Lara Gross looked more polished than the rest of the judges. Erin felt like a country bumpkin next to her, though she wasn't even sure what it was that made Lara seem that much more distinguished. She wore a chef's jacket with black accents. Her hair was gathered in a neat bun, like it would be for working in a kitchen. She worked in a steakhouse in the city, and looked cool enough to juggle knives without breaking a sweat. Because she was brought into the judging panel late, her bio wasn't included in any of the contest promotional material. Erin would need to look her up online to find out anything else about her.

She pulled her attention away from the new judge as the first round of drinks were distributed for tasting. She had a job to do, and that didn't include investigating the other judges.

Erin was surprised to find that she could tell the drinks that had been fermented for carbonation from those that had been carbonated with a CO_2 canister, which she could tell from those carbonated with dry ice. There was something about the dry ice beverages. It wasn't a scent exactly, Erin knew that dry ice didn't leave taste or smell behind, but the drinks just had a different quality from those that had been carbonated with machines or fermentation.

She savored each drink carefully, letting it sit in her mouth and bubble for a moment before swishing it around and eventually spitting it into the bucket next to her. There were a couple that she swallowed. They were just so inviting that she had to test the 'finish' that she wouldn't get except by swallowing.

There were ninety-seven beverage entries. They seemed endless. It took a couple of hours to get through them all. Erin carefully scored each one, although she knew she wasn't taking the same care on the later entries as she had on the earlier ones. After having tasted so many different offerings, some of them just didn't make the cut, no matter how generous she tried to be. And it took more to impress her. That unevenness in scoring would be evened out in the head-to-head comparisons. Any inferior entries that had squeaked in because they were among the first the judges had tasted would soon be compared to the handful of late entries that had stood out over everything else.

When they scored their final cards, there was a round of applause and they were allowed to leave the judging table and mingle with the audience for a time.

If any of the contestants revealed which of the entries was theirs at that point in an effort to curry favor and get a judge to endorse their entry, they would get an automatic expulsion. Erin hoped that no one tried to talk to her about their entry. She would hate to have to rat someone out and have their entry canceled.

As soon as she left the judges' table on the raised stage, Terry was at her side, taking her arm. He and K9 guided her through the crowd. Despite all of the security measures that the contest had in place, neither she nor Terry had the confidence that Erin would be completely safe. A weapon could be missed by metal detectors and x-rays. Or someone could have already visited the room and planted a weapon to be used later. Or they might use an improvised weapon or their bare hands.

Erin felt better with Terry and K9 at her side. Their eyes all sharp and bodies held alert for any sign of trouble.

Nothing would happen during the contest. The organizers promised. But Erin was sure they would have promised that no one would be harmed right from the beginning, and yet Beryl still had been, and so had Charley and Kirschoff.

As Erin greeted the various people who came forward to smile and shake hands and introduce themselves, her mind wandered again to Chef Kirschoff.

He was the one who had dropped the CO_2 canister in the restaurant, resulting in the explosion. What if it hadn't been an accident or a canister that had been tampered with, but something intentional on Kirschoff's part? Neither of them had been seriously injured, but either of them could have been. Everyone kept saying that they had been so lucky.

So he couldn't have detonated it on purpose.

CHAPTER 43

When she could sneak away from the festivities, Erin went to the Whitewater Junction Public Library and looked for Beryl's book. She had already checked their online catalog to confirm that they had a copy, and it didn't look like it was out on loan. She wandered the aisles, reading the Dewey Decimal designations on the ends until she found the section the recipe books were in.

She had jotted down the call number for Beryl's book and hunted down the shelf for it. When she arrived at the right shelf, she ran her finger along the spine labels, looking for the BAT designating Beryl Batcombe's book.

It wasn't there.

Erin double-checked the call number and looked for it again. She tilted her head and read the titles and authors. Maybe it had been mislabeled. It should be there if it wasn't out on loan.

But it was missing from the shelf. Erin took a step back and let her eyes wander over the rest of the shelves. She loved cookbooks, and she recognized a number of the titles, though there were still many that were new to her. She resolved to go to the library in Bald Eagle Falls and be sure that she read every cookbook they had there. Then she could ask for the ones at Whitewater on an interlibrary loan. Who knew what recipe gems she might find.

Her eyes rested on a thin volume with the title *Recipes from Mawmaw's Kitchen.* Erin bent down and snatched it up. Beryl's book was there! It had just been mis-shelved. That happened all the time. People pulled a book off the shelf and put it back in the wrong place. Librarians were forever trying to identify books that were out of place and to put them back, but it was a losing battle; there was always another one just down the row.

Erin wandered over to the nearest soft chairs and sat down. She opened the book and started to browse through the recipes.

There wasn't much there that was interesting or unique. They were mostly recipes she had seen before. Some weird sixties and seventies stuff, but the really traditional stuff was pretty straight-forward. Basic recipes that could be found in any grandma's recipe collection.

There were some interesting recipes for home-brewed sarsaparilla, rubdown, meatloaf, sausage patties, fried green tomatoes, moon pies, even a stack cake, which was what she had entered into the Country Fair to win the Alaskan cruise. Hers, of course, had been gluten-free.

Erin took a few more minutes to look at the dessert recipes in the back. Desserts were her specialty, after all. There were a few that had interesting local twists. There were even a couple of ice cream recipes, which she stopped to look at in light of the contest. But traditionally, ice cream had been vanilla, so Mawmaw didn't have any inspiring ideas.

She looked up from the book and saw Charley walking toward her.

"Someone said they'd seen you coming in here," Charley said. "Are you hiding from your responsibilities? Aren't you supposed to be schmoozing?"

"I schmoozed. Now I'm taking a break before I have to get back to the judging."

"Yeah, 'cause the judging looks so hard. All of that sipping must get tiring." Charley grinned to show that she was joking.

Erin rolled her eyes. "You try sitting up there with hundreds of people watching you take a drink and write down scores a hundred times. It's actually pretty nerve-racking. What if there was something stuck in between my teeth?"

Charley made a show of examining Erin. "Nope. You look perfect, like usual."

"Like usual?" Erin couldn't help wondering what Charley was buttering her up for. Like a kid getting ready to ask a parent for money. "Usually, I'm a hot mess, hair coming out from under my cap, spills and fingerprints all over my apron, flour on the end of my nose…"

"Like I said, perfect. That's just how a baker should look. Would you buy treats from a baker who looked absolutely polished, without a hair out of place? You'd think they must be fake. A baker can't make all of those different things without spilling something."

"Nice save." Erin took one last look at Beryl Batcombe's book, then put it down on the little table next to her chair. "So, what's up, Charley?"

"I've just been talking to Hans," Charley said, the laughter leaving her eyes. She spoke carefully. Not exactly like she was upset, but as if she needed to make a plan to form every sound.

"Yeah? How's he doing?" Erin couldn't make herself feel the same level of warmth and concern for him as she'd previously had.

She straightened suddenly, remembering.

"Oh. So, uh… what were you talking about?"

"About Beryl," Charley confirmed.

Erin let out a sigh of relief. "So he told you?"

"Not like I didn't guess as much before," Charley said with a shrug. "I couldn't see any other reason he would have made her a judge. Or picked Whitewater as a location. But he wasn't with her anymore. Just doing a favor for an old flame."

Erin pursed her lips. Kirschoff had put a good spin on it. "I'm not sure she was an old flame. I think they were still involved."

"Doesn't matter. She's out of the way now. I don't need to worry that she's going to come back into his life."

No, that much was a certainty. "Did he... tell you anything else?" Erin was fishing for confirmation that Kirschoff had also told her about his wife and family back home. That no matter what they had shared, he would leave her behind and go home to his family when everything was done.

Charley sat down in the chair next to Erin. She readjusted its position so that she and Erin could see each other's faces and body language. Charley leaned forward in her seat, lowering her voice even more than she had out of respect for the library.

"Yeah, I guess he did. He didn't just give Beryl the position because they used to be together."

"Oh...?" The conversation was going in a different direction from what Erin had anticipated, but she rolled with it.

"He didn't come out and say it in so many words, but I think... she was blackmailing him."

CHAPTER 44

*E*rin's surprise must have shown in her face. Charley gave a little laugh and settled back.

"Yeah. Can you believe it? Everything I hear about this woman… everybody who talks about her has something different to hate about her. You know how they tell you not to speak ill of the dead? I don't think that applies to Beryl Batcombe. Lots of people around to talk about what a jerk she was, sticking her nose into things that weren't her business, saying rude or racist crap, and now this! Blackmail!"

"So she told him that if he didn't appoint her as one of the judges, then…?" Erin trailed off, waiting for Charley to pick up the narrative.

"I'm not sure exactly what she threatened him with. Like I said, he didn't tell me in so many words, but I guessed."

"She threatened to do something that he wouldn't like. Reveal something about him that he didn't want other people to know."

Charley nodded and waved her hand at this. "Lots of people have things that they'd rather not have spread around. Everybody's left fingerprints somehow. You can't hide things in today's world."

"You didn't ask him what it was?"

"No. I don't need to know what it was."

So Kirschoff had only done the job halfway. He had told Charley that he and Beryl had been together, but not that he was going home to his wife when the competition was over.

Erin chewed on her lip, looking at Charley's open, comfortable expression. Was Erin really going to break the spell and tell Charley Kirschoff's secret? Charley wouldn't be looking quite so comfortable and smug then.

"Charley..."

"You're going to tell me anyway, aren't you?" Charley scowled. "Why do you gotta rain on my parade?"

"I'm sorry. But I think you should know..."

"Look. We're not that serious. I know that when he leaves here, he probably never calls me again. He travels. He doesn't live anywhere near Tennessee. It's the first and probably the last time that he's stopped here. So what does it really matter?"

"I just think... he should be honest with you. He's only telling you half the story."

"And is it really important for me to know the rest?"

Erin nodded. "I would want to know."

"Yeah, you probably would. But you live a different kind of life than I do. We're not the same."

"Then maybe you won't care. Maybe you'll be happy to just take him as he is. But he really should have told you."

Charley growled. "You'd better not be telling me that he's dying."

"No!" Erin puffed out a breath of laughter. "No. I think the closest he's come to that is the explosion of the CO2 canister."

"Me too. And I don't plan to come any closer in the next few years."

"I thought you were the one who likes to live dangerously. Go ahead and try risky things. Live a full life. Live fast, die young..."

"No. I've never said that." Charley rolled her eyes.

Erin couldn't imagine being as wild and carefree as Charley and, maybe subconsciously, she was looking for a way to knock her down. She needed to just take Charley as she was.

"So tell me whatever it is about Hans," Charley said, clicking the button on her phone to see what time it was. "You have to be back in your seat in ten minutes, so we should be heading back."

Erin looked down at her purse as she got ready to return to her judge duties. "Well… it's just that he's married."

"What?"

Erin had been half-expecting Charley to say that she already knew that, and to object to Erin being so dramatic about it all. But Charley's voice was shocked.

"Chef Kirschoff. Hans. He has a wife and children."

Charley shook her head and swallowed. "A wife and children? Estranged?"

"No. He just likes company while he's on the road."

"So he's going back to them after this is over? All of this is just… a little fling while he's away from home?"

Erin nodded silently. She felt terrible to be the one to break it to Charley, especially since Charley seemed to be upset about it. She didn't just take it in stride.

"Yeah. I'm sorry."

Charley swore.

"That's probably what Beryl was holding over him," Erin said. "Make me a judge, or I'll tell your family about us."

"Yeah. Sheesh. He seemed like a nice guy, didn't he?" Charley looked earnestly into Erin's face. "Tell me you thought so too. Maybe you weren't interested in him romantically, but you liked him and thought he was a good guy. Right?"

Erin nodded. "Yeah. I really enjoyed working with him and I thought he was a nice guy. I never thought… that he had another side like this."

"Okay… well…" Charley stood up and took the first few steps toward the door. Erin followed quickly behind her. "Okay, so that's the news about Hans. We still have the rest of the competition to get through. It isn't like I didn't know we only had until the end of the contest together. I knew it would all be over soon and he would be pulling out again."

Erin nodded, knowing that it didn't make Charley feel any better. They made it to the library doors before Charley made the second connection. She turned and looked at Erin.

"You don't think he had anything to do with Beryl's death, do you? You don't think that he got tired of her making demands and threatening to expose him and decided to... get rid of the problem permanently?"

"No, I'm sure it couldn't have been him." Erin tried to recall the details of the night that Beryl had died. "He would have to have been in the conference room when Beryl was poisoned. He's the big name. People would have noticed if he had just walked out. Especially when they found out later that Beryl had died. Wouldn't they?"

"The police haven't released any details of how and when she was killed, though. And most people wouldn't know that... there were issues between the two of them."

Erin bit her lip. It was getting sore and swollen from her anxiety. "I don't think he left the conference room before the conference let out. So he couldn't have had anything to do with her death."

Charley raised her eyebrows. "You'd have to talk to the cops. Until they release what her time of death was... you don't know if he had time to meet with her and kill her after the conference let out. You don't know where he went after that, do you?"

"No." Erin felt like there was a lead weight in her stomach. It was a good thing she hadn't swallowed all ninety-seven different samples of soda. She might have brought them all back up. "I don't know where he went. But I'm sure he couldn't have had anything to do with it. He isn't that kind of person."

"Before this, I would have said he wasn't the kind of person to marry and have kids. I would have told you he was a permanent bachelor. Maybe a bit of a player, but not a cheater."

Erin sighed. Charley patted her on the arm.

"Don't think about it right now. You have a job to do."

CHAPTER 45

It was difficult to concentrate during the second stage of the competition. Erin tried to focus on the two drinks that were placed in front of her, ignoring the spectators, the war going on inside of her head, and everything else. Just two drinks. Taste them both, decide which she liked better, and wait for the next head-to-head.

After a few minutes, she fell into a rhythm. She was sure she was right. There was no way that Kirschoff had killed Beryl. There was no need for her to agonize over it. The drinks were pleasant. She could just focus on one sense, and put everything else out of her mind. It was a sort of dissociation, but it was the only way she could continue to judge the contest and not be derailed by Beryl's death and the latest revelations.

She focused on the taste of a pleasant, fermented root beer. It had made it past the first round of head-to-head tastings and was back in the second round. Erin sampled the drink it was up against, a surprisingly refreshing watermelon soda. Mixing memories of eating watermelon on a hot summer day with the Snapples they consumed in large quantities. She had a hard time deciding which drink should go on to the next round.

Lara muttered something next to her. Erin looked at her.

"What?"

"That root beer. Reminds me of something, but I can't put my finger on it."

Erin considered. She tried to identify each of the flavors. If she were trying to recreate it, what ingredients would she use? As a young child, Erin had shown off her excellent senses of smell and taste in identifying the teas that Clementine sold in her tea shop. She could tell most teas simply by scent, picking out the different herbs and spices or recognizing the full bouquet as one of the commercial blends.

"Judges?" Kirschoff prompted, voice booming over his lapel microphone. "Place your votes as to which of the drinks will be in the final round."

"Most root beers used to be made from sassafras root," Erin told Lara. "But there are health risks, so they switched to using artificial flavoring or other roots or barks."

Lara looked over at her. "What do you think of this one?"

"Doesn't taste like artificial flavoring to me. It's been brewed and fermented." She closed her eyes, taking another tiny sip and swishing it around her mouth. She smelled the glass. "It's a blend. There's birch in there. Ginger. Sarsaparilla. All blended together."

"So can you call it root beer if it has all of those things in it?"

Erin hadn't thought much about the names of the contest entries. Some of them had fanciful names, others were quite generic.

"Ginger and sarsaparilla are both roots. So if it is a fermented concoction of ginger and sarsaparilla, then by definition, it is a root beer."

Lara nodded. "Even if it doesn't contain the ingredients that commercial root beer is made with."

"Right."

Lara marked her choice on her ballot. Everyone else had passed in their ballots and were waiting for Erin's vote. She marked her choice and dropped it into the ballot box. There was applause. One of the scrutineers moved forward to open the ballot box and count the votes.

Erin was happy for a break while they waited for the votes to be counted and for the three drinks that had made it to the final round to be announced. She shut out the crowds, closing her eyes for a few moments of peace before the pressure of the final round. The audience was chattering excitedly.

"You from around here?"

Erin didn't want to be pulled out of her thoughts, but it was too late. Once she had processed the question, she couldn't return to floating behind her eyelids in a state of suspended animation. She opened her eyes.

It was Lara, of course, sitting beside her and making small talk while they waited for the next round. Their mikes were shut off, so they were able to talk to each other without it being broadcast to all of the spectators.

"Well… yes and no," Erin admitted.

"How can it be yes and no?"

"I have kin on the mountain…" That was enough for most of those in the area to accept that she was 'one of them' even though she hadn't spent her whole life there. She went on, giving Lara a little more detail. "I lived here as a young child, spent some of my time in Bald Eagle Falls. But after my parents died, I migrated north. Eventually ended up in Maine before coming back here. It's been a long journey."

"Ah, that makes sense," Lara acknowledged. "Someone said that you were native Tennessean, but you don't have the accent and I don't remember hearing about your family before."

"Yeah. There were Prices here, but it's been a long time since there were very many of them. End of the line."

"You could always have a passel of kids and bring the name back," Lara laughed.

"I don't think that's going to happen," Erin said with a tolerant smile. She didn't even know if she were going to have kids. "And even if I did, they'd have their father's name, not Price."

"Of course. I didn't mean it seriously."

"I don't think we've met before," Erin said. She put her hand out to shake. "You were a last-minute addition, and I don't remember hearing your name before either."

"Gross? There are still some around. But I'm more of a transplant too, like you. My grandparents came from the area, but my dad grew up in South Carolina, and my mom was French. I didn't settle here until a couple of years ago."

"Where did you grow up?"

Lara's eyes were on the crowd rather than on Erin. "Can't believe the amount of publicity this little contest has gotten."

"A quarter of a million bucks. That's not chicken feed around here."

"No. Lots of poor folks that would make a real difference to."

"So where did they find you? Are you associated with someone in the contest?"

"I used to work for one of the sponsors. Someone gave the organizers my name with a bunch of others. I don't know how they made the decision, but they decided to invite me to be a judge. I figured I have the time and wouldn't mind the honorarium, so I said yes."

Erin chuckled. "Well, I hope you're enjoying it."

"I am, actually. Which three do you think make it to the final judging?"

"The last one was a toss-up. I don't know which way it will go. The others... the vanilla cola was nice. Really smooth, lots of depth." Vanilla always made Erin feel warm and cozy. It would be a good scent for a candle to light close to bedtime. "And... let's see... the cherry."

Lara nodded. "Could be. And out of those three, which would you choose as the winner."

"Really hard to decide. They're all delicious, with just the right amount of fizz."

"If you could have a case of one of them in your basement, which would it be?"

Erin thought of the finalists she had suggested. "To be honest, I think… the sarsaparilla."

"Ah. The root beer."

Something jiggled in the back of Erin's mind. Something about sarsaparilla. She closed her eyes, trying to picture it. Another of the drinks? Something someone had said to her? Something she had read?

She pictured Beryl's book in her hand. There had been a sarsaparilla recipe in the book. That must have been what made Erin feel like she'd already been talking about sarsaparilla. She had flipped past it pretty quickly. What had the ingredients been?

Erin touched Lara on the arm like she needed to stop Lara from talking, even though she hadn't been saying anything. She waved for the attention of one of the organizers, standing nearby, waiting for the results. The tall man stepped closer and bent over.

"Miss Price? What can I help you with?"

"We need a recess. Can we break for a few minutes? Just make it an extra-long commercial break?"

"We're just about ready to announce the finalists." He looked at Erin, waiting for her to say that she didn't need a break. She could hold on until the winner was announced. But Erin couldn't go on, she needed to talk to someone.

"I just need five minutes."

He looked at his watch. "This has all been carefully timed. We really can't step off of the schedule."

Erin looked at the spectators. She couldn't see anyone familiar.

Vic was sitting on the other side of Lara. She reached behind Lara to touch Erin on the shoulder. "What is it, Erin? What's wrong?"

"I need to talk to someone."

"Who?"

Erin looked at the wings of the raised stage and spotted Terry. He was looking concerned, standing just at the edge of the stairs, leaning forward, K9 at his side.

"Erin?" Vic prompted.

Erin motioned for Terry to come to her. He was up the stairs and past the hired security in an instant. He stood at her shoulder, looking around tensely for any threat.

"What's up, Erin?"

"We need a break. I need to talk to…" Erin tried to think of the best solution. "Umm, Chef Kirschoff and Deputy Coleman. I guess that would be the best…"

The tall man was shaking his head. "That's not possible. We are ready to proceed with the final judging. We can't put that off. You can talk to whoever you need to after."

"It needs to be before."

CHAPTER 46

There was a buzz of activity. The spectators clearly wanted to know what was going on, but Erin was careful to keep her voice down. Her mike was turned off so that her words wouldn't be broadcast over the whole crowd. Erin wouldn't back down. The staff were forced to bring Chef Kirschoff over. Terry was standing behind Erin on his phone, and she could hear him over everything else, calling for Deputy Coleman to join them on the stage.

Chef Kirschoff wasn't nearly as jolly as usual. His face was red, and he hovered over Erin, trying to talk her into just proceeding as planned. Erin covered her mike even though she knew it was turned off.

"I know the recipe for the sarsaparilla."

Kirschoff rolled his eyes. "We don't require that entries are unique recipes created by the entrant. There are probably a number of them that were made from exactly the same recipe."

"But this is one from Beryl's book."

He looked at her, brows pulled down. "I guess you found a copy. But it doesn't matter where it's from."

Erin looked around. Deputy Coleman was mounting the stairs and joined the scrum around Erin.

"Beryl published a cookbook," Erin said quickly, trying to get everyone up to speed. "It was supposed to be her family recipes. But after it was published, there were allegations that she had stolen recipes from other people. They weren't her family recipes. She had taken other people's recipes and not even bothered to reword the directions. Straight up plagiarism."

"We already know about that," Coleman said. "After the accusations, her sales fell off completely, they were pulled from stores, and she couldn't sell the books as firewood. No one would buy them. No stores would sell them. Eventually, none of the people who claimed she had stolen their recipes bothered to prosecute. If the books were no longer being sold, that was enough. And a sight cheaper than trying to sue her."

Erin wasn't really concerned with why there had been no consequences to Beryl. She looked at Lara and then around the others gathered close.

"The root beer. I don't know whether it is going to the final round or not. But if Beryl was up here judging, she would have known that was a recipe from her book."

"Why does that matter?" Coleman demanded.

"Because Beryl wouldn't have wanted it to make it to the final round. She would have blocked it before it could make it there and get any publicity."

"One judge couldn't keep an entry from advancing."

"If she gave it low scores in all categories, she could. There's no way it could make a high score overall if she didn't grade it fairly. Or she could say that there was something that should disqualify it. We're allowed to talk among ourselves and decide if an entry violates the rules."

"Like what?" Kirschoff asked. "She could not have disqualified it."

"Lara and I were just discussing whether it qualified as a root beer when it used sarsaparilla for flavoring. Because traditionally, root beer and sarsaparilla are two different things. If it uses sarsaparilla root, it is sarsaparilla, not root beer."

"Are you saying you want it disqualified?" Kirschoff ran his fingers through his hair worriedly.

"No. We would have said so. It also uses ginger root, not just sarsaparilla, so it can technically be called root beer. But if Beryl had been here, and it got through the first round, she could have had it disqualified for misrepresentation."

"And she would do that so that someone else would not win with her recipe?" Terry asked. He shook his head, a very slight side to side gesture. "Why wouldn't she want it to win? Wouldn't that be good publicity for her?"

"It would bring up the whole plagiarism issue all over again. Whoever entered it would make it known that she had stolen it from them, and all of that stuff would be out in the public again. This time with a much bigger audience." Erin nodded toward the crowds in the audience waiting for them to finish their discussion, and to the TV cameras that were broadcasting to the even larger virtual audience.

"So, you think that whoever entered this sarsaparilla is Beryl Batcombe's killer," Coleman said slowly.

"Yes."

"Thinking you've got the killer is all well and good... but there's no proof. It's completely circumstantial. Having a motive doesn't mean that the contestant was the one who killed her. Lots of other people had motives too."

"And then there's Chef Kirschoff."

Kirschoff's eyes widened. He held his hands up in protest. "I didn't have anything to do with killing anyone."

"No!" Erin nearly laughed. "I didn't mean that. I mean, you were the next one who was targeted. Because you had picked Beryl as a judge. The contestant thought that you were being unfair. That you were showing favoritism toward Beryl just because... the two of you were close."

He shifted uncomfortably. "I can pick whoever I want as judges."

"Yes. But you picked someone who has a reputation for being

a cheat, plagiarizing other people's hard work. Someone with a background like Beryl's should never have been picked as a judge."

He was uncomfortable, making a face and looking down at the table as if he were fascinated with something there.

"Why did you pick her?" Coleman asked.

No one answered at first. Erin tried to catch Chef Kirschoff's eye and raised her eyebrows questioningly. Did he want her to tell Coleman, or was he going to step up and admit the truth? Hans sighed, shaking his head.

"I picked her because she was blackmailing me."

There were no gasps of shock. Terry and Coleman were cops, used to people doing underhanded and illegal things. And Lara hadn't been around for long enough to be shocked by anything. Maybe she had already sensed some of the undertones and knew that there had been something strange going on with Kirschoff and Beryl.

"The fact that Beryl was getting publicity for an opportunity that never should have been given to her and that Chef Kirschoff was unfair in his selections and put her in that position give motives for both Beryl's murder and the explosion when Chef Kirschoff was handling the CO2 canisters," Erin reiterated. "And as soon as Beryl tasted that sarsaparilla, she would have known it was the recipe she had stolen, and she would have known who had entered it. Maybe she wouldn't have eliminated it, but the contestant couldn't count on that."

"It all fits together neatly," Coleman admitted. "And the food poisoning on opening night? Who was your contestant trying to get even with—or rid of—with that little caper?"

"I don't know," Erin admitted. "Maybe it *was* just an equipment malfunction and we jumped to conclusions. Or maybe it was to distract us from the killer, to make us think that they just wanted to get the contest shut down, not that Beryl and Chef Kirschoff had been targeted."

"But it's still all circumstantial. We need actual evidence. Chef

Kirschoff, can you check the entries and let me know who submitted the drink in question?"

"They're supposed to be blind. I can't reveal it now, before the final judging."

"But if it wins…" Erin protested. "It can't win if the contestant killed Beryl to keep it in the running. And if it doesn't win, then what's to stop him from killing again in order to disqualify the winner?"

"I need the name," Coleman said firmly. "This isn't about the contest, this is about solving a possible murder."

Kirschoff scowled, thinking about it. "You can wait a few more minutes. It won't make any difference to whether or not he is convicted."

"Are you obstructing an investigation?"

"If you wait, you may get the evidence you need… the contestant's reaction to the results of the judging may give you what you need to arrest him."

Coleman shook his head. "Get me the information now. Then I can have eyes on him. I won't reveal it to the judges, so that it won't affect the contest results."

How was Erin supposed to ignore the fact the contestant who had entered the sarsaparilla might be a killer and judge the drink on its merits?

Eventually, Kirschoff and Coleman went off to look at the entry details. Terry stayed with Erin, though she started to feel a little self-conscious with him standing protectively over her.

None of the other judges had bodyguards.

"It will be over soon," he promised.

"Yeah." Erin breathed out slowly. "And then I can really enjoy the ice cream tomorrow and not worry that someone will try to poison me. Or that something else dreadful will happen. I know lots of people here, and I don't want anything bad to happen to any of them."

"Of course not. Think about the ice cream tomorrow. And about going home to Orange Blossom and Marshmallow."

Erin looked down at K9, nodding and trying to keep from tearing up. Soon everything would be back to normal.

CHAPTER 47

Finally, everything was settled and they were ready to move on. Terry moved to the wings again, K9 at his side, both of them ready to run to her aid if needed. Erin waited, stomach tense, for the big reveal as to which drinks were the final three.

Kirschoff rambled about the sponsors, how great the contest had been, and the talent represented, before finally getting to the entries.

"The finalists for the beverages competition are…"

Erin held her breath. A strawberry cream soda that she had really liked. A carbonated mint tea that was remarkably refreshing.

And the sarsaparilla root beer.

Erin tried to keep her expression pleasant and not show any reaction to the news. She looked around at the audience, looking for someone who was too happy about the advancement. Someone with a much deeper reaction than seemed normal. But everyone was clapping and whooping, encouraging the three finalists on. Some disappointed faces, but Erin wasn't worried about them. If the sarsaparilla maker was the killer, he was going to be happy at this news. The anger would come later when it didn't make it to first place and win a huge windfall. Or maybe it wasn't even the money, but just the fact that they hadn't recognized the brilliance of the recipe.

Three glasses were placed in front of Erin this time instead of just two. She looked at them, preparing herself.

Should she go with her conscience, picking the one she felt was the best even if it might trigger a reaction from the killer? Should she intentionally advance or block the sarsaparilla?

"I've never faced a decision like this," she murmured to Lara. "What do we do?"

"Taste them," Lara said simply. "And then you will know."

Erin looked sideways at her. Lara was an unknown entity. Picked at the last minute. Chef Kirschoff was the only one who knew her background. And so far, his track record was not great. What if *Lara* were the culprit? She could easily have entered the sarsaparilla under a different name. No one was checking people's ID against the entries. Her challenge to Erin to just try the drinks felt wrong. How would Erin know when she tasted them? She was still going to be in exactly the same dilemma.

Unless the sarsaparilla was poisoned.

She'd already drunk it twice, so she didn't think that was possible. Lara hadn't moved from her seat or tampered with Erin's glasses. An accomplice? A volunteer working the contest?

It didn't make any sense. But she was suddenly paranoid. The killer was still out there, watching her and the other judges. Maybe planning to take Kirschoff out. Or to harm one of the rest of them. There was no reason for anyone to target Erin, except that she was a friend of Kirschoff's. Maybe the killer didn't care about collateral damage.

Lara picked up the first of her glasses and tasted the entry. She set the glass down again, and nodded at Erin.

Go ahead.

Erin cleared her throat and looked at the drinks. She picked up the strawberry cream soda. She admired it in the glass for a moment, the delicate pink color and tiny bubbles. She had already tasted it twice and knew that she liked it. She took a tiny sip. Hardly enough to wet her lips.

She put the glass down. She looked over the crowd. Nothing looked wrong. Everybody was doing exactly what she would have expected them to. Smiling, waiting with interest for the final results. A few tears from people who had probably just been ousted in the last round. There were a few familiar faces. Charley. Terry. Bella. Vic's friends.

Erin picked up the next glass. She and Lara both took a sip of the carbonated mint tea at the same time. Erin forced a smile and nodded. It was not a beverage she would have tried outside of the contest, but it came together very nicely.

Lara picked up her root beer. She tipped it in Erin's direction, toasting her. Then she took a mouthful and let it sit in her mouth before swallowing.

Erin licked her dry lips and looked at the root beer. She'd already had it twice. She knew it was fine. She liked it, and it hadn't caused her any ill effects. It was just someone's old family recipe, left over from the days when there weren't commercial sodas around and it was brewed as a health tonic.

She lifted the glass to her lips, mimed taking a drink, and put it back down.

Erin picked up her scorecard. She had only to assign a one, two, and three in the order of her preference. She set it in front of her and picked up her pencil.

She saw a sharp movement out the corner of her eye and turned her head quickly. It was just Vic's friend, Clayton. Erin was jumping at everything.

Clayton called something out to her. Erin couldn't hear him over the chatter of the crowd. She leaned forward, shaking her head and frowning. Clayton shouted again, repeating himself a few times before Erin could see his lips and hear enough of his voice over the crowd to understand what he was saying.

"You didn't drink it!"

Erin looked down the table toward Vic to see if she had heard.

Vic looked back at her, eyebrows raised. Her facial expression clearly asking whether Clayton was right.

Erin's face warmed. She wanted to hide it, knowing she was turning bright red. She looked down at her score sheet, ignoring both of them. She had tasted all three entries twice before. She knew exactly what each of them tasted like. She would rate the strawberry cream soda first, then the mint tea, and last the root beer. She liked it, but it really was sarsaparilla, and there was no special twist to make it the entrant's own. It was nice, but it didn't take a risk like the mint tea. And the strawberry cream soda was just so perfect in every way, making her think of warm summer afternoons spent picking wild berries as a child.

And if the person who had entered the root beer in the contest really was Beryl's killer, then there was no way Erin was going to play right into his hands.

$\mathcal{E}$rin put her ballot in the box. Lara also put hers in through the slot. She looked at Erin. "Are you okay?"

"Yeah. Fine."

"You're just looking a little… I don't know. Anxious. Frazzled."

"It's been a long day. That's all."

"And a bit stressful," Lara contributed with a smile.

"Yes. But that's it for today. Then we can relax until the ice cream tomorrow."

Lara nodded cheerfully.

But Erin knew there was still more drama coming before she could relax. They weren't just going to announce the winner and all retire to their hotel rooms.

Each of the judges had put their ballots in the box. The scrutineer went through each of them, entering the scores on a clipboard and making a show of tallying them up and then of double-checking his results. There were shouts from the crowd, pushing him to announce the results. Finally, the scrutineer handed the clipboard to Chef Kirschoff.

He cleared his throat, made a little speech about the importance of the results, and thanked the various sponsors by name, making everyone groan with impatience.

"And the runner up is… entry sixty-eight, Summer Strawberry Cream Soda!"

Bella squealed and made her way up to the stage. She was presented with her runner-up ribbon, pictures were taken, and then the spotlight turned back to Chef Kirschoff. Erin couldn't help grinning like a proud parent. Her Bella had made it to runner-up! And the cream soda had been really good.

But everyone was waiting for the news of the grand prize winner. They clapped politely for Bella, but were waiting for the real news.

"And the winner of the beverage portion of the Great Tennessee CO2 Cool-off contest and winner of $250,000 is…"

Everyone held their breaths.

"Entry thirty-four, Mint Tea Fizz!"

A cheer went up. Erin didn't know the man who walked up to the stage to receive his recognition. His name was announced as Eugene Bath. More posing, handshakes, and pictures.

"And that means that third prize goes to entry fifty-seven, Traditionally Brewed Meemaw's Root Beer," Kirschoff announced genially, looking out at the crowd.

Erin watched as Clayton pushed his way toward the stage. For a moment, she thought that he was approaching to talk to Vic, believing that everything was over and he would be allowed up onto the stage. Her hand made an involuntary movement to shoo him off.

Vic rose partway out of her seat, face pale. Chef Kirschoff studied Clayton, maybe wondering where he had seen the young man before.

But pretty much everyone's eyes were still on Eugene. He was smiling and bowing and posing for pictures as people held their phones out at arm's length to try to avoid getting all of the other phones in the picture.

Clayton broke into a run and vaulted up onto the stage, avoiding the guarded stairs completely, and with a yell of rage, charged directly at Kirschoff, bowling him over. They both fell to the ground in a tangle of arms and legs, Kirschoff letting out a yelp of surprise.

Erin was on her feet, not sure when she had actually stood up. Everyone was pressing forward, trying to see what was going on. Erin tried to see everything that was happening in slow motion rather than the quick and violent blows exchanged between the two.

Was there a weapon? A knife or a gun? She couldn't spot anything. No blood blossomed from Chef Kirschoff's snow white chef's apron.

Clayton was screaming and yelling something incomprehensible, Kirschoff's words sharp and cutting like a knife, guttural German she couldn't understand.

She was holding her breath as the policemen and hired security men rushed in to separate the fighters. She leaned over the table watching, her whole body tense.

They hauled Clayton back and he yelled in protest.

"You both deserve to die!" Clayton bellowed, spittle flying everywhere as he tried to pull himself free of half of the Whitewater Junction police force. "You're like two snakes breeding in the grass! You're both as bad as each other, pretending to be honest, upright citizens when you're really rotten to the core! Stealing people's property, manipulating the results of this contest, thinking you can just ride into town and take over everything and shape this town to do your will!"

"Clayton!" Vic said faintly from her place at the judge's table.

He couldn't have heard her over his own shouts, but he turned and looked at her. "*You* were supposed to be one of us! How could you turn your back on us and consort with the likes of him? Both of you! Pretending that you care about other people, and then letting Kirschoff and Beryl Batcombe walk all over us, grinding us into the mud! Just because he has money. And we don't, we're just no-account hillbillies. He thinks we're not even human!"

Vic shook her head in protest, as white as a sheet.

"I couldn't believe that you accepted the judgeship from him.

You should have known how corrupt he is! How could you look at someone like him and not know that he was corrupt all the way through?"

Vic didn't say anything. The police continued to wrestle Clayton around to secure him in handcuffs, search him, and eventually get him back to his feet. He continued to spout more accusations and bile in the direction of Kirschoff and the judges as they hauled him away.

When they got him out into the corridor, Erin heard yapping and growling and a howl of protest from Clayton, and caught a glimpse of Willie working to detach Nilla from Clayton's leg.

Then he was gone. Things seemed suddenly too quiet, a black void of silence in the landscape.

Others who were closer to Kirschoff helped him to get to his feet and brush himself off. He made a few weak, laughing comments into the mike that no one understood. He turned the mike over to one of the other organizers. In a clear, concise voice, she apologized for the disruption and gave everyone directions to the next event, where they could taste samples of some of the entries and fill their stomachs with hot dogs.

erry waited until people were on their way, then climbed the stage stairs to smile at Erin, pat her on the back, and nudge her to her feet.

"What do you want to do? I assume you probably don't want…" he gestured to the crowds headed to a hot dog orgy. "All of that."

"No. I don't think I can look at food right now."

She knew that there was going to be an eating contest. One of those competitions where the entrants tried to gobble as many hot dogs as they could in the space of three minutes. She didn't feel like eating, and she certainly didn't feel like watching anyone else gorge like that.

Terry nodded. "Why don't we go somewhere quiet, then. You don't want to eat?"

"No. If you want, we can go somewhere. I just don't think…"

"It's fine. I don't need to be social right now."

"They have a nice library here."

"You want to go to the library? Not to the hotel room?"

"Yeah. Unless… if you've got a headache and want to go back and lie down."

"No. The library is fine with me."

They walked for a few minutes in silence. Erin's arms were wrapped around her body, as if she were cold or trying to hold herself together. She wasn't sure which. Just that she didn't want to let go.

"Do you think they'll have enough to charge him? Like Coleman said, it's all circumstantial."

"They've got him dead to rights on assault. That will hold him while they gather more evidence. They'll get his fingerprints, search warrants issued... we don't know what they'll find until they look."

"I always thought... you know, you watch TV crime shows and murder mystery movies... and you think that once you've identified the killer, that's enough. Everything is neatly tied up in a bow and you can put him away for the rest of his life. But that's... I'm finding out that's not really true."

Terry held the library door open for Erin. She went in and wandered toward the recipe books.

"I can't believe that it was one of Vic's friends. They were always so... friendly and welcoming. They seemed open. But..."

"Just like anyone else... people wear masks. A public face that keeps other people from knowing who they really are and protects them from judgment."

Erin nodded. "I guess. You do things to protect yourself, and forget that other people do too. You think that you're seeing the other person as they really are when, in reality, we're all wearing masks."

Terry looked at the shelves that Erin was standing in front of. "Hmm. I wonder what you're in the mood to read today."

Erin grinned at him and grabbed a handful of books on traditional Tennessean cooking.

Vic poked her head through Erin's back door. "Yoo-hoo. Everyone decent?"

"Come on in," Erin invited.

Vic let herself in. Orange Blossom got up from the warm little nest he was curled up in on the couch and marched over to see her, stopping once on the way to stretch out his front and back legs and to arch his back.

"Morning, Blossom! Are you glad to have your mommy home?" Vic crooned, picking him up. He sniffed at her suspiciously, probably smelling Nilla on her. So far, no one had come forward to claim the dog, and Erin suspected he'd already found his long-term home.

"At least he didn't give me the cold shoulder like last time."

"Well, last time you were away for weeks, not just a few days. And maybe he's realized that you still come back even when you've been away for a long time. That has to be stressful to an animal. You can't explain your plans to them."

"Yeah. I'm glad Adele could look after him. I know that witches aren't actually anything mystical, but… she does seem to have a certain understanding with animals that I can't explain."

"She's gentle," Vic said. "She doesn't move suddenly or make loud noises."

"Yeah. Maybe that's it."

Vic cuddled Orange Blossom against her face. "Terry's working?"

"Yes." Erin smiled. "He's been feeling pretty good. I hope it lasts."

"Oh, me too. It's been long enough. He deserves to be able to get back and feel good about himself again."

"Yeah."

"Have you heard anything from Detective Coleman? About Clayton?" Vic grimaced. "It's so weird wanting to catch a killer, but not wanting my friend to be punished."

"It's a strange position to be put in," Erin agreed, thinking of how she had felt about Roger Cox's arrest. "I guess Clayton was pretty eager to talk about Beryl and Kirschoff and everything they had done to hurt him and his family, at least to begin with. I was right, that recipe in Beryl's book was from him. Passed down from his grandma. That's the name that he wrote on the entry form, so when Kirschoff and Coleman looked at it, they didn't know whose it was."

"Isn't it weird that he would end up on a cruise where Kirschoff was the chef? What a bizarre coincidence."

"I don't think it was a coincidence." Erin shook her head. "I think that's why he was on that cruise to start with. He knew about Kirschoff and Beryl. Wanted to get a look at him. Maybe he even intended to attack Kirschoff while he was on the cruise."

"But with everything else going on he got spooked?" Vic filled in. "Huh. I wonder. It just seems so strange to think of him that way… I just thought he was a fun guy to hang out with. Kind of… carefree. Someone who knew how to have a good time."

Erin remembered what Terry had said about people wearing masks. Everyone trying not to let their own mask slip…

The doorbell rang.

"I wonder if that's Adele," Erin guessed, looking at the kitchen clock. It was a little late in the morning for Adele.

But it wasn't Adele.

Mary Lou stood on Erin's doorstep, looking uncomfortable.

Erin was surprised but tried to act as if she weren't. If Mary Lou were ready to make up, Erin was happy to do her part. She hated the rift that had developed between them.

Mary Lou looked past Erin to see who else was there. "Erin. Victoria."

"Hi, Mary Lou." Erin opened the door farther and motioned her in. "Would you like to come in?"

"No."

They stood looking at one another.

Mary Lou held out a folded newspaper. Thin, like all of the

editions of the Bald Eagle Falls weekly. Erin had seen more substantial school papers.

"I wanted to see Joshua's article," Mary Lou said. "You know he wrote an article for the paper?"

"Yes!" Erin thought about how Joshua had approached her against his mother's wishes. She knew that Mary Lou would not be happy about it. "I haven't had a chance to look at it yet. Is it good?"

Mary Lou unfolded the paper and opened it up to the appropriate page. She passed it to Erin.

There was an upside-down-L-shaped hole where an article had been cut out of the newspaper. In its place was a sticky note with something scribbled on it. Erin brought it closer to her face. The handwriting was jagged and difficult to decipher.

If you want to know where your son is, maybe you should ask Erin Price.

Did you enjoy this book? Reviews and recommendations are vital to making a book successful.

Please leave a review at your favorite book store or review site and share it with your friends.

Don't miss the following bonus material:
Sign up for mailing list to get a free ebook
Read a sneak preview chapter
Other books by P.D. Workman
Learn more about the author

Sign up for my mailing list at pdworkman.com and get Gluten-Free Murder for free!

PREVIEW OF CHANGING
FORTUNE COOKIES

CHAPTER 1

$\mathcal{E}$rin invited Mary Lou into the house, and at first, it looked like the older woman was going to refuse. She hadn't been happy with Erin recently. This latest development wasn't going to make her more likely to forgive Erin for past mistakes. But then Mary Lou nodded her head, patted her gray bob, and entered. Erin motioned toward the couch, her brain spinning, trying to sort things out.

Vic stood in the kitchen doorway, her long blond hair tied back in a ponytail, her mouth open slightly. She knew how Mary Lou felt about them lately, so she was surprised by Mary Lou coming into the house. Vic looked at Erin, her brows coming down.

"Erin? What's wrong? Is everything okay?"

"No." Erin shook her head. She couldn't explain it. She pointed at Mary Lou for her to explain to Vic. "Tea? I'm going to put on the kettle." She passed Vic in the doorway and started to get the tea things ready. She turned on the electric kettle and gathered teacups, an assortment of tea bags, and the other items she needed.

"What is it?" Vic asked Mary Lou, her tone anxious and uncertain. "Did something happen? Is it Roger?"

But it was not about Mary Lou's husband. As far as Erin knew, he was still safe in the facility where he had been held since he'd been arrested for murder and assault. Not jail, but somewhere they would, hopefully, be a little more compassionate and be able to handle his brain injury.

Nor was it about Campbell, Mary Lou's older son, who had been in some trouble in the past.

Erin listened for Mary Lou's answer, but she didn't explain to Vic. She probably handed Vic the same paper that she had shown to Erin. The Bald Eagle Falls weekly newspaper, which had included a news article written by Mary Lou's younger teenage son, Joshua. But the article had been cut out and there was a sticky note in its place.

If you want to know where your son is, maybe you should ask Erin Price.

The kettle started to whistle. Feeling numb and distant, as if she was enclosed in a bubble, Erin poured the steaming water into the teapot and then took the tea service out to the living room. She set it on the coffee table and sat on the couch beside Mary Lou. Not too close—she didn't want to impinge on Mary Lou's personal space—but close enough that they could talk and Mary Lou would know that Erin was there to help and support her. Vic sat in one of the easy chairs across from her, looking as pale and horrified as Erin felt. Mary Lou herself, appearing composed as she always did, smoothed wrinkles in her pantsuit and didn't immediately help herself to a teacup.

"Can I pour for you?" Vic offered. "What kind would you like?"

Mary Lou seemed far away. It took her a few extra seconds to process Vic's question and focus on the tea bags in the basket.

"Earl Gray," she said eventually. "Thank you."

Vic busied herself with preparing a cup for Mary Lou, then

passed it across to her. She poured for herself and Erin, and let Erin choose and add her own teabag. They sat there, looking at each other. They looked like three friends gathered for a gossip session. But that wasn't how it felt.

"I don't know anything about where Josh is," Erin told Mary Lou. "I hope you know that. I don't know what this note means, but… I don't know anything about where Josh is or what he is doing. I haven't seen him since he came to Whitewater Junction to interview me."

That had been days before. She remembered him coming to her hotel room, notepad in hand, eager to act the part of a mature reporter. Erin assumed that Joshua had gone home after that interview, had carried on his life as usual through the remainder of the cooking contest. And he had, of course, handed in his report to this English teacher and submitted it to the newspaper.

And then…? What had happened? And why did the note say that Mary Lou should ask Erin, when she knew nothing of Joshua's whereabouts?

"He isn't home?" Vic asked the obvious.

Of course Josh wasn't at home, or his mother would not be concerned about a note that implied something had happened to him.

"No. He was home yesterday… everything was normal. I thought… everything was even better than normal. But something happened. This morning… he didn't come down for breakfast. When I looked in his room to wake him up… he wasn't there." Mary Lou's gaze sought out Erin's. "His bed hadn't been slept in."

Erin's stomach clenched into a tight ball. She felt like she was being strangled. What could have happened to Joshua? If his bed hadn't been slept in, he hadn't just gone for a walk or to visit a friend or pick up a cup of coffee that morning. Something had happened to him the night before. He had left the house without Mary Lou being aware of it and he had not returned.

"Have you called the police?"

"No." Mary Lou shook her head. "I haven't talked to anyone. I just... I called him on his phone, but there was no answer. I was going to call you, but... I just came over."

"Yeah. This is really crazy. But I... I don't know where he is..." Erin trailed off. She didn't know how to explain the note. Someone was trying to throw suspicion on her, but she hadn't had anything to do with Joshua's absence.

"But maybe if you thought about it, you would have some idea," Mary Lou said. "Even if you haven't seen him or heard from him, you must know something about what is going on. Why would the note say that if it wasn't anything to do with you?"

"But it isn't. I don't know anything."

"Where would he go? You two have been involved in everything going on around here. You must have some idea."

Erin felt lost.

"What about Cam?" Vic suggested. "Maybe he went to visit his brother. And this note is just... I don't know. Some kind of joke."

Mary Lou had her phone in her hand. She stared at it as if it was something foreign to her. Or might blow up any minute.

"Have you called Campbell?" Erin asked. It was probably the first thing Mary Lou had done.

"No. He won't be up yet. He stays out late. Sleeps half the day. He wouldn't wake up."

"But if Joshua is with him... they must know you'd be looking for him. Or if he's not, won't Campbell want to help look for him? He would want to know right away."

Mary Lou shook her head. "There's no point, Erin. I said he won't wake up. I can't ask him or tell him anything if he is asleep and doesn't answer his phone."

Erin understood this, but still felt like Mary Lou should at least try.

"If he really is missing, we should call the police," Vic said.

"Yes," Erin agreed. "The earlier they can start looking for him, the better the results."

"I don't think they'll look if it hasn't been forty-eight hours, will they?"

"No, they'll look sooner than that," Erin assured her. "If you think something has happened to him, you should tell them right away. The first few hours can be critical. We don't want to lose them."

"I don't *know* that anything has happened to him. This could just be... a joke. Someone being silly. He's a teenager. They do stupid things without realizing what the consequences could be."

"But if he was just out with friends, wouldn't you be able to get him on the phone?" Erin pointed out.

"Maybe. Maybe not. There are a lot of places in these mountains where you can't get a signal. If he's out of range of a cell tower, or in a canyon, or spelunking, I wouldn't be able to get him."

"Spelunking," Erin repeated. Just thinking about being underground in a cave was enough to take her breath away. Still. "He wouldn't go into a cave without friends, would he? And without letting someone know where he was?"

"N-no..." Mary Lou drew the word out, and even though she said he wouldn't do it, she immediately contradicted herself. "Like I said... he's a teenager. And teen boys do all kinds of crazy things without understanding the dangers. As you well know." She gave each of them a hard stare. Erin looked down at her cup, her face hot with embarrassment. "You try to tell them something they need to be careful of, a decision that could bring them to harm, and you just get 'I'll be fine, Mom. I promise.' As if they can control the consequences." Mary Lou took a sip of her cooling tea. "I don't know how many times I've told them you can't choose the consequences. You can only choose your actions."

Erin looked at Vic. "Well... we can look around town. See if he's at the school or any of the regular hangouts. We can't check out all of the caves in the area, of course, but maybe Willie could drive by a couple of the more popular ones. See if there are cars parked outside."

Vic nodded. "If you aren't sure yet if there's really a problem and want to look for him first, we can help with that."

Erin remembered the search party for Roger when he had wandered off on his own. It was different for Roger because of his brain injury. He wasn't just a teenager off having a good time. He was easily confused and could have hurt himself. The whole town had shown up to help look for him and to comfort Mary Lou. Should they send out the call for help with Joshua?

But Erin could see that would not go over well. If Mary Lou made a big fuss about him being missing and it turned out that he'd just taken a day off to mess around, the police and everyone else would be irritated, Mary Lou and Joshua would be embarrassed. Tensions between them would increase instead of decreasing.

"Do you want us to help look?" Erin asked Mary Lou.

Mary Lou sipped her tea, looked around, a small crease between her eyebrows. Then she finally nodded. "Yes. I suppose so. We can at least do that."

Erin and Vic nodded their agreement. Auntie Clem's Bakery was covered for the day, so they were free to spend the day as they wished. Erin had been planning to do some business planning and later to run some errands, but those things could be put off. If Joshua was missing, it was an emergency. She needed to be flexible and concentrate on what was most important.

"With this mention of you," Mary Lou said, motioning to the newspaper lying on the coffee table, the sticky note incongruous in the sea of black print, "do you think... that he's back in Whitewater?"

Erin looked at Vic. She didn't feel like driving back to Whitewater, and once she got there, where specifically would she look? But the notes said to ask Erin where he was. That implied that something Erin had done had resulted in Joshua's disappearance. And lately, all she had done was to be a judge at the cooking contest and to help solve Beryl Batcombe's murder.

A murder that Joshua had been asking questions about.

In Whitewater.

"I guess," she said reluctantly. "If it has something to do with me… that's really the only thing unusual that I have done lately. And Joshua interviewed me about it."

Vic nodded her agreement.

"I don't have a vehicle, though," Erin realized. "Willie took his truck and Terry took his."

"You should have gone with Jack to look at cars when they were here," Vic pointed out. "They had their eye on a few good deals."

"I know. But there was so much going on with the contest and everything else." And Erin hadn't wanted to go with Jack. She'd felt pressured before even getting near a car lot. She didn't want to be pushed into anything. She would buy a new car when she was ready. On her own. Without someone else pushing her into it and spouting facts and figures at her.

"Is Terry actually using the truck?" Vic asked. "Could we borrow it?"

"I'll check." He was often on foot patrol around the town, his truck just parked in the lot at the Town Hall, where the police department was housed. It was only a short walk to get there from Erin's house.

$\mathcal{M}$ary Lou raised her hand to stop Erin as she slid out her phone and looked down at it to dial Terry.

"What are you going to tell him?"

"That I need the car to go to Whitewater and…" Erin trailed off. She could see the warning in Mary Lou's eyes even before she said anything. "And… you don't want me to say anything to him about Joshua?"

"I've told you before that you need to watch what you say to him. If I wanted the police involved, I would call them myself."

"Okay." Erin looked at Vic. "Then I guess… tell him that I decided that my errands might take longer than I had originally planned, so I want to get started. And after we check out White-water, we'll have to run into the city to take care of them, so it doesn't look suspicious."

Mary Lou gave a brusque nod.

Erin swallowed. "Okay." She didn't like the subterfuge, but it was really just a lie of omission. She really would do her errands as she told him.

"Should we split up?" Vic asked. "I suppose I should stay here and look around, we can cover more area if we split up."

It was a sensible plan of action, but Erin bit her lip and shook her head. "I'm not sure… I don't want to go by myself."

Vic cocked her head. She raised her eyebrows in query. "It's just for a few hours. You wouldn't be staying there alone."

"I know. But since the accident, I don't really want to drive the highway by myself. I can, but… I just would feel better if I had someone with me. So that if anything happens…"

Nothing would happen, of course. Just because she had been followed and forced off the road once, that didn't mean that it would ever happen again. It was a once-in-a-lifetime occurrence.

Not something that was going to happen to her again.

"Oh, hon'," Vic leaned across the coffee table and touched Erin's arm. "I didn't realize."

Erin squirmed. She wasn't looking for pity or even just attention. She wasn't doing it to be the poor, damaged little girl. She'd filled that role too many times in the past, the only survivor of the rollover that had killed her parents when she was just a child.

"I *can* go by myself," she asserted, looking at Mary Lou. "It's just… safer with two people in the car."

Mary Lou nodded. "If you could see if there's any sign of him in Whitewater Junction, that would help," she said, without comment on Erin's weakness and the inconvenience it caused. "I think I should stay here, in case he comes home, or in case… I don't know. The police call me with news."

Erin was about to ask why the police would call Mary Lou if she didn't report Joshua missing, but then bit back her response.

If they found Josh's body, Mary Lou meant. If they found him injured or dead, Mary Lou would be the one they called and she would want to be close at hand. Erin tried to blink back tears and not let the lump in her throat change her voice.

"Yeah. If he's in Whitewater, we'll find him."

If he was in Whitewater.

If he was alive.

If someone hadn't kidnapped him and hidden him away somewhere.

Erin managed to borrow Officer Terry Piper's truck without giving away that she was running over to Whitewater to see if she could find a missing teenager. There had been a couple of awkward pauses during the call. Like he knew that Erin was keeping something from him. Like he was trying to figure out how to ask her what was really going on but was afraid to ask.

Or maybe she just imagined it.

"He said it's fine," Erin told Vic. "He and K9 are just out on foot patrol, and he'll either walk home or get Stayner to drop him, depending on how he's feeling at the end of his shift."

"He's been doing better lately," Vic contributed. "It's nice to see him looking bright-eyed again."

It had been a difficult few months, a hard recovery after Terry had been attacked, hit over the head, and choked out. The damage went a lot deeper than she had expected. Nothing like TV cop shows where people got knocked out all the time and seemed to go on with barely even a headache or moment of vertigo. Things had been much worse for Terry.

But he had seemed to be doing better the last few days. She could only hope that he would continue to feel good and not relapse back into migraines, insomnia, and nightmares. And the irritability and mood issues.

"We'd better head out pretty quickly," Erin suggested. "If we're going to look for Josh and try to get our most urgent errands done, we can't waste any time."

"Yep," Vic agreed. "We'll be quick as two winks. Do you want me to make some sandwiches so we don't have to stop for lunch later?"

"Good idea. I'll check the animals' bowls"—she had two pets home, Orange Blossom the cat and Marshmallow the rabbit —"Then, why don't I walk over and get the truck while you make the sandwiches. I'll make sure it's gassed up, and then we'll head out."

"Sounds like a plan," Vic agreed. She shook her head and *tsked*. "Poor Mary Lou. If we end up finding Joshua and this was just some kind of joke or ill-conceived teen prank, I'll whup that boy myself."

Erin had seen Vic's father try to beat her. He did not approve of her being transgender or getting together with a man from a rival clan—and she knew that Vic was only blowing hot air. There was no way she could do the same to another teen, no matter what he had done.

"I don't think it is a prank," Erin said. "I can't see Joshua doing something like this. He loves his mom and he knows all the stuff that she's been through. He wouldn't do something that might hurt her more just as a prank."

"No. I don't think so," Vic agreed. "Okay. I'll see you in twenty minutes or so."

After checking the food and water dishes, Erin grabbed her purse and headed over to the police department at a brisk walk.

Erin didn't run into anyone who slowed her down on her way to the Town Hall, so she was able to get Terry's truck and top off the gas tank in the allotted time. She picked Vic up at the house, and they were on their way to Whitewater.

Erin didn't want to keep going over the same ground when they hadn't found out anything yet. They could speculate all day long on where Joshua had gone or why he had disappeared, but they wouldn't know until they'd had some time to turn up some clues. Erin looked around for other things to talk about as she drove the highway. She didn't want to admit how anxious she was about being followed again, and she wouldn't be calmed just by listening to the radio. She needed something that took enough of her attention that she wouldn't constantly be thinking about the cars and trucks on the highway behind her.

It was a busy highway, not like the secondary road she'd been on the day that she'd been forced into the ditch. Nothing was going to happen to her out in the open where everybody could see.

"I did a few trials of recipes for the fortune cookies," she told Vic. "A few other people have done gluten-free fortune cookies. Mostly based around tapioca starch or cornstarch. They are pretty simple, actually. Just a matter of rolling or pressing them, cutting them into a circle, and then folding them while they're still warm. Then they get crispy when they cool."

"I always wondered how they baked them with paper inside," Vic laughed. "Because you would either have to bake them at a really low temperature, or the paper would light on fire. And I'd never even seen a scorched fortune."

Erin smiled and nodded. "I always wondered too. It's a bit of a letdown to realize that they insert the fortune and fold the cookie after they are baked. Removes some of the mystique."

"Won't it be great for the Chinese restaurant to offer gluten-free fortune cookies for their clientele? It's such a nice touch. I can't wait to see Peter Foster try his first gluten-free fortune cookie."

Erin was determined to keep her smile from fading, so she kept it firmly in place even though it made her sad that Mrs. Foster had decided Peter would not be visiting the bakery in person any time soon. Like Mary Lou, she was upset with Erin for mentioning Peter's name during a police investigation, resulting in Peter being interviewed by the police. Not just once, but twice.

It wasn't Erin's fault that he'd been a witness in both cases. He'd told her key clues that had led to her figuring out what had happened, but which also led to him being questioned.

It wasn't like he'd been a suspect, like Joshua. It was understood right from the start that the little boy had only been a witness, and one who didn't even realize what it was he had seen.

"I thought we should do some kind of care basket for Mrs. Foster," Erin said, changing the subject. "She'll be having that baby any day now, and it would be nice if she didn't have to be on her feet coming around to the bakery for a couple of weeks. We could take or deliver her the things that she normally comes around for… bread, muffins, afterschool snacks…"

"What a great idea," Vic enthused. "You're always coming up with such creative plans."

"You don't think she would be offended, do you? Thinking that I was saying she wasn't capable of looking after her own family, or that I was just trying to get closer and interfere with things…"

"Of course not. It's a lovely thing to do. No one could find fault with you for helping a customer out during a challenging time."

"Okay." Erin wasn't always sure. People did seem to find fault with her for the littlest things. Even when she was doing something she thought people would approve of, doing something nice for someone just to be nice, they would criticize or put some kind of negative spin on things.

"Don't worry about the old gossips," Vic said, reading her mind. "Some people are negative no matter what. You're not going to change that. You have to just ignore them and live your life."

Erin nodded. "Yeah. I will. I just feel sometimes like I missed out on a bunch of etiquette lessons because of the way I was raised. There are all of these little rules that I never picked up on."

"That's just the south for you. And small-town living. There *are* a bunch of special rules. But you can never do them all, so you have to just develop a thick skin about the rest of them."

Changing Fortune Cookies, Book #14 of the Auntie Clem's Bakery series by P.D. Workman can be purchased at pdworkman.com

If you enjoyed this book, please take the time to recommend it to other purchasers with a review or star rating and share it with your friends!

facebook.com/pdworkmanauthor

twitter.com/pdworkmanauthor

instagram.com/pdworkmanauthor

amazon.com/author/pdworkman

bookbub.com/authors/p-d-workman

goodreads.com/pdworkman

linkedin.com/in/pdworkman

pinterest.com/pdworkmanauthor

youtube.com/pdworkman

ABOUT THE AUTHOR

Award-winning and USA Today bestselling author P.D. (Pamela) Workman writes riveting mystery/suspense and young adult books dealing with mental illness, addiction, abuse, and other real-life issues. For as long as she can remember, the blank page has held an incredible allure and from a very young age she was trying to write her own books.

Workman wrote her first complete novel at the age of twelve and continued to write as a hobby for many years. She started publishing in 2013. She has won several literary awards from Library Services for Youth in Custody for her young adult fiction. She currently has over 60 published titles and can be found at pdworkman.com.

Born and raised in Alberta, Workman has been married for over 25 years and has one son.

Please visit P.D. Workman at pdworkman.com to see what else she is working on, to join her mailing list, and to link to her social networks.